Lines

Cira Mozos Ansorena

Lines

Kosmovisiones acknowledges the Traditional Owners of the Country on which this book was created, the Wurundjeri People of the Kulin Nation, and pays respect to their Elders past, present, and emerging.

www.kosmovisiones.com
Kosmovisiones
Melbourne, Australia

LINES
First published by Kosmovisiones, 2026
ISBN 978-1-7641445-0-6 (paperback)
ISBN 978-1-7641445-8-2 (hardback)
ISBN 978-1-7641445-2-0 (ebook)

A catalogue record for this book is available from the National Library of Australia.

We are not alone.
We are threads of the same quipu.

KNOTS

KNOT I

THE LINE THAT UNFOLDS

The cry of a bird awoke Ikan. He stood quickly, stirred by the message woven into the bird's call, and stepped out of the cabin. A sensation swept through him, a summons to embark on another journey of power.

The first tremor beneath his feet made him run. Pushing up the hill with unshakable determination, he reached a rocky ledge rising above the sea. There he paused, breathing in the air thick with salt and electricity. Lightning split the horizon, briefly illuminating the shadows looming over the Outer Reserves. As if performing an ancient rite, he opened his hands and pressed them slowly against the damp ground. Carefully, he moved a heavy rock, fixing his gaze on the *quena* resting beneath it. He looked at it with reverence and humility. Feeling its permission, he lifted it in his hands, elated.

The taste of cane tuned his breath, and with unwavering *Intent*, Ikan drew a new sound from the quena—a deep melody offered to the wind. Suddenly, a strong tremor ran through his bare feet. He staggered as he watched rocks break free and tumble into the ocean below.

Ikan, watching as the storm drew closer, continued playing the quena, feeling himself part of the chaos descending upon the Outer Reserves. On that cliff, he tested whether he possessed enough power to sustain the entire battle, making the sound a bridge between worlds. The earth itself answered him with distant echoes.

Then, he noticed a surveillance device emerging from between the rocks: a sphere, spinning. The metallic orb positioned itself at his level, observing him through its many lenses. Another unexpected tremor shook the rocky terrain. In that instant, seizing the opportunity, Ikan swiftly grabbed a nearby stone and hurled it at the vigilant sphere. The impact landed with a dry thud. The camera fell and vanished into the furious sea.

He brought the quena to his lips once more and kept playing. His defiant eyes lifted towards the distant lights of Sector B, gleaming like a constant threat.

They're like those black clouds, he thought, heavy, oppressive, covering the horizon of the Outer Reserves like a storm of technological domination.

From a higher vantage point, Elías watched in silence. His serene posture and steady gaze revealed the wisdom of a life spent in search of understanding. Amid the roar of the wind and distant thunder, Elías perceived something else—a deep and steady heartbeat. It was as if the storm itself were the drum of the cosmos echoing through the cracks in the veil separating the different *Pachas*, those invisible threads where past, present, and possibility touch in a spiral.

When he felt the third tremor, he knew the nocturnal spectacle had come to an end. With a slow gesture, he pulled a condor feather from his belongings and released it to the wind, a sign of gratitude and acceptance of his role in the weaving of time. He descended calmly to where the boy was.

'Ikan,' he said in a deep yet gentle voice, 'we are gathered in the cave. Nuna wants you to join the assembly; she knows you have played the quena.'

Ikan, with the quena as his instrument of communion with the mystery, knew that through its sound he had joined the shifting currents of reality. Though he couldn't yet see the purpose in its entirety, he was certain of one thing: in that battle, he had gained enough power for another encounter with the unknown.

Naran watched between the buildings as the pale winter light faded away. She walked slowly, her steps heavy after hours of wandering through cobbled alleys. In one hand, she held a photo of her father, wrinkled and worn by time; with the other, she timidly approached passersby, pointing at it and asking if they had seen him. She barely lifted her gaze, afraid someone might notice her youth and vulnerability. Every few steps, she raised the photograph again, but the hurried crowd ignored her or dismissed her with a gesture. A drop of rain blurred the image, and Naran wiped it clean with her blackened hand. She tried showing it to a woman, but the woman silently shook her head and walked away.

Hopeless, she leaned against a building, letting its cold façade support her sadness. Another day with no news. With a brusque movement, she tried to wrap herself more tightly in her jacket, but the freezing wind sent a shiver through her. *I should have grabbed warmer clothes when I escaped the centre,* she thought, scolding herself. She had already run off in search of her father several times that month, and now she blamed herself for not having learned to pack her backpack better. She barely had any clothes and, even worse, they were wet. If she didn't find shelter soon, she knew she wouldn't survive the night's frost.

Sheltered beneath the building, she watched as heavy raindrops seeped into her worn shoes. Her attention, however, was far away: it wandered, lost among the images unfolding in her mind, triggered by the smell of soup wafting through a nearby window. *What are they having for dinner?* she wondered, as memories of the centre returned to her. Nothing seemed more distant from the cold, hostile street than the metallic atmosphere of the youth shelter. The caregivers' indifference, the disconnection between the young people… everything was cold. And yet, in that darkness, that coldness had felt like a kind of safety. *Maybe I should go back,* she thought, feeling like a solitary tree on a frozen plain.

A noise made her tense. She looked to her left and saw a man, a vagrant, approaching as he dragged a shopping cart full of broken objects. The man stopped in front of her, his gaze vacant, and offered her an old, tattered blanket.

'No, I'm fine, thanks,' Naran replied, turning her head to avoid the musty smell of the garment. She didn't want to strike up a conversation with a stranger.

The man looked at her with an expression she couldn't decipher and whispered,
'Dark times are coming.'

He handed her a pamphlet before continuing, dragging his cart.

Naran looked down at the paper and shrugged, not really knowing what to say. Her need was primal, too immediate to worry about times to come.

'These streets have borne the weight of several empires. There was a time when countries claimed to have brought civilisation to the millions of indigenous people they enslaved and killed,' the man said without stopping. 'Now, the central sectors do the same with our minds.'

'What does that have to do with Karanza?' asked Naran, reading the name on the pamphlet.

'Karanza is a refuge. It's our only hope to resist. Look there; maybe you'll find the answers you need.'

'Have you seen him?' she asked then, showing him the photograph. 'He's my father, and I haven't heard from him in over a month.'

'Look in Karanza.'

'How do I get there?' Naran insisted, searching for directions in the pamphlet that might point the way. When she looked up, the man was already turning the corner of the alley, shouting as he disappeared.

'Remember!' he whispered as he retreated. 'Every coloniser has their cracks. No empire lasts forever.'

His words, heavy with bitter truth, struck something deep within her. For years, she had felt in tune with those ideas, carrying them like a burden. But she had to admit they hadn't brought her answers—and now the weight of her circumstances made her crumble. The vagrant manifested something that terrified her: the possibility of being so marginalised herself. If she were connected to the system, she wouldn't be in this situation. *I need to find my father quickly*, she thought, staring at the pamphlet in desperation.

She hadn't been able to locate him; mobile lines were cut for civilians, and only communications through MIO remained active. Which meant she was in the same situation as that man—banished from everything she once considered hers, wandering, divided, bitterly recognising that a part of her still longed to access that newly established reality. A wave of rejection and anger washed over her, and she raised her voice: *Why is it my fault I can't access that wretched program?!* she shouted, as tears soaked the dark strands of hair clinging to her skin. She wiped her eyes with her arm, clearing her greenish, slanted features, and looked again at the pamphlet, wondering what she could do.

The pain in her chest intensified. The cold air slashed her lungs and she could barely feel her hands. The temperature was dropping fast. She couldn't return to the youth shelter— the metallic atmosphere of that place gave her chills. The young people there didn't know what was really happening. *Why are we kept there? Have they turned us into prisoners just because we're incompatible with the system?* she thought with a mix of frustration and anguish. But she couldn't go to the police either; they would send her back to the centre, where they would tell her the same thing as always: that Alan, her father, was busy with the research project and that, due to the state of emergency, she had to follow orders. But she could no longer accept that situation—she had to find him.

The pamphlet in her hands was a fragile object, but now it felt like an anchor. Naran needed to know if the latest system update was safe, if with it she could finally become compatible. She looked again at the printed words… *Karanza might be a solution if I can't find my father,* she told herself, trying to soothe the uncertainty devouring her.

A cold wind blew something against her hands. Startled, Naran grabbed a feather. *How could a bird survive in this inhospitable climate?* she wondered. For a moment, that condor feather, so simple and light, evoked distant, warm landscapes where nature still offered refuge. She could almost feel the lushness of the trees and the deep green of their canopies, and a fleeting peace enveloped her. But the past was only an echo—a voice lashing her mercilessly like the gusts of wind, a song of faded memories and broken hopes. In that moment, the present terrified her: desolate streets, abandoned buildings, neon lights screaming colours and repetitive messages about MIO—that artificial reality projecting horizons that promised everything and offered nothing. Those landscapes were virtual confines she feared but also longed for, and to which she couldn't gain access because she was incompatible.

With those thoughts, she wandered distractedly for a while, roaming with sleepy eyes through the shadows of the night. Another freezing gust snapped her from her trance and reminded her again who she was: Naran, a seventeen-year-old girl who had witnessed a reality vanishing beneath the imminent confinement of the population, destined to hibernate in bunkers connected to the MIO system during the glaciation. That thought brought her a pain as real as it was useless. Upon realising it, she shook off the nostalgia she used as her only shelter, and an impulse urged her to survive: she had to find a place to spend the night.

The wind blew fiercely as Naran stumbled through the desolate streets of the peripheral sector. Amid the gloom, disoriented, she barely recognised the echoes of her own footsteps. Her legs hardly obeyed her; exhaustion weighed down her every movement. To shake off the numbness, she jumped a couple of times, though the relief was fleeting. Her drowsy eyes caught a glimpse of space beneath the stairs of an old building—a hidden spot that promised some respite to survive the endless night. With the last of her strength, she dragged herself there, pulling cardboard boxes from a nearby dumpster to seal the entrance to her improvised refuge.

But upon arrival, reality struck harshly: the floor was soaked from the recent rains. A puddle became a mirror, and her gaze shifted to the surface, where her thoughts projected the same results from the graph, repeated endlessly after each test, alongside the blinking words: *incompatible*. A breath of cold air pulled her back to the present. Shaking her head, she tried to dispel those memories, those burdens chasing her like persistent shadows.

The image of her warm home, the one she once shared with her parents, crossed her mind, bringing a moment of fleeting comfort. A shiver ran down her spine and she let the memory go with a sigh, though its departure left a painful void. With tears in her eyes, she headed to the dumpsters to search for an alternative. A sudden cramp shot through her legs, tensing her body to its limit. She knew she couldn't afford to linger in that emotional state; she needed to gather strength to survive. *There's no time*, she repeated as she looked at her hands, purple from the cold.

Suddenly, distant shouts broke the silence. She turned her head towards the sound and saw two teenagers running at full speed, crossing a main avenue. To her surprise, the kids turned a corner and entered the alley where she was. A van approached behind them, trying to cut them off.

As they raced past her, Naran stepped back, startled by the uncertainty. She was too exhausted and absorbed in her thoughts to react. *I just want to rest*, she thought, wishing to escape the anguish consuming her for a moment. But something inside her snapped to alert; her senses sharpened, and her body reacted instinctively. With a leap, like an animal on guard, she broke from her lethargy and recognised the van approaching. *It can't be*, she murmured, astonished.

The hum of patrolling drones filled the air, accompanied by the shrill echo of alarms. The van advanced fast, and Naran, driven by instinct, followed the two teenagers. Though her body was at its limit, something within gave her strength. Suddenly, a cramp brought her down, but a hand quickly appeared to help her up. The boy pulled her back into action, and Naran looked at him with gratitude, too breathless to speak.

'Hurry!' shouted the girl leading the escape as she climbed an exterior staircase.

'Follow her!' the boy exclaimed, still holding her arm. 'You can trust her; she's my sister, Maia.'

The boy's voice was urgent. Maia motioned for them to enter the building through a broken window. As they climbed the façade stairs, Naran observed the girl's agile, determined movements. Maia, strong and fast, wore a black hood that concealed her features; her loose, functional clothes reinforced her air of resolve.

But at one point, Naran slipped and fell backwards. Instinctively, she grabbed the boy's leg to prevent a worse fall, and that fleeting contact made her realise he wore a prosthetic. The small detail led her to glimpse the relationship between the siblings: Maia was her brother's protector. Her strength and determination came from her need to keep him safe—and that somehow made Naran feel safer too. That perception became an anchor amid the chaos.

For the first time in a long while, she felt connected to someone, even if they were complete strangers.

Finally, they slipped through the broken window, and Naran collapsed to the floor, gasping. She closed her eyes for a moment, trying to process everything that had just happened. But her mind was a whirlwind of images and emotions. *How did I get here?* she wondered, overwhelmed by the past few days of fleeing and despair. Exhaustion overtook her, and she slipped into darkness for a moment until a sudden shake woke her abruptly. The boy was calling her, his voice thick with panic.

Naran opened her eyes and felt reality slipping through her fingers, blending with what seemed like a dream: heavy footsteps echoed through the building, and through a gap in the staircase, they saw one of the security men climbing, getting closer.

'Néstor!' shouted Maia, irritated to see her brother moving aimlessly. 'Focus!'

'What do we do now?' he asked, nervous.

'Wait here!' Maia darted off to find another way out. Within moments, she returned and pointed in a new direction.

'We'll go down the exterior stairs on the other side.'

Naran, however, suddenly stopped. Her thoughts turned inward, and before her, different possibilities unfolded. She could see how each choice would affect her destiny and that of her companions. Reality, malleable before her eyes, turned into a fan of potential futures. Though she couldn't guarantee the certainty of what she saw, her intuition sharpened with each perception.

'Wait!' she exclaimed firmly. Her tone stopped the siblings, who looked at her in surprise.

'What is it?' asked Maia, her anxiety evident.

'Not that way,' said Naran, convinced. The images and sensations she had just experienced reinforced her decision. Though she couldn't fully explain it, she knew continuing down the exterior stairs would be a mistake.

'How are you so sure?' Néstor asked, sceptical.

'I've considered the possibilities—another vehicle is coming that way. If we go there, they'll trap us in the alley.'

The siblings exchanged a glance, doubting Naran's certainty, but the growing noise of the door being forced pushed them to act.

'There's no time, let's go!' said Naran with determination.

Despite their doubts, Maia and Néstor followed her. They exited through the back door and quietly descended towards a dark basement car park. They searched the vehicles for somewhere to hide. After several failed attempts, Naran noticed that a van's window was open. They slipped inside and huddled on the van floor, holding their breath as the security men passed nearby.

When they finally heard the sound of the patrols moving away, the group let out a sigh of relief. Naran, still trembling from the weight of her decision, pressed the photograph of her father to her chest. In the darkness, her mind tried to find clarity.

Even though doubts persisted, one thought clung to her heart: there was still hope.

Alan, his eyes glazed with tiredness after another long day, listened to Nelida speaking, as if from a distance. Fatigue was etched on his weary face; his mind wavered between the responsibility of the project and his personal worries. The past weeks had been exhausting for everyone at the Research Centre, but he felt particularly drained.

'So, Alan, with what we've accomplished today, do you think the report will be ready by the deadline?' asked Nelida, her voice thick with anxiety. 'You know we have until next week at the latest.'

Alan slowly released a device connected to a computer by several cables and pushed his chair back to recline. The bright light of the office irritated him, and he squeezed his eyes shut while stretching in an attempt to relieve the strain.

'Are you alright?' she continued, unable to hide her concern for her colleague's state.

Alan's silence was answer enough: the Incompatibles were about to arrive at the Centre, and everything had to be ready for the project's final phase to be approved. The pressure was immense, fuelled by Margot's constant interference. The coordinator, fearful of being dismissed by the central sectors, kept changing the plans. The atmosphere was thick with tension.

'You know I got into this project because of my daughter,' Alan finally responded, lowering his head as if speaking more to himself than to Nelida. 'Well, I mean… for a whole generation of young people, to believe in their possibilities. Even if the circumstances are against them, whether socially, environmentally, or financially, everyone should have the chance to become who they want to be, not be relegated by the force of something bigger than them.'

Nelida nodded slowly, hoping the conversation wouldn't stretch on. It was late, and they had a crucial meeting the next day where they had to show solid progress. The results needed to convince all parties; otherwise, the project could be doomed. However, Alan's fatigue seemed to push him to voice the doubts he had been repressing.

'Do you think each of those young people can find that sliver of luck—that second that can completely change their life?' he asked, pausing to exhale and release some of the pressure he felt. 'Do you think, being connected to a machine, they can still find their destiny? Or are they doomed to do what we adults want from them? Worse yet, what a program decides for them.'

Nelida watched him, her concern for him growing with every passing moment.

'I think you've gone too long without sleep, Alan,' she replied gently.

Alan leaned forward, covering his face with his hands. His voice trembled slightly when he asked:

'Do you think I'm a good father? I'm so deep into this that I feel like I'm drifting away from her.'

His colleague placed a hand on his shoulder in a silent gesture of support.

Alan knew she was right, but the weight of his thoughts kept him trapped. He felt like he was struggling to keep a ship afloat, trying to balance the expectations of everyone involved in the project. But if things didn't go well in the next day's meeting, he would have to make a difficult decision—perhaps even abandon everything he had worked for.

That night, after weeks of failed attempts, he tried to contact his daughter, but communications were down. The feeling of helplessness overwhelmed him, and uncertainty became his shadow. Despite it all, the scanner was complete, and Alan trusted that his work would be worthwhile. He believed that, in the end, the project's leaders would understand why some teenagers couldn't be connected to MIO. Yet deep within his exhaustion, a doubt persisted: was he truly doing the right thing? Could this effort prevent the project—and all the young people he was trying to protect—from sinking into a system that seemed inevitable?

'You need to rest,' said Nelida firmly.

The morning light reflected from the van's rear-view mirror, illuminating Naran's face. The sun's glare woke her with an uncomfortable blink, and Maia, urgency clear in her voice and movements, pulled her from her drowsiness.

'Wake up, we have to go quickly!' she exclaimed, shaking both Néstor and Naran. 'Someone could come into the garage at any moment!'

The recent events still reverberated in Naran's mind like a confusing tide. The images of the past hours—full of running and tension—faded as she forced herself to focus on the present. Still dazed by the abrupt change in her surroundings, it took her a moment to process where she was. Maia, seeing that Naran was still disoriented, leaned towards her.

'Are you alright? We need to move now,' she insisted, her tone firm but not aggressive.

Naran nodded slowly, feeling reality pressing from every direction. Néstor, his face still sleepy but curiosity awakening in his eyes, broke the silence:

'How did you know there was a second car coming from the other side of the building?'

The question pulled Naran out of her trance. She remembered how she had seen those images in her mind, how her intuition had caught something the others couldn't foresee. But she hesitated before answering, unsure how to explain it.

'I think I… followed my intuition,' she murmured, almost in a whisper. 'My name is Naran.'

Saying her own name made her falter. Speaking it aloud forced her to face a part of herself that seemed blurred, fragmented by painful memories she couldn't piece together. The words seemed to get stuck in her throat, each syllable heavy with crushing uncertainty. Maia watched her carefully, trying to decipher something more in the young woman's face. Yet Naran lowered her gaze, unable to hold eye contact.

The tension in her chest was suffocating, and though she wanted to trust them, a part of her remained alert, unable to stop seeing them as strangers. Finally, she found a possible way to connect with them, even if it came from a shared wound.

'I escaped from a youth centre two days ago, and I don't want to go back. I'm looking for my father.'

The words hung in the narrow space of the vehicle. Maia and Néstor exchanged a brief but loaded glance of understanding. After a short silence, Maia spoke and shared her own story: the siblings had also escaped from a centre for Incompatibles, and now they were trying to reach the suburb of Karanza, where they hoped to reunite with their parents.

Maia was older than Naran, and her presence carried a maturity beyond her years; her shaved head and sharp features gave her a combative air, reinforced by her tall build and broad shoulders. She hadn't yet turned eighteen, which meant she hadn't been implanted with the device for permanent connection to MIO, and she bore no integration mark at the base of her neck.

Néstor, younger, was around sixteen and contrasted with his sister in many ways: his frame was thinner, more delicate, with slanted eyes that reflected a mix of curiosity and fear. Maia clearly led the duo, and he seemed to find refuge in her strength.

'Karanza…' Naran repeated, letting the name echo in her mind. An image of the pamphlet she'd been given the night before crossed her mind. 'What's happening there?'

'In Karanza, all those who disagree with the new MIO program update are gathering. There are people who refuse to connect or those who simply can't. It's our last chance,' Maia answered, her tone blending determination with worry. She shifted her posture, her face hardening as she continued:

'Besides, our father is sick. Our mother is with him, and with all this chaos, we decided the best thing would be to take refuge with them in Karanza.'

Maia's revelation left Naran deep in thought. The idea of Karanza, until recently nothing to her, was beginning to take on deeper meaning. The option presented to her the previous night started to feel less abstract and more urgent.

'Are you sure this is really happening in Karanza?' she asked, searching for some certainty.

'Yes, part of the population is rebelling against the central sectors' orders,' Néstor affirmed with unexpected conviction.

'They're tired of Sectors A and B being used as a social laboratory by the system's controllers. Sector A was the first to connect to MIO, and in Sector B almost the entire population is already connected. Now we know those in the system are beginning to experience adverse effects...' Maia's voice carried the weight of anger.

Something within Naran shifted. The air around her felt heavier, charged with meaning. Finding others with a purpose made her feel less alone in the search for her father.. The idea of joining Maia and Néstor on their journey to Karanza began to solidify in her mind.

'I'll go with you to seek refuge in Karanza if I don't find my father along the way,' she announced, her voice tinged with gratitude and resolve.

Maia nodded without surprise. It seemed she had expected it.

'Then let's go now,' she said decisively. 'They've started cutting communications between the suburbs to prevent people from moving; they don't want more people reaching Karanza. We have to leave before it's too late.'

The urgency of the moment pushed them to act. Together they began gathering what little they had, preparing for the next stretch of their uncertain journey towards the place of resistance.

Maia led the group, discreetly signalling for them to head towards the square as they exited the garage; it was crucial to avoid the main avenues of the sector.

Néstor, with the cunning of someone who had learned to survive in scarcity, veered off towards a row of abandoned shops and returned moments later with several cans of food. The faint clinking of metal in his hands sounded, for a moment, like a small victory in the midst of uncertainty.

The first rays of sunlight filtered between the buildings, casting a dim light that barely pierced the stubborn morning fog. In the distance, the peaks of the mountains wore their first dusting of snow—a quiet but relentless reminder of the coming glaciation.

'How much time do you think we have left?' Naran asked, her voice a blend of curiosity and fear.

Maia answered without taking her eyes from the horizon, her tone steady but laced with a certain melancholy.

'In a few weeks, these streets will be completely frozen. Life on the surface won't be possible anymore.'

'And in Karanza? Do you think people will survive?' Naran pressed, her worry clear in every word.

Maia sighed, her gaze fixed on the glow of the distant central sectors.

'They've built a network of underground galleries. Even so, it'll be a challenge to spend so many months locked away. But I'd rather that than be connected to MIO—cut off from what truly matters: my family.'

Néstor, walking a few steps behind, added in a heavy tone,

'We're worried about our father.'

Naran nodded silently, taking a moment to absorb Maia's words. There was something in the siblings' quiet resolve that unsettled her. They didn't want to be connected to the system, while for her, connecting to MIO still felt like the only possible way out, a final, desperate attempt to fit in and escape the shadow of being incompatible.

She had worn that shadow for so long, it no longer felt like shame—it felt like skin.

A distant cry broke the monotonous rhythm of their march. From a higher ground, the group watched as a brigade of police officers evicted several families from their homes. In the square, a bus waited with its doors open while the agents forced the last people remaining in the suburb to board. Sector

B was on alert, and evacuation orders were merciless. Most people obeyed as an escape from the crisis, knowing they had to enter suspended hibernation in the bunkers—enclosed facilities beneath the city designed for months of artificial sleep, disconnected from each other, from the surface, from what truly mattered.

The buildings, stripped of humanity, stood like monuments to the sterile logic of technocratic control. Their interiors had become empty cells while the inhabitants were moved like numbers in a system shielding itself from the glaciation with algorithmic efficiency.

One family waited until the last moment before being separated: a weeping mother tried to drag her small children towards the bus, holding a baby in her arms, carrying a few belongings. Her face reflected the helplessness of having to choose between obedience and destruction by the system. The children clung to her legs, screaming, while the father tried to calm them. And finally, the family said goodbye in a heartbreaking embrace. The woman with the baby was taken to special housing. The father and children were forced into the vehicle.

Naran watched it all with a mix of anguish and helplessness. The pain of that reality seemed to pierce her chest. She wondered how many families, how many children, were facing a similar fate. The sense of helplessness paralysed her for a moment—until she felt Néstor's hand pulling at her arm.

'We can't stop,' he said, his tone firm but understanding.

Naran's legs wouldn't respond. Her body trembled under the emotional burden of everything she had witnessed, but she knew she had to keep moving.

Maia and Néstor quickened their pace, anxious to reach Karanza and reunite with their family. They crossed several neighbourhoods and stopped at an abandoned shopping centre.

The flickering screens still projected MIO ads, promoting the safety and comfort of connected life.

Maia, hiding her face beneath her hood, rummaged through a nearby dumpster and returned with some food containers.

'We have to keep going,' she said, nodding towards a tunnel that connected to the outskirts of the sector.

As they moved through the passage, Naran once again felt haunted by uncertainty. In the past century, the world had changed in unpredictable ways: first came the floods that submerged most countries, then the establishment of the central sectors and the confinements caused by epidemics. Now, the imminent glaciation threatened to impose a long isolation that would erase the few remaining traces of humanity.

Was it easier to live back in the age of nations? Naran wasn't sure, but something in her longed for the illusion of stability those times seemed to offer—before the sea swallowed the coasts and the sky froze over the cities. She wondered in silence, watching Maia and Néstor swiftly crossing an avenue. She hurried her steps, realising she had fallen behind, her heart racing with fear and adrenaline. Though the shadows of past and present pursued her, she couldn't afford to slow down. She had to move forward, even if it meant facing a destiny she still didn't fully understand.

Without warning, a fierce tremor shook the asphalt beneath Naran's feet. She stumbled, her heart racing from the jolt, her limbs suddenly heavy, as if gravity had turned against her.

A dizzying sensation overtook her mind; the world seemed to fold and unfold before her eyes, revealing a tangle of interwoven flashes and lines, like a fractured tapestry.

Reality tore open before her.

Disoriented, Naran perceived alternate dimensions collapsing and intermingling in her stunned consciousness. It was as if all the possibilities that had ever existed unfurled at once, flooding her with a cascade of impressions. And there, in the midst of that whirlwind, an unexpected figure emerged: a white llama, adorned with vibrantly coloured ornaments on its ears and neck. It walked forward with serene steps, radiating inexplicable calm.

Something in its presence awakened echoes of Naran's childhood. Buried memories surged back with force, stirring a fragile blend of nostalgia and confusion. But the animal was not alone. Beside it, on the edge of a mountainous landscape that felt like another reality, stood an older woman with grey hair cascading in waves and dark, piercing eyes shining with logic-defying intensity. Her sun-weathered skin and the deep lines across her face spoke of ancestral wisdom. Solid and ethereal at once, her figure moved between unseen layers. The Pachas—the invisible threads of time—vibrated with her.

Naran felt both presences, the llama's and the woman's, intertwining in a symbolic dance that transcended understanding. For a moment, time and space ceased to exist. It was as though the fabric of reality had torn open, offering a glimpse into something vaster. Silence filled her within, as images, sounds, and emotions wove together in an impossible symphony.

A screeching noise—cars, brakes—tore her from the vision. Urban chaos crashed back into her awareness like a slap. Naran was in the middle of the road, surrounded by vehicles skidding, stopping, accelerating, barely avoiding her.

'Naran! Get out of there!' Maia's voice, sharp with alarm, snapped her from the trance.

Néstor, from the side of the road, shouted her name too, bewildered. How had she ended up in such a dangerous place? Naran, dazed, tried to move, but her body lagged behind her mind. Maia ran to her, seized her arm, and dragged her to safety with strength that defied her frame. Néstor joined them, incredulous.

'What were you thinking!? You almost got yourself killed!' Maia exclaimed—furious, but also clearly shaken.

Naran, without replying, turned her head towards the road. She searched for something, any trace of the llama or of the woman, but everything had disappeared. The mountains, the vivid colours, even the sense of wholeness she had experienced —all had completely faded away. Only the cold grey of the city and the oppressive noise of the engines remained.

'Are you okay?' Néstor asked, his voice soft with concern.

'Yes…' she whispered, though she wasn't sure it was true. The enigma pulsed in her chest, spinning like a persistent echo.

Maia, still pale, steadied herself and adjusted her backpack.

'We have to keep going. We can't stay here.' She tried to sound calm, but her trembling hands betrayed her.

Naran nodded slowly. But her thoughts were still anchored in the vision. Was it a dream? A hallucination? Something in her said no. Whatever it was, it had marked her.

As they walked, the experience replayed in her mind. Time had cracked. Reality had opened. The woman's eyes, the llama's steps—they lingered. She couldn't recall the words, but she felt their weight.

Something inside her had stirred. Something long dormant.

After a long silence, Maia said, 'Whatever happened back there, let it go. Right now, the important thing is getting to Karanza.'

Naran didn't respond, but clenched her fists tightly, aware she couldn't ignore what she had seen. Though the meaning still escaped her, something within sensed that the encounter was a key—a threshold to something deeper. Her perception of time and reality had begun to crack, hinting that nothing would ever be the same.

That woman, that animal… What is happening to me? she repeated in a frantic inner dialogue. The enigma lingered like a whisper from another time, wrapping her in a journey through uncharted territories belonging to both the world and her own mind.

The teens jumped over a railing and crossed the muddy fields where several rusted train cars, once part of freight convoys, lay abandoned. The damp ground soaked their shoes and made each step difficult, but Maia, determined, stopped to point them in the right direction.

'On the platform to the right are the trains heading north, to Karanza,' she said quietly, turning to the others. 'We can circle around and reach the platform through the open field.'

Naran tried to keep up with Maia and Néstor, but her mind remained trapped in a whirlwind of images. The perceptions that had unsettled her on the road kept resurfacing, disrupting her focus and blending fragments of past and present into a confusing tangle.

'Wait a moment,' she said suddenly, stopping. There was a warning in her voice. 'A patrol is entering the station. It's heading for the next train bound for Karanza. We'll have to wait until nightfall and get on one of the freight cars.'

Néstor scoffed, his irritation unmistakable.

'Again with your visions, Naran! We don't have time for this. Let's go!' he exclaimed, pulling at his sister's arm to keep moving.

But Maia's face changed instantly. Concern made her stop.

'What is it, Naran? What did you see?'

'She didn't see anything. She just wants to slow us down,' Néstor interjected, impatience creeping into his voice. 'She's not sure she wants to come with us to Karanza and needs more time to think or to wait for her father to show up...'

'A patrol is heading for that train,' Naran warned urgently.

Maia, granting her a measure of trust, responded:

'The station is almost empty. We'll stop here for a moment and see if what you're saying is true.'

Néstor shook his head in disagreement and kept walking.

'I'm tired. I need to get on that damn train. If you don't come with me now, I'll see you in Karanza.'

'Wait,' Maia warned, pointing to the patrol that had just entered the station. 'Naran's right... we'll wait until nightfall.'

They passed the time eating in silence until Néstor broke it, taking advantage of his sister stepping ahead to see if the way was clear.

'I would have preferred to stay connected to MIO instead of having to go to Karanza, but...'

Naran looked at him intently, wondering about the source of his discontent.

'It's because they used to disconnect us from the program when...'

'What do you mean? You mean you couldn't connect?' she interrupted hastily, not wanting to show her concern and fear about the subject.

'You know, when you're inside the system...' Néstor moved closer to her and almost whispered, as if he didn't want anyone else to hear. 'We have certain skills for inserting information. That's why they ended up cancelling our access to the program, calling us Incompatible.'

'Incompatible... that cursed word,' Naran exclaimed.

'I want to keep trying,' he clarified, 'so I don't have to think about this anymore, at least for a while.' He pulled up his pant leg, showing her his prosthetic. 'Lately it bothers me when I walk,' he continued, 'and it's a limitation. But inside the program, I felt, in a way, free.' He made a gesture of frustration as he adjusted the prosthetic straps. 'First, I want to take my sister to Karanza, but after that I'd connect to the system... with conditions.'

Naran felt surprised by Néstor's openness about his incompatibility. He leaned even closer to her and whispered softly:

'And what skills did you have inside the program?' he asked. 'I imagine you didn't follow the rules either.'

Naran was confused by his words. She longed to piece together her experience within the program, but her memories surfaced vaguely and distantly, as if they had been lost in some corner of her mind. Her frustration grew and, in silence, she admired Néstor and his ability to show himself as he was. *He can speak freely, while I strive to fit in, hiding what makes me different, hiding my limitation*, she reflected. Her thoughts consumed her, prolonging her answer once again.

'I don't have any...' she finally answered, as if trying to protect herself.

Néstor held his penetrating gaze on the girl's fearful eyes, and his thin face was sharpened by an ironic smile.

'After freezing up in the middle of the road, I thought you had escaped from one of those places where they lock up those who don't fit in.' His words slid out slowly. 'But I know...' He paused briefly. 'I know you're scared, I know you want to be compatible, and it's very unfair that they've labelled us with that damned word, as you say.' He moved closer slowly, trying to earn her trust. 'We're in the same situation, Naran, and we need to connect to that program. During the hibernation period, it's MIO that determines reality, and we don't want to be isolated from it. But we also have the right to set our own conditions...'

Néstor stood with a slight jump and stretched his numb body, continuing to move and speak as if he were playing a role that, this time, was no longer secondary. Without his sister in front of him, he seemed more relaxed and decisive.

'That's why you were in a youth centre, because of incompatibility, and therefore, you also have certain abilities within the system.'

Néstor nodded as he pulled out a crumpled piece of paper.

'We decided to escape because someone gave us this message, distributed by Karanza.'

Her eyes showed the impact the information had on her.

'Do you really want to know what's going on?' Néstor continued, looking at her with a hint of irony and superiority.

Naran nodded. Despite her indecision, she needed to clarify the whole situation somehow. And Néstor began to read until his sister approached, and he quickly tucked the note into his pocket. The boy's words penetrated her mind and sparked an internal struggle that left her speechless. Before she could respond, Maia returned with urgent news.

'The patrol is already pulling out,' she announced, pointing towards the open field. 'We have to move now. There's a freight train leaving in a few minutes.'

The three moved quickly and quietly, but soon noticed a new danger: a pack of dogs began barking in the distance, their eyes glowing intensely as they approached. Torches switched on behind them, and the voices of their pursuers filled the air.

'Crouch down and follow me!' Naran ordered, her voice firm and determined.

Through the darkness, the young woman spotted a gap in the fence and, without stopping, slipped through the narrow space, followed by Maia. When Néstor tried to pass, his prosthesis got stuck and one of the dogs leapt at him, sinking its teeth into his prosthetic.

'Help!' Néstor shouted, struggling to free himself.

Maia pulled her brother with all her strength as Naran ran towards them. With combined effort, they managed to free the prosthetic from the fence and close the gap before the dogs could get through. Exhausted but driven by fear, they sprinted across the open ground until they reached a freight car that was about to depart. When they finally managed to climb onto the train, all three collapsed onto the floor of the car, panting and drenched in sweat. As the train began to move, a sigh of relief washed over them. For the first time in hours, they felt they had a small advantage.

Naran, however, remained silent, watching the landscape rush past through the slats of the car. Her thoughts returned again and again to Néstor's words: though she couldn't clearly remember, part of her knew there was something in her past she still didn't understand, something that connected her both to the siblings and to the mysterious presence she had seen on the road.

As the train advanced towards Karanza, the young woman closed her eyes and allowed herself, for the first time in a long time, to slip into a state of reverie that enveloped her like a refuge.

Naran was only seven years old when her imagination and curiosity began to manifest in astonishing ways. Her mother would watch her playing alone in her room, laughing enthusiastically and speaking out loud as if she were accompanied by someone invisible. There were moments when the girl's behaviour changed radically: she would become completely still, her gaze fixed on the wall or the window, as if in a trance. Despite her young age, she could remain in that position for long periods. In those moments, her mother approached cautiously, because even though Naran was physically present, it felt as if her daughter was travelling somewhere distant, perceiving something beyond the visible. Sometimes, it seemed as if she could see an entire universe reflected in her daughter's pupils—a world she herself had left behind as an adult. When Naran returned from those contemplative states, she would share stories that made her mother understand she had inherited her grandfather's gift: her voice could weave tales as if threading colourful strands on a loom. She tried to capture those moments in drawings as well; however, her sketches were a chaotic mess of shapes defying interpretation—figures that might be horses, deer, or something different.

One afternoon, because of the intensity of these experiences, her mother decided to share her concerns with Alan. He was seated in the living room, reviewing his research notes, when his partner, Unay, approached him.

'Naran's been in one of those states for almost two hours today,' she began, her voice carrying a mix of awe and concern. 'I sat beside her without disturbing her, and when she came back, she spoke of animals and people she'd been with. She even mentioned, for the second time, a woman named Illa. She drew her and an animal she plays with. It's such an unusual name… I doubt she's heard it here.'

'I think all children have fantasy worlds and imaginary friends. It's part of development, a natural stage of growth and exploring creativity,' Alan replied, not looking up from his notes, speaking with calm, almost indifference.

She watched him for a moment before responding. Her dark eyes, an inheritance from the mountainous lands of the Outer Reserves, shone with a mix of tenderness and resolve.

'Alan, yes, it's imagination, but it's also something more. I know what's happening because it's part of me too: she's Dreaming while awake.' Her voice was soft, but each word carried weight. 'In my community, we were always taught that Dreaming isn't just play; it's a way to connect with parts of ourselves beyond time and space.'

Alan finally looked up, his sceptical and calculating gaze meeting Unay's. He closed the notes in his hands and leaned back in his chair.

'I know you grew up surrounded by those traditions, and I'm glad Naran grows up with that legacy, but we also can't let her get lost in these... experiences. She could disconnect from reality.'

His words hung heavy in the air. Naran's mother took a deep breath, trying not to let frustration take over.

'Disconnected from reality? What reality are you talking about? We're not isolated fragments; we're part of a weave. She feels it, and instead of ignoring it, I'm going to help her to understand it.'

Alan frowned and crossed his arms.

'What you call a weave, I call imagination. And I don't deny it's powerful, but it can also be dangerous if left unchecked.'

Unay stepped closer to him, her gaze full of determination. She felt certain that Naran wasn't imagining... she was remembering.

'Are those worlds as real as this one? My father used to say that time isn't linear, that realities intertwine like threads in a weave. And Naran is seeing it, Alan. I don't know how to explain it in a way you'll understand, but I know she's living it. And if we don't support her now, she might close that door.'

Alan remained silent, his expression undecided. Though her words hadn't convinced him, he could feel the passion and certainty in Unay's voice. There was something in her conviction that was hard to refute.

Still drowsy, Naran gazed at the image of the strange creature that had appeared before her. Something stirred within—a distant, half-buried memory whispering that it was the same animal she used to draw as a child. The train lurched abruptly as it changed tracks, jolting her from her reverie.

She sensed the lines of the past weaving into the present, giving way to new directions, a constant and unexpected flow of events. The images resonated in her mind like echoes from a distant place, and for a moment, she wondered what was truly happening to her.

'Mother, I miss you,' she murmured softly, lost in her thoughts.

These images…perhaps they are the way you return to me, through that animal, through this reality now emerging…

Suddenly, the train decelerated sharply, and the screech of the brakes shattered the heavy silence, filling the car with a deafening noise. The sound pulled her back to the present moment. *I need to focus on my immediate reality*, she thought, shaking her head, trying to shake off the thoughts. She couldn't afford to drift off; as her father used to say, she needed to survive.

'This can't be happening now!' Maia exclaimed in desperation, watching as a security patrol positioned itself on the tracks, halting the train.

Maia shook Naran's and Néstor's shoulders, pulling them out of their drowsiness.

'They're inspecting the train; we need to get off now. We'll walk the last few kilometres to Karanza.'

Naran watched apprehensively as several security officers climbed onto a couple of cars, dangerously close to theirs. Then, fleeting images crossed her mind, flashes of possible paths unfolding before her eyes. An intense tension sharpened her perception and, while she tried to decipher these visions, Maia pushed them towards the door of the carriage. Without warning, the three of them fell roughly to the ground, rolling over gravel and mud. They barely had time to get up before the train resumed its journey, and their hope of going unnoticed quickly vanished; a patrol spotted them, and the voices of the agents echoed in the air, ordering them to stop.

'Run!' shouted Maia, taking the lead.

Néstor led the group, guiding them through the underbrush flanking the tracks. The three ran with all their strength, zigzagging between shrubs and fallen trees as the sound of a police vehicle and barking dogs followed close behind. Amid the chase, they spotted a rusty sign that read: Karanza, 1 km. A spark of hope ignited in their hearts: they were close. The wind, heavy with the scent of damp earth, seemed to whisper that the end of their journey was within reach. Yet the pursuit did not relent.

Drones hovered overhead, adding tension to the chaos. And from a distance, they could make out the rusted towers of an old factory marking Karanza's entrance. Maia pointed with a shout:

'There's the wall! Just a few more metres!'

Naran was exhausted but the urgency drove her on. She felt the world begin to warp. Multiple realities seemed to overlap; the known world mingling with others that seemed to surface from deep inside her.

As she ran, two paths emerged. In one, a wall of shadow rose ahead, and she perceived in the distance the figures of an animal and a woman who seemed to be calling her. In the second, she raced towards Karanza, but a police van blocked her path

'No, not now!' she cried out in confusion, feeling her perception split between these two realities.

Then, the two worlds merged into a sudden clarity, if she could overcome the obstacles ahead, other realities would be within reach. In the subtle world, she managed to cross through the wall of shadows threatening her. At the end of the path, she saw the animal and the woman, whose figure radiated a profound calm. The woman looked at her intently and, in a whisper that seemed to come from the mountains themselves, spoke her name:

'Naran.'

With a start, the young woman began to remember.

'Illa.'

Back in tangible reality, a security agent caught up with her and, after a struggle, managed to seize her. Naran's consciousness refocused once more on the few metres separating her from the village, on the words that had accompanied her throughout the journey, spoken by that strange vagabond: *Karanza may be our only hope.* For a moment, all the effort of the past days seemed to have been in vain. Yet, without fully realising it, she had managed to cross the most difficult of all barriers, the one that separated her from herself and from the world concealed beyond her fears, beyond her shadows.

Maia and Néstor were also intercepted, pinned against the hood of the van. An officer ran a scanner over Néstor's back, frowning at the results.

'Both are outside the normal frequency range,' he murmured, consulting with his partner.

When it was Naran's turn, the device vibrated differently. The agent looked at the screen, visibly puzzled.

'And with her... the deviation range is even greater,' he said, almost as if he couldn't believe it.

'Are you sure?' asked another officer. 'Run the scan again.'

They repeated the procedure, confirming the results. The agents exchanged tense glances before contacting the base for instructions.

Naran, Maia, and Néstor were forced into the police van. Maia protested loudly, while Néstor, defeated, simply lowered his gaze. Naran watched everything with a mix of anger and resignation, in silence; she felt once again marked for being different.

The van started and drove them away from Karanza's wall. As the landscape blurred quickly behind the windows, Naran closed her eyes: the image of Illa and the animal remained alive in her mind, like a persistent flame that refused to die. A chill ran through her body upon hearing that their destination was the Research Centre; a sense of helplessness and defeat overtook her, casting a shadow over her thoughts. *What if I fail in my last chance to connect?* The question reverberated inside her, repeating like a persistent murmur. *Why do I keep spinning around the same circle over and over?* It felt as though the whole world stood against her every time she dared to step forward. As the van rolled on, she sat in silence, trying to make sense of the chaos. She could not rid herself of the sense that something remained concealed.

KNOT II

THE MIRROR AND
THE THREAD

'Wait a moment, Alan,' a voice echoed from the hallway of the Research Centre.

He turned his head and offered a brief greeting, but continued walking in haste. Margot, the project coordinator, quickly caught up with him and regarded him with her usual severity, a blend of authority and urgency that seemed to have intensified in recent days.

'We were worried, we've been looking for you for hours. The sponsors and directors are waiting in the boardroom.'

'I'm picking up some documents from my office, then I'll join you.'

'I'll go with you, there's no time.' Her tone left no room for argument.

They walked in silence, keeping a certain distance, but the atmosphere between them was tense. Margot, with her rigid posture, asserted her authority even in her stride. Though accustomed to the rigorous demands of the project, her expression betrayed the weight of accumulated pressure.

'Look, Alan,' Margot continued as they walked, 'the sponsors have arrived. Therefore, we'll focus on the results and their practical application, no detours. Today we need to be concise.'

Alan nodded slightly, though his mind was elsewhere. His thoughts lingered on the perspective he had gained after his visit to the Outer Reserves. He knew that what he was about to present would generate discomfort, but he could no longer unquestioningly follow the project's traditional course.

When they entered the boardroom, the anticipation was palpable. More than twenty people were seated around a rectangular table, while others stood around the edges of the room. Alan didn't allow himself to pause and recognise familiar faces; in his mind, he perceived only an atmosphere charged with impatience and tension.

'First of all, I want to thank you for the trust you've placed in this project,' he began, removing his jacket with deliberately measured movements.

He tried to project serenity, though inside he was filled with doubts.

'These have been challenging weeks.'

He paused, using the images from his visit to the Outer Reserves as an emotional anchor. He took a deep breath and continued:

'I want to apologise for the setbacks with the new device. And, with humility, I can say we were wrong during Phase 1… Believing that the adolescents had a synchronisation problem with MIO, or that there was an attention deficit within the network. We placed the responsibility on them, but it was ours.'

He fixed his gaze on the representatives of the educational materials companies, ensuring he had their attention.

'In Phase 2, the adjustment and implementation of the new educational material also did not yield the expected results. This has led us in a new direction.'

Before he could elaborate further, Nur, one of the Centre's directors, interrupted him with a sharp tone:

'We expect, then, that you can confirm the implementation of Phase 3 with this segment of the population.'

Rain and wind lashed against the windows, adding a layer of tension to the atmosphere. The attendees, visibly exhausted, shifted impatiently in their seats. Alan felt the weight of expectations on his shoulders, but this time he wasn't there to satisfy them. The moment to change course had come.

'The flaw, I believe, lies within the program itself,' he declared firmly. 'The MIO system cannot comprehend the neuroplasticity of this group of adolescents. Labelling them as Incompatibles was, in truth, a mistake—for it is through them that we are now uncovering the limitations embedded in the system's own algorithms. Rather than being the problem, they are the challenge that reveals the way forward.'

The door to the room suddenly opened, and Elías entered with a discreet greeting. His presence immediately altered the atmosphere. Alan returned the gesture, thanking him with a glance full of recognition and gratitude.

'I'd like to introduce Elías, an anthropologist from the Outer Reserves,' he announced. 'His perspective and the wisdom of these communities can offer us integrative approaches for Phase 3.'

Elías, with his serene demeanour and measured voice, thanked them for the opportunity to collaborate.

'I believe this project has the potential to become a synergy,' he began, 'a bridge between technological knowledge and ancestral *cosmovisions*. We can no longer ignore the richness of human diversity. The Incompatibles are not a failure but a wake-up call about what we need to integrate.'

Though he knew he had stirred discomfort, Alan felt he had opened a door, and all that remained was to wait for reactions and prepare the next move. After what he had come to understand in the Outer Reserves, the project had to pivot so that the Incompatibles would no longer be seen as the problem, but as the possibility.

A reddish twilight split the horizon. Alan was leaving behind the coast of the central sectors, a world that had forgotten the simplicity of the tides and the circular flow of life.

In the Outer Reserves, time was not measured by clocks or digital calendars, but by the shadows cast by the sun on the *Intiwatas* and the cycle of the stars. There, the elders taught that technology was merely an echo of knowledge already existing in the weave of the universe, like the patterns of Aztec codices or the Incan *huacas* that still resonated in the mountains. In contrast to the central sectors, where everything had to be measured and controlled, the reserves lived by the principle that everything was interconnected, like an invisible network linking all living beings.

The boat approached the dock quietly as a pair of seagulls cut through the dawn with their cries. He watched the choreography of the waves, waiting for them to recede so he could disembark. From a distance, Elías observed Alan—a researcher of distant realities—stepping awkwardly, trying to avoid the foam that was already washing away his footprints.

Alan felt the tension of the journey dissipate as soon as he set foot on those lands. He had crossed from the artificiality of Sector B to the rawness of the Outer Reserves, seeking respite and the refuge of his people's wisdom. He left behind his fatigue and, with it, the weight of centralised control.

He quickly found relief in seeing how the different communities resisted the dominance of the sectors. Despite rising sea levels, glaciation, and the dangers all this entailed, these communities refused to relocate.

Among them was Elías, an anthropologist deeply rooted in his people, resisting both climate collapse and political encroachment.

But above all, he was a grandfather to his people, a guardian of his people's ancestral wisdom.

'Welcome, Alan,' Elías greeted him with a slight nod, but with warmth in his voice. 'Thank you for building this bridge of understanding. And I am very sorry for the loss of Unay.'

Elías' deep tone resonated within Alan. The mention of his deceased partner stirred emotions he had tried to suppress. Unay, with her ancestral bond to these lands, had always spoken to him of the vital force that dwelled within the reserves.

'Thank you, Elías. This place has always been special to me. Now, more than ever, I feel the need to understand it better.'

'I'm glad your old paradigm didn't give you the answers you were searching for—and that it led you here. Sometimes, it takes chaos to discover something new.'

Elías met his gaze steadily. He seemed to be connecting with something deeper than the project that had brought Alan there.

'Alan, in the Outer Reserves we have not allowed the waters that submerged the world to carry away our roots. After the flood, when most countries disappeared, many thought our stories, our narratives, our cosmovisions would vanish as well. But that wasn't the case. We gathered here, in these reserves, not merely as survivors, but as guardians of something far deeper… Our texts and the stories of our communities remain alive among us.'

As he spoke, Alan recalled Elías's controversial articles, those that openly challenged the MIO program and its implications. The Outer Reserves, along with Karanza, had become a beacon of resistance, a place where the Incompatibles and dissidents found refuge and purpose. This trip was not just an academic visit, it was an act of reconciliation with Unay's roots, with her legacy, and with the questions he himself had avoided answering.

Elías walked slowly as they passed a group of women weaving colourful fabrics. He nodded, inviting his new companion to walk along a path lined with trees. As they advanced, Alan couldn't help but notice the vitality of the place: women weaving under the shade, children playing and filling the air with laughter, elders gathered in circles, sharing stories. Life flowed there without the haste or shadows of the central sectors.

'What you see here is not just resistance,' Elías said, breaking the silence. 'Across the various reserves we have woven a crucible of knowledge. It doesn't matter whether different communities or *Ayllus* call it *assemblage point*, *Nagual*, *Teotl*, *Dreaming*, or even *Ayni*.' He paused for a moment and observed the geometric patterns of the weavings. As you can see, Alan, this is not just an interlacing of abstract ideas. Here we weave community, we raise our Ayllu. We thread our differences together, creating a fabric that unites us and strengthens us against any narrative that seeks to confine us.'

His companion contemplated the weavings with new eyes. For the first time, he understood they weren't merely decorative, they were living stories, a way of narrating and preserving the essential. *She used to speak to me about this weaving, but I didn't understand… until now.* He watched the children playing, the adults laughing and conversing. Unlike the climate of anxiety and rush in the central sectors, there seemed to be no fear of glaciation here. Then, with sadness, he realised that unlike the technocratic model, where control restricts, here the social fabric connects. Where fear reigned, here trust guides.

Elías sensed the weight in Alan's eyes, stopped, and looked at him gravely.

'By coming here, to the Outer Reserves, you are interlacing something too, Alan. You are seeking to integrate cosmovisions, to understand our ways of seeing and inhabiting time. You are opening doors that closed long ago. This act of union is not just for the Incompatibles. It is an act for everyone. Because only by weaving our stories together can we find new answers to MIO… and to the reality imposed upon us.'

He pointed to the sky visible through the trees.

'We teach our people that the cosmos is an infinite fabric. Each one of us is a node.

Each story, a thread.

And now, Alan… You are part of this weaving. And together we can make even MIO tremble before that which we can create.'

Finally, he led him towards the slope of a cliff. The light of sunset played with the shadows, creating shapes that seemed to move with a life of their own.

'We must climb these stones. We're heading towards a cave. This is not just a place, Alan, it is a resonance. You are about to see something that will change the way you perceive reality. But remember, what matters is not what you understand, but what you choose to do with it.'

His companion nodded. A weight on his chest, but also the certainty that this step was necessary.

Alan refocused his attention on the room, carrying with him the way of seeing he had embraced in the Outer Reserves.

'As I was saying, it's a flaw in the system.'

He looked again at all the representatives gathered there with the directors. The atmosphere in the room was tense, a mixture of curiosity and rejection. He knew this meeting at the Centre would be difficult, but also essential—a crucial moment to propose an alternative approach to the latest update of the MIO system.

He pulled a scanner from a box beside him, and Margot, the project coordinator, volunteered for the demonstration. As Alan moved the device over her back, he pointed out the shoulder blades.

'This particular point is key,' he said as the data began to project onto a screen. His voice was calm but firm. 'Here is where a connection to a subtler reality occurs. Through this connection, millions of data points pass through us continuously, but we can only encode a fraction of them. This information is interpreted according to our perceptual point and ultimately projected as the reality we experience.'

The attendees watched the screen with a mix of astonishment and scepticism. Alan continued, anticipating the doubts that would arise.

'When users connect to MIO, the system captures their attention and fixes this perceptual point. That means they can only interpret reality according to the data the system provides. However, the so-called Incompatibles are different. Even when connected, their perception remains fluid and open to broader bands of information.'

Alan took a step back, letting his words settle in the room. Elías took the floor with the serenity that characterised him, measuring each phrase to give it the necessary weight.

'That group of the population labelled as Incompatibles possesses a special ability within the system.' He paused, letting the words sink in.' They not only perceive more, thanks to the fluidity of their perceptual point, but are also able to project this information into the network.'

A murmur spread like a wave through the room. While some attendees exchanged incredulous looks, the corporate representatives seemed increasingly tense. Alan raised a hand, asking for calm.

'I understand your doubts,' he said resolutely, 'but this explains why they are disconnected. The Incompatibles can expand perception within MIO, and this is not a flaw. It is an opportunity for the whole system.'

The atmosphere grew more hostile when one of the attendees slammed a glass down on the table. Alan drew a deep breath, trying not to lose his focus.

'We propose that instead of using this device to homogenise the entire population under a single pattern, we respect the specific abilities of this group. We believe that, during the hibernation period, the Incompatibles could perceive new solutions within the network. We have been trapped in a loop for years; they might bring the possibility we have yet to see.' With those words, he uncovered the virtual immersion helmet developed with his team. 'This device would allow the Incompatibles to interact with MIO without being treated as interference or error.'

Voices began to rise again, this time with more intensity. While some argued about the risks of this approach, others defended the need to explore alternatives. Finally, one of the corporate directors stood up abruptly.

'We have already approved changes in the educational program for these youths; there is no room to implement another approach at this stage. Negotiations are closed.'

Nina, a representative of the tech companies, added with an ironic smile:

'The perspective of the Outer Reserves is not suitable for this project. The idea of living in another layer of reality, as described in your studies, is just as limited as the system you criticise.'

Elías, with his usual calm, replied:

'It's easy to judge what one does not understand. I'm not here for you to label the Outer Reserves as 'the others,' but to offer an integration of perspectives—so this project doesn't become a process of socialisation, a game of winners and losers. If we can set all that aside, we have the opportunity to create a new game, where the only essential thing—the only thing that truly matters—is the growth of consciousness.'

Alan, discouraged, glanced away from the table and thought of the cave paintings he had seen in the Outer Reserves. Elías had told him they represented a struggle of perceptions, of competing realities. He recognised, with dismay, a similar struggle taking place around him, one with stakes that would determine their future.

The first time Naran saw Ikan was when she arrived at the Research Centre. The room was filled with young people: some sank into resignation, while others shifted restlessly in their seats, their eyes fixed in fear. The air was heavy with the weight of expectations placed upon this group of Incompatibles. With a sigh, she felt the pressure in her chest, realising where she was: trapped alongside Néstor and Maia in an experimental facility. It resembled less an educational centre than a labyrinth of uncertainties.

Amidst it all, Ikan stood out. His relaxed yet untameable presence contrasted sharply with the anxious unease of the others. He seemed to belong to another world, perhaps to the Outer Reserves, where freedom and connection with nature still endured.

After the initial shock of her arrival, Naran sat at a table, opened her notebook, and began to draw. Immersed in the movement of her hand, she sought to disconnect from the hostile atmosphere. Each stroke was not only an act of concentration but also a quiet defiance against the order that confined her.

Ikan watched her with curiosity.

'For this place, such a thing already feels a little anachronistic,' he said, breaking through the room's taut, nervous silence.

The young woman half-closed her eyes and fixed them on him. Although his dark hair concealed part of his face, his presence overflowed the room, as if he still carried with him the breath of nature. There was something about him that did not belong to that Centre. He lingered… like someone who had never fully left the mountains.

Their eyes met.

A barely perceptible tremor ran through Naran. Images began to well up in her mind: a cave, a distant drum, a voice that was not her own… and yet it called to her. As though, in looking at him, he had returned to her a forgotten part of herself.

And for an instant, she understood: Ikan was not merely a stranger.

He was a mirror.

A reflection of possibilities.

A bridge towards the subtle.

But the void that opened upon feeling it was too much. Faced with that fissure in her perception, she sought refuge in the familiar. She returned to her walls, her lines, the drawing she could still control.

With a sweep of the room, she confirmed that nothing had changed. *Why were they being kept waiting so long?*

There were around thirty teenagers. Some conversed coldly; most bore on their faces the desperation and gloom that spoke for them. Naran wondered if they had had an experience similar to hers, if they too had felt so misunderstood.

Did they all know we are here because of the new update? That this might be the last chance for the Incompatibles to access the program? What will they do with us if we fail? Keep us asleep through hibernation?

She clicked her tongue and looked for Néstor and Maia, clinging to something familiar. *We can still escape to Karanza.* The thought made her shudder: she remembered the trials she had already overcome, and those still awaiting her.

Ikan perceived her turmoil. He knew how the system tried to mould them, how each one fought against the inward parts of them that had not been accepted.

'It's not the first time a social system has failed to value what a teenager can offer,' he said aloud. 'In MIO we are not what we are, but what others want us to be. In the system, there is no option of rebellion; our identity will be defined by algorithms, trapped in an artificial structure.'

The image of being imprisoned by the program crossed Naran's mind. Fear made her shrink, and she looked at him in irritation.

'The inability to connect is what makes us alike,' Ikan whispered. 'And what may set us apart, perhaps, is the fear of accepting what we are.'

Something awoke in her, though she kept her eyes lowered.

'What do you propose, then?' she asked timidly, unwilling to enter into confrontation.

Ikan observed her from a certain distance, with a mixture of curiosity and pride. There was something in her, yet her constant refusal to accept her own shadow kept her trapped in a limited perception. He knew it. His earlier words were true: she no longer remembered who she truly was.

He had infiltrated the group of Incompatibles with the hope that, together, they might prevent MIO's artificial line from destroying the other connections. But frustration overwhelmed him as he saw them bound to a linear vision of time. None had learnt to still the mind enough to perceive the other time. The system had branded them with a single word: Incompatibles. And that label had ended up defining them, conditioning their thoughts and actions.

Naran felt Ikan's critical gaze, but instead of facing that abyss, she took refuge in her drawing. The pencil outlined an animal she had seen in Karanza, a being that carried a meaning deeper than she herself could grasp.

Ikan stepped closer and looked at the notebook. On seeing it, he wondered whether Nuna's and his help during the Dreaming had enabled Naran to reach other lines.

'Where have you seen that animal?' he asked.

Naran hesitated. She did not want to expose herself before a stranger. She lowered her eyes to the drawing, denying what she had glimpsed in her visions. *None of that matters anymore,* she told herself. She only wanted to remain unnoticed, to leave that Centre behind, to escape the nonsense.

'It's just a drawing,' she replied, her voice uncertain.

Ikan had expected that answer. No matter how much they helped her, she still refused to open up to other ways of perceiving. Everything had been in vain, he thought. He laughed inwardly, asking himself: *What was he meant to learn from her? What was he supposed to accept from this reality that she still rejected?*

'Very well, keep drawing that llama,' he said with a sigh, as he stepped away.

The word struck her.

Her hand moved of its own accord, tracing the outline of a llama.

With that simple stroke, the boy's world collided with hers, opening a new perspective. Her finger moved slowly along the sketch and she understood that she could do the same with her memories. Just as she had shaped the lines into a defined figure, perhaps she could apply that same retrospective lens to her own life.

She lifted her eyes and met the boy's deep gaze. For an instant, she felt his eyes stretch beyond the present, slipping into another time. If she could learn to walk backwards, she might join the dots that had brought her to that very moment. To see every fragment of her story, the turns that had drawn her destiny, and begin again at the origin.

If she could glimpse the whole picture, perhaps a single corrected stroke would be enough to redefine it all. Then her present might open, free itself from confinement and lead her towards the possibility of finding her father, and even herself.

She did not know whether that inquiry was only another trap to escape the confinement of the Centre, but she hardly cared. Her mind travelled in every direction, trying to reconstruct the events. Something eluded her—she sensed it. In that enigmatic puzzle, scattered pieces awaited to be joined. If she could succeed in linking them, new possibilities would emerge on her path. Perhaps in this way she might break the destiny others had drawn for her and free herself from the strokes that kept her prisoner.

Among all the flashes evoked in her memory, she chose to linger on one. And then the images surged with the force of an overflowing current:

A cave.

A distant drum.

A community gathered around the fire.

And there he was. The boy with wild eyes who now stood before her. He was there, seated close to her.

A faint pulse ran through her body. A formless certainty, scarcely a whisper, as though something—or someone—was trying to break through her thoughts. But it was not the moment: the hall was still full of teenagers trapped in their silences. Naran, with the pencil still in her hand, took refuge again in the strokes, convinced she was not yet ready to see what was being asked of her.

Close by, Ikan watched her in silence.
She does not open her hand.
She does not release the stroke.
She does not see the lines.
Yet the first thread has been laid—still unnamed, but already woven.

A metallic clang burst from the loudspeakers, followed by a monotonous voice ordering the youths to go to their rooms. The sound tore through the haze in which Naran had been immersed, pulling her out of her daydream. The sensation of being trapped between two realities left her disoriented. She blinked, looked around… but Ikan was gone. His absence was a tangible void.

For a moment, she thought that everything she had experienced had been a dream, a manifestation of exhaustion and the chaos ruling her mind. Doubt followed her as she made her way to her room, dragging her feet as though the weight of what she had seen had materialised in her body.

Upon entering, the first thing she noticed was the narrowness of the space: grey walls that seemed to close in on her and a dim artificial light that barely softened the coldness of the place. And yet, there was something comforting in the solitude that little room offered.

At least here I can rest, she told herself, dropping her few belongings onto a metal table in the corner.

She lay down on the bed with a deep sigh, feeling fatigue spread through every fibre of her being. She closed her eyes, but her mind did not quiet. The storm of thoughts and memories kept her awake. Her hands instinctively searched for the notebook she had taken with her.

She held it up, letting her eyes follow the lines that seemed to carry their own life. It was more than a sketch: it was a map of decisions, of the points that had brought her here.

A sudden flash crossed her mind. The image of her father emerged from the shadows like a fragment lost from a dream.

Where are you now? she thought, with a mixture of longing and despair.

The question lingered inside her, amplifying the emptiness that had accompanied her since she had lost contact with him. She closed her eyes again, pressing the drawing to her chest as if, by doing so, she could reach him across time and distance.

At last, exhaustion overtook her and dragged her into a restless sleep. Yet even in sleep, the lines of the drawing seemed to shift in her mind, weaving the scattered fragments of her past in search of an answer she was not yet ready to grasp.

KNOT III

THE FRACTURE OF THE CENTRE

Alan followed Elías, who, despite his age, moved with surprising agility. The old man leapt from rock to rock with ease, while Alan, more hesitant, struggled to keep pace. The sweet aroma of plants mingled with the salt of the churning sea, and for a moment, Alan allowed himself to disconnect from his relentless inner dialogue. He saw, astonished, how the lush vegetation of the cliff seemed to defy the harshness of the environment. That contact with nature, so strange to him, rekindled a spark of wonder he hadn't felt in years. However, that sensation quickly faded, and his mind sank back into its usual worries. *Will this flora and fauna survive the imminent glaciation?* he thought as his gaze wandered across the landscape.

The anthropologist pointed to a rocky formation rising ahead, and they had to climb over slippery boulders to reach the entrance of a cave. As Alan crossed the threshold into the gloom of the hollow, he left behind the outer light—and with it, part of his certainties. Once inside, a young man awaited them with a pair of flashlights. Elías briefly introduced the boy, and together they began advancing through a narrow passage. The roar of the sea filtered through the cracks in the rocks, and small streams of water dripped inside, intensifying the sense of otherworldliness that clung to the corridor.

Finally, the passage opened into a wide, circular space. Beams of light seeped through the upper cracks, faintly illuminating the interior. Elías lit a few oil lamps, and Alan, exhausted, leaned against one of the walls. From there, he could appreciate the singular beauty of the place: an internal lake reflected the glimmers of light, while hanging vegetation added an almost otherworldly atmosphere. In the centre, a flat stone area held the remnants of a bonfire, evidence that the space was used for gatherings.

Elías pointed to one of the walls. Alan approached, intrigued, and discovered inscriptions and paintings depicting human figures surrounded by lines radiating from their bodies. The images seemed to vibrate with a meaning that escaped conventional logic.

'What do these figures mean?' Alan asked, striving to understand.

Elías traced the inscriptions with his hand, following the shapes upwards.

'They might be showing different times, perceptions, bands of information… possibilities each person can connect to.' His voice was serene, as if speaking from ancestral knowledge. 'Look at these lines,' he continued, pointing to a thick band branching into various strokes. 'These connections represent perceptual routes, paths leading to interconnected realities. However, notice this black stroke shaped like a serpent. It represents a shadow, a force trying to prevent us from accessing those routes.'

Alan observed the paintings in silence, trying to find the connection between those representations and the project he was working on.

'I don't understand how this is related to MIO,' he finally admitted, uncomfortable.

Elías turned towards him, his gaze heavy with meaning.

'MIO is more than a technological system. It's an artificial line—a serpent that coils around perception, limiting access to other realities. It traps us in a dream, in a unique and rigid reality.'

Alan felt the cave walls closing in on him. The weight of Elías's words added to the pressure he had been enduring for months. He thought of Naran, of the Incompatibles, and of the responsibility that weighed upon him; and a wave of anxiety overtook him. For a moment, he wished he were back in the central sectors.

'I don't know what you mean,' he faltered, trying to process what he was hearing. 'I think it's better if we go back.'

Elías interrupted him with a direct question:

'What do you think MIO is, if not a mechanism to fix the assemblage point of the population?' His tone was direct but not accusatory.

Alan began to feel dizzy, as if Elías's words unearthed fears he had been repressing. Before Alan could react, Elías struck him sharply on the shoulder blade. The force of the blow destabilised him, and Alan collapsed to the ground.

When he raised his head to protest, he realised everything had changed.

After a long silence, Elías's voice filled the room, bringing everyone back to the purpose of the meeting:

'I remind you of the weight of your power and your responsibility in this game: you have the ability to direct and control the attention of users, and with this program, you control the perception of the entire population.'

Alan, silent until then, noticed the intensity in Elías's eyes. Though he hadn't planned to speak about Sector A, the anthropologist's desperation pushed him to act.

'Our proposal might not only be a solution for the Incompatibles but for the entire population.' Alan paused, aware he was about to reveal information that was not yet public. 'We know what's happening in Sector A: the MIO system is generating serious mental health problems. Therefore, this is not just a technological issue… it is a corporate and governmental responsibility to protect the health of the users.'

The announcement sparked a wave of murmurs and whispers among the attendees, many of whom struggled to process what they had just heard.

'In our ordinary lives, when we reach our twenties, existence stops feeling new,' Elías intervened with a calm yet heavy voice. 'The mechanisms that govern society—work, health, family—become routine. The point of perception or assemblage point becomes fixed, and with it, our life becomes mechanised.'

He resumed quickly before being interrupted:

'MIO is designed to overstimulate cognition; it creates dependency and consumes users' attention. In ordinary life, it takes twenty years for our point of perception to become fixed. Within MIO, we've recorded it happening in just months—even weeks. The constant information overload accelerates this process, locking perception prematurely and causing an alarming rise in mental illnesses.'

Alan exhaled deeply, as if shedding a burden long held.

'Our proposal is not a threat; it is an opportunity. The Incompatibles have a unique capacity: their perceptual point is not rigidly fixed, which allows them to perceive beyond the system's limitations. If we give them a controlled margin, they could help us introduce new perspectives that the system would otherwise never consider.'

One of the representatives stood up, trying to be heard over the murmurs.

'Are you suggesting they be allowed to introduce new data? That's already implemented; they can program within certain limits.'

'I'm not referring to that.' Alan looked at him with determination. 'I'm talking about going further, about allowing them to introduce information outside of the existing program. No more than 5%.'

The atmosphere grew tense, and Jitesh, one of the most influential executives, tried to close the debate:

'Alan, let's allow the latest update to proceed as planned. The Incompatibles will be able to connect but without the ability to modify the system. We can't risk that 5% causing chaos.'

Alan muttered to himself, recalling Elías's words:

'Without chaos, there is no creation.'

Margot spoke up to reinforce the executives' point: the risk was too great. She handed the floor to Inma, a representative of the entertainment companies.

'We have developed various gaming applications within the network. We could design a specific one for the Incompatibles, with accelerated images and information speed to capture their attention and avoid conflict.'

Margot nodded in agreement with the idea:

'The Incompatibles cannot continue to hinder Phase 3 of the project. The update will proceed as planned.'

Elías, watching as Margot and the other executives exchanged looks of mutual approval, raised his voice like a taut string:

'Governments have created reformative structures, institutions of control. They are perpetuating a ridiculous illusion—a mirage—that they hold power over the young. But the young are not the problem; they are the breach through which the real might finally return.'

His words hung in the air, but the room remained indifferent. Erik, one of the executives, stood up without a word, signalling the meeting's end.

'There is no time for experiments,' announced Nur. 'The update will be implemented in a few days to ensure all users adapt.'

Elías watched as most left the room, his words dissipating like smoke. He knew his fight was not against the people in that room but against something much larger, the artificial line that, by homogenising perception, became a repetitive and unquestionable mechanism.

Alan remained behind, motionless, as the shadows of Margot and the director receded. Their complicit glances had summarised the core of it all: power. On this gameboard, the battle was not merely technological; it was about perception itself, about controlling the reality of the population.

Elías turned to him with a serene gaze, as if seeing him beyond time.

'The fight is not about data, Alan, nor about the program.'

'Then what is it about?' he asked softly.

'About attention,' his companion replied, 'because attention is energy. And whoever controls it... controls consciousness.'

Alan remained silent. The words were not new, but this time he felt them cut through his mind and body like a sharp blow, striking the very centre of his perception. *Who decides what is real?* he thought, his gaze fixed on the screens reflecting the cold precision of Phase 3. *They see the Incompatibles as an error, something to be corrected. But perhaps they are not. Perhaps they are the only piece capable of tipping this game towards a reality without artificial horizons.*

And for the first time, instead of seeking answers, he chose to stop observing from the outside and began to look from within. His body remained there, but his consciousness did not.

The weight of his companion's words kept seeping into his mind: *the struggle is for attention… and whoever governs it, controls consciousness.*

Something had shifted within him, for he was no longer observing from the outside but from another place. Deeper. More real. As if a veil had silently torn, and what once had been interpretation now unveiled itself as living presence.

The cave of the Outer Reserves surfaced in his mind—not as a memory, but as a tremor that ran through him. He recalled the blow to his shoulder blade, how that small impact had destabilised his perceptual point, had fractured it… and had freed him.

Where before there had been only darkness and emptiness, he now saw people gathered around the fire. Among them, his daughter, Naran.

And he knew it was not a vision. It was recognition. He was not dreaming of the future. He was stepping into it.

There is another line, another time.

KNOT IV

THE LIVING MEMORY

'Come on, Naran, jump to the dock!' Unay's voice, warm and cheerful, reached her as she extended her hand. The little girl, still dizzy from the boat trip, hesitated for a moment before taking the leap.

Years had passed since their last visit to the Outer Reserves, delayed by Unay's fragile health. Her daughter, unaccustomed to the rocking of the boat, felt immediate relief when her feet touched solid ground. Several relatives awaited them with smiles and embraces, filling the air with a festive atmosphere. Naran, soon surrounded by other young ones, quickly forgot her seasickness and ran through the cobbled alleys, their laughter echoing off the stone walls until they arrived at a large square. There, the celebration of Ayni was in full swing.

An improvised stage hosted musicians playing ancestral melodies on quenas and *charangos*; women dressed in traditional attire danced to the rhythm, their colourful skirts spinning in harmony with the beat. Naran stood entranced, her eyes drinking in every detail. Exploring the stalls around the plaza, she found a group of women weaving; their skilful hands shaped complex patterns that seemed to come alive. The little girl sat beside them and watched how each stitch had purpose, how every figure—triangles, llamas, suns—told a story. *Everything is connected,* she thought, feeling a peace rarely found in the central sectors.

Later, she joined the other children at the centre of the plaza, sharing sweets and laughter. One of her aunts handed out *alfajores,* and Naran delighted in their flavours. In that moment, she felt she belonged to that place, to that community. She glanced sideways, searching for her mother, and was glad to see her laughing and chatting animatedly in a group. Yet, the shadow of her father's absence crept into her thoughts: a scientist from the central sectors who had always refused to move to the Outer Reserves. The girl felt torn between sadness and belonging until she felt her mother's hand brushing hers. Unay, as if sensing her daughter's thoughts, approached and stroked her hair.

'We'll return soon, Naran,' she whispered, her tone reflecting her own mixed feelings. Then, pointing towards the stage, she added, 'For now, enjoy. The music and poetry are about to begin.'

The soft melody of a quena filled the air and revitalised Naran's heart. Quietly, she and her friends squeezed through the crowd of adults gathered around the stage until they secured front-row seats. The young man playing the quena paused his performance to greet an elder woman. With contagious joy, the woman addressed the children:

'What shall the poetry be about?'

A timid voice whispered something about the *Apus,* while another child shouted eagerly about the condor.

The quena sounded again, this time with a nostalgic rhythm, marking the beginning of the verses:

> *On the high peaks of the Apus,*
> *where Hanan Pacha meets the skies,*
> *the sacred flight of the condor*

reveals to me the infinite horizon,
woven into an eternal tapestry.

Along the serpent's winding path,
I slide through the Uku Pacha,
finding hidden wisdom,
and the infinite cycle of rebirth.

The elder woman paused, and the young man resumed his quena playing. Then she continued, deeper, more intimately:

Ayni, sacred principle,
reciprocity in every act,
what you give returns to you.
The threads connect me to the Pachas,
weaving my steps through the Great Path.
Oh, Apus, guardians of the mountains,
protect our journey.
In Ayni we shall live in harmony
with all that I am,
in harmony with all that is.

The words lingered in the air, and Naran let herself be carried away by the images that emerged in her mind: the Apus, the condor's flight, the serpent's cycle… everything seemed to come alive within her. Suddenly, a voice from the audience exclaimed:

'Nuna, now let Ikan recite!'

Naran looked at the young man who had played the quena, and when their eyes met, he smiled before beginning his own poem.

Condor who soars through the Hanan Pacha,
guardian of the skies,

teach us to fly beyond illusion,
to break free from the perception imposed upon us.

In Ayni we find truth,
in giving and receiving, balance.
Each knot in the quipu is living memory:
what was still remains.

We are not trapped forever.
By connecting to our roots,
we weave the possibilities of what is yet to be born.
May each step reflect reciprocity,
may we recognise light within every shadow,
and in the meeting of opposites,
may the true Chawpi awaken.

When Ikan recited the last verse, Naran rose, and as their gazes met, time seemed to suspend. That crossing of eyes awakened a bond: a silent thread, a latent memory, traced in a meaning vaster than her understanding.

The sound from the loudspeakers wrenched her from her reverie and returned her to the Research Centre. As the images of the Outer Reserves faded from her mind, Naran recognised that something within her was beginning to remember, that she was reclaiming what had once belonged to her.

Margot introduced herself to the group with a calculated smile, subtly pausing after each sentence as if measuring the impact of her words. Her face attempted to project warmth, but her rigid, unmoving posture betrayed hidden tensions. Naran observed how the coordinator struggled, unsuccessfully, to capture the attention of the teenagers in the training room. Their faces reflected their lack of interest, although the air in the Centre felt dense, heavy with an invisible pressure weighing on them all. The woman stepped forward, moving closer to the group in an attempt to reaffirm her authority.

'We're running out of time,' she began, her tone firm yet measured. 'For those of you who have been here for a week, you've already received orientation on the MIO simulation program. For the newcomers, let me tell you that we're at a critical point: you must access the latest update of the device. This is the first step for Phase 3 of the project, and it's crucial that you all cooperate in the homogenisation trials—not only for the success of the simulation but also to ensure your integration into the MIO program.'

Her words hammered in Naran's head. She knew Margot was talking about them, those who had not yet submitted to the system—the Incompatibles. But her mind wandered, unable to fully process what was being imposed on them. The certainty of being inside a controlled experiment deeply unsettled her.

'Today, due to recent changes, I've decided to accompany you in person,' Margot continued, flashing her rehearsed smile once more. 'I will supervise the training sessions and coordinate everything from here. Nélida, our technician, is also with us to ensure that the perceptual unification tests are carried out optimally.'

Nélida spoke with a tone that was more approachable and precise:

'As you know, due to the extreme conditions of recent years, underground bunkers have been built so the population can hibernate and remain protected. This has ensured our survival, although we recognise it continues to be a difficult and uncertain time for each of you.'

Naran scanned the faces around her, searching for reflections of her own unease. A technician interrupted her thoughts:

'Thanks to the team's efforts, we've not only advanced with the MIO program but also reduced environmental impact by minimising energy consumption and pollution. In doing so, we hope to ease the burden on the planet and give it time to recover.'

'It's a bit late to worry about that now,' Néstor murmured sarcastically, provoking a few nervous laughs.

Naran leaned back against the wall. She understood the meeting would drag on unnecessarily, but something inside her remained alert—because they couldn't simply accept everything without question. As her thoughts tangled, she glanced to her left and saw Ikan beside her, his sharp gaze always assessing, always doubting.

'Does anyone want a chocolate ice cream?' Margot asked suddenly, changing the tone of the conversation.

The air in the room slightly relaxed. Some teenagers gave involuntary smiles, imagining the taste.

'When you heard those words, most of you visualised the ice cream; some even tasted it. Do you think we all imagined the same ice cream?'

'No,' the group murmured.

'Then, why does each of us imagine a different ice cream?' she insisted.

'Each one remembers the last they ate,' said a boy, while others added it could also be the ice cream they would like to try.

'The brain does not distinguish between what is real and what is imagined,' Margot clarified, observing them. 'The same happens in MIO: the brain believes what it experiences in the program is real. And this is a key point, because when you connect to the main system, even while hibernating, your brain will keep learning and experiencing, as if it were in reality.'

Naran felt a knot in her stomach. *Were they being trained to accept a false reality? What other choice did they have?*

Nélida, noticing their attention fading, intervened in a more conciliatory tone.

'We know MIO is not reality, but being in the network is better than the loneliness of past winters.'

Margot tried to adopt her same tone:

'The goal is for everyone to be connected. The system will update based on shared experiences; an algorithm will analyse perceptions and create a consensual vision of reality. Thus, what the majority sees will be considered valid within the program.'

'So an algorithm decides what is real?' Ikan whispered to Naran with a tone soaked in distrust.

Nélida attempted to offer a more philosophical twist.

'Reality is not outside of us, but within our thoughts, in our convictions and beliefs. When these change, so does what we perceive as real. The same happens in MIO: reality must be shared… If we all imagine the same ice cream, the system accepts it as truth.'

'And if we disagree?' Maia interjected defiantly. 'What will happen if we accept that reality? Will we lose our individual perception? And after the glaciation?'

Margot held back her irritation and replied coldly.

'What matters now is uniformity. Without this homogenisation, you won't be able to connect to the main program.'

'There's always the option of Karanza,' Maia retorted. 'I prefer to be with my family. I'm not interested in being part of this.'

Naran hesitated. *Connecting during hibernation seemed the safest option, but what if they couldn't connect after all?*

What if it was all a trap for their attention? What if the real program wasn't in the system, but in what they chose to see?

The image of an endless cycle unsettled her, and she heard herself shouting:

'I don't want to do any more tests!'

Silence fell over the room, followed by nervous murmurs.

'They have us here because we can alter the program,' Ikan whispered to Naran, 'but what they really want is for us to stop seeing what's happening. The ice cream is the nut.'

'Nut…?' Naran asked.

Ikan leaned slightly towards her, as if sharing a secret.

'They place dried fruits or nuts inside a jar like this. The monkey puts its hand in and closes it to grab the food… but it can't pull its hand out with a closed fist. So it stays trapped. The trap doesn't hold the monkey—its own grip does. You are free, Naran, you always have been. But as long as you cling to your perception of how things should have been, you'll be like the monkey. The pain isn't in what happened, it's in still clenching your fist.'

Naran saw clearly that she was still clinging to the pencil, to the drawing, to the lines. It wasn't just understanding—it was perception unravelling. She was still holding onto the very strokes she herself had drawn, the ones that had kept her reality trapped; strokes where her perception had unknowingly become entangled.

Ikan looked around and saw all the Incompatibles holding onto the nut. He then made a decision: he would meet with Nuna again and seek another possibility. He knew she would reproach him for his arrogance and indifference towards those who had yet to develop the perception of other lines. However, he would explain everything he had seen and the reason for his choice; he would no longer waste his energy on a Dream that didn't belong to him.

Naran felt, with astonishment, a force emerging from the depths of her being, leaving traces in its wake.

It was a pulse, it was memory.

And there he was. Ikan. Not in the hall, but in another place, in another time.

She no longer knew whether she was dreaming, remembering, or imagining: it was all a current flowing through her.

Her body shuddered at the vision of a cave, of a community gathered around a great fire, and Ikan, seated close by, as if he had always been there.

'Wait, Ikan, don't go. What does *Chawpi* mean?'

Naran thought that the firm voice that had stopped the boy wasn't hers, but something beyond herself asking the question.

Ikan stopped abruptly: the word struck him like an echo of something he had been trying to ignore. Chawpi, the centre, the balance between polarities... He himself had forgotten what it meant. For the first time, his gaze moved beyond that distance, that feeling of being above the situation; Naran had confronted him with something he too needed to remember.

'Chawpi is the point where opposing lines meet,' he said in a lower, almost reflective voice, 'it's the balance between what you believe you are and what you truly are. What we remember when we return to the centre.'

Ikan understood that, for a moment, she had been aware of her own connection to the Intent, and that's why she could perceive this had been a sign: Naran was present at the gathering in the cave, she remembered herself in that word. Now he couldn't leave, he had to continue with Nuna's plan, and he was there to help her strengthen that bond.

Why, by helping each other, could they reach a balance for the community? Strange indeed are the challenges of the infinite, he repeated to himself. He looked back and didn't respond to the part of her still identified with the program, but lowering his head, he wished to acknowledge the spirit, the double that dwelled within her and had spoken to him through that word: Chawpi.

'I know who you are, Naran. I remember you from many Dreams. And if you remember me too… then we've already crossed the threshold that needs no words.' The young man took an instrument from his pocket. 'If that's your desire, to remember and inhabit what already lives within you… I'm here to help you,' he said, pausing as he brought the quena to his lips.

And then, through the sound, he opened another line, another possibility, another time.

The boy began to play a melody, something Naran had not expected at all: a melody that did not come from outside, but from an echo already dwelling within her. The music hurled her into an abyss, as if reality itself had split in two and her consciousness had slipped into a vast ravine. It was as though everything were happening for the second time, or perhaps had never ceased to happen.

What if time did not move forward, but turned upon itself, repeating the dream until someone remembered it?

'I will help you perceive cyclical time.'

Naran opened her eyes, though not completely. She was in the Research Centre, she was in the cave, she was within herself. All at once.

And in that crossing she understood that attention was a threshold, and that she had just crossed it.

A faint light filtered through the fissures in the stone, filling the air with a quiet strangeness. Flickering glimmers revealed the natural shape of the cave; stalactites hung from the ceiling, composing a symphony of angles and curves that defied gravity. Something in that scene felt familiar: as though she had already been there, but also as though she had not yet arrived. Time did not advance: it curved, it opened like a spiral.

Naran moved forward cautiously. Her footsteps spread like a murmur over the damp rock. The atmosphere seemed to whisper expectation, as if that space itself were trying to reveal ancient secrets. Each glimmer slipping through the cracks was a message from another world. As she ventured deeper into that place, she felt the sonorous silence enfold her: a heartbeat in a realm where time seemed suspended. She felt immersed in a different reality, where the tangible yielded to the subtle. Curiosity urged her on.

The trembling light cast moving shadows, figures that danced with every flicker of the fire burning further ahead. Her sight adjusted to the half-light, and she distinguished a group of people gathered in a circle: in the centre, one figure addressing the rest.

The sense that something extraordinary was about to happen grew with each step. In that gathering, those present seemed to guard ancestral mysteries, secrets passed down through generations.

Hypnotised by the singularity of the moment, Naran sat among them. She sensed that all shared a common longing: to explore the unknown. But her immersion was abruptly broken when she heard her own name.

Suddenly, Ikan rose and voiced his discontent aloud:

'I don't think it's fair, Nuna. Why must I connect with her while she is in the Centre, inside that program? Why does it have to be me? I expected greater challenges.' He lowered his head and whispered, 'She no longer remembers this time, she is no longer one of us...'

The elder woman, with the serenity granted by wisdom, approached him calmly.

'Ikan, did you feel that tremor before this gathering? 'she asked, as her steps opened space among those present. 'The lines clash when it becomes imperative to integrate other perceptions.' Her voice floated, not pressing for answers. 'Even if you say that Naran does not belong to this group, if you looked beyond the form, you would understand she is already here.'

'She too Dreams.'

'She too weaves.'

Silence settled like a soft mantle, and Naran, absorbed, felt something expand within and around her, for Nuna's words were no longer words: they were echoes.

Nuna paused. Her eyes looked at him, yet it was as if she saw through him.

'Naran is beside you, even if you do not yet perceive her. She is part of the same quipu as you. And the key is to remember that we are all threads of the same weave.'

The awicha stepped forward and leaned slightly towards them, as if revealing a secret sown beyond time.

'You are here to recognise and inhabit a Chawpi,' she said, her voice serene as it moved through the gathered circle, 'a point where love ceases to be projection and becomes Munay: conscious, resonant love revealed as a shared vision. Until you can sustain it,' she continued, 'each of you will see your shadow reflected in the eyes of the other. And you will not truly see—you will be Stalking your own reflection.
The journey is towards the abstract.
Towards what cannot be named, but can be remembered.
Towards love when it ceases to be image and becomes vision. And then, you will bring to the community what is already unfolding on another plane, that which can only be perceived from the centre.'

Ikan, surprised, turned towards where Naran was sitting. Their eyes met, and in that instant she felt an inexplicable vertigo, as though her perception had suddenly expanded. She rose at once, unsettled by the sudden attention and the enigma enfolding the moment.

Then the jolt came: the vision began to fragment as if an invisible force were pulling her elsewhere; the cave, the gathering, Nuna's words… all dissolved like a gust.

A buzzing sound shattered the stillness of the Dream, followed by a sharp, repetitive tone emerging from the Centre's loudspeakers. A monotone voice announced that the Incompatibles were to proceed to the testing hall.

She looked around, but Ikan was nowhere to be found. Once again she thought that everything she had experienced had been only a dream. Doubt pursued her as she walked towards the hall, with the sense that, for a moment, she had managed to step beyond the imposed lines. But her perception was returning to them.

The system was claiming her, the new device awaited her, but something within her no longer answered from the same place.

She had touched another line. And though invisible, it still passed through her.

KNOT V

THE POINT THAT OBSERVES

Alan and several directors were in the program room on the second floor. Through the glass windows, they watched the teens gathering to begin the tests. Jitesh, one of the directors, thanked Alan once more for having completed the device on time. The helmet, he said, would enable the teens to connect to the system through the homogenisation of perceptions.

'So basically, we just need to adjust the emission speed,' summarised the director, brushing off the implications.

Naran's father remained silent, weighing the entire situation. One of the technicians on the team responded in his place:

'Now, through the new device, the program will send double the data per second, capturing the attention of the Incompatibles and overriding the information they were projecting into the system.'

Alan observed the adolescents gathered around Margot and Nélida, inspecting the new helmet. Perhaps it had never been about the helmet or the program itself, but about their attention—or the absence of it.

'Let's see if everyone manages to make the connection,' the technician murmured, cautiously.

'I trust they will,' the director replied, unshaken.

But Alan couldn't shake off his concern:

'I insist,' he said gravely, 'it's a mistake to treat these adolescents' abilities as a threat, as a virus infecting the system.'

'I understand your point, Alan, but I also need you to understand ours. We're under immense pressure: political, corporate, entangled with third-party interests, the glaciation, and countless other factors.' Jitesh paused, attempting to show Alan that, in truth, he was merely a pawn on a much larger board.

Naran's father saw how the director's gestures ensnared him in his own rhetoric; he skilfully evaded responsibility, diminishing his perceived influence.

'We're exposing these teens to uncertain technology. We still have no studies on the effects of doubling the system's frequency.'

'I believe you've done solid work, Alan. Try not to worry so much.'

'As I mentioned in the meeting,' Alan began, locking eyes with Jitesh, 'one of my top priorities is the wellbeing of these adolescents. That's why I'll continue the research. Perhaps in a few weeks, we could open the 5% protocol...'

'Forget that line of inquiry, Alan,' the director interrupted firmly. 'We need this version of reality disseminated among the population. We don't know how long the glaciation will endure, and we can't afford to destabilise the system. The program serves as a virtual homogeniser, just as networked devices always have. Now more than ever, we need social cohesion—and that can only be achieved through MIO's virtual narrative.'

What if what they called 'cohesion' was nothing more than shared hypnosis? Alan wondered.

'Today's dominant narrative is woven inside an oppressive virtual regime,' he finally whispered, voice laden with concern. 'Are we talking about cohesion—or perceptual control?'

'We offer a coherent narrative for a fractured reality,' Jitesh replied, his gaze fixed with satisfaction on the group of Incompatibles examining the device.

Alan sensed that the director still failed to grasp the gravity of the situation.

'Do you want chaos taking root in their minds, or in the system itself?' Naran's father pressed, watching the teens' body language: resistance, fear, disheartenment. 'Have you read the latest reports from Sector A?' he continued, his deep voice casting a shadow across the room. 'They indicate rising levels of depression and anxiety. And more disturbingly, there are anomalies in brain regions tied to creativity, attention, and emotional processing.'

Jitesh, visibly distant, looked at his watch, already thinking about his next meeting.

'That also happened outside the system,' he answered evasively. 'Don't persist in the notion that MIO is the villain and you are the saviour of these kids. Trust the project, Alan. We cannot afford chaos taking root in the program. The priority now is to capture this group's attention, to ensure they connect and discover their identity within the system. That is your contribution, and theirs.'

Alan remained silent. He sensed the project had always been heading that way, disregarding the wellbeing of the young. He no longer cared about Jitesh's words and was unwilling to prolong a sterile discussion. He would continue his investigations, doing everything possible for them. Meanwhile, his thoughts troubled him, and he instinctively distanced himself from the painful feelings the whole situation generated.

He looked once more through the window, watching the group of teens prepare for the tests, and a new unease overcame him upon spotting a familiar figure. He squinted, uncertain whether his eyes deceived him—but no, Naran was really there.

His heart skipped a beat the moment he recognised her; a wave of dizziness swept through him, and he longed to press his palms against the glass, letting the weight of his emotion press there.

Naran was there, yes—but it was as if he couldn't reach her. Not because of distance, but because they were both suspended within the same crossing, perhaps resonating at the same frequency, yet unable to find one another.

What if it wasn't her drifting away... but him, still not daring to see himself?

Naran arrived home with her usual routine in mind, grab something from the fridge and lock herself in her room. But to her surprise, her father was waiting for her.

'Come, Naran, I have something to show you.'

She frowned, her expression guarded. The living room had been transformed into a small laboratory; cables stretched in all directions.

'What's going on? Are you going to interrogate me?' the teenager asked distrustfully.

Her father looked at her with a faint smile.

'Yes, with a polygraph, to ask you what you do all day locked up in your room. But no, this is for something more important.'

'Of course. Your stuff is always more important,' she replied dryly.

Alan ignored his daughter's sarcasm and answered calmly:

'I'm trying to demonstrate scientifically what I've witnessed. I need to validate my hypothesis with this device.'

Naran nodded. They hadn't talked much lately, but she could sense the urgency behind her father:

'Okay, I'll let you use me as a guinea pig.'

'I want to make some records and better understand why you can't connect to MIO.'

Naran lowered her head. She hadn't told her father about the situation at the new Centre, but she suspected he already knew.

'Have you talked to my teachers?'

'No, I haven't spoken with them,' he answered, downplaying the matter. 'I've been immersed in the project research, and now I have a broader perspective.'

The girl felt her father wasn't being sincere; she was convinced the Centre had contacted him about the difficulties she continued to face in virtual learning.

Alan looked at her with a hint of sympathy. He couldn't let her carry the blame. Since her mother's death, she had been struggling, and it hurt him deeply to see her locked in her room, wasting away day by day in her sadness and lack of interest in the world. He had to find a solution, not just for her, but for all the Incompatibles.

His daughter glanced at him distrustfully. Though they'd drifted apart, a part of her still longed to reach him; *they couldn't go on like this*. Finally, Naran relaxed her attitude and tried to express what she truly needed.

'I'm not going to continue with the treatment.'

'It's for your own good,' he replied with a disapproving grimace. 'The doctors have said your mind is very scattered, that you're always daydreaming without being able to concentrate. Also, you've been very sad since your mother...'

She felt her father was trying once again to confine her to his view, first through his scientific reasoning, and then by bringing up her mother's death. He wasn't truly listening; he only pushed her into those two frames, leaving no space for her own voice. She was about to turn seventeen, and everything remained the same.

'Dad, if the treatment had worked, I would already be connected to that blasted program. I'm Incompatible, and you have to accept it.'

Her father looked at her intently and understood that she had grown enough to see the truth. Without saying a word, he inserted other cables into the device.

'I agree with you,' he whispered as he continued with the adjustments.

'I don't know if you say that because you really believe it or just to get me to leave you alone,' Naran replied resentfully. 'Sometimes I think I'm a burden to you because things don't go the way you plan.'

'It's been hard for both of us.'

'And yes, of course, I miss Mum a lot. These last few years I've followed your way of seeing things. But now,' she began, pausing to look at her father sincerely, 'I've thought about the possibility of moving to the Outer Reserves. I'll be with my relatives and won't have to worry about all those tests, those devices.'

Alan, recalling what he had seen in the cave, passed the scanner over his daughter's back at the height where Elías had struck him. When the light blinked beside the left shoulder blade, the data began to project on a monitor.

'Dad! Are you listening to me!?' Naran shouted, demanding his attention. 'I don't want more cables, virtual systems... I want all this to end.'

Tears began to roll down her cheeks. She felt that he didn't care about anything. She just wanted to feel connected, for her father to listen to her and accept her as she was.

'I've been to the Outer Reserves,' Alan said, looking at the analysed data. 'I also feel there's another possibility. I'm developing a new device; give me just one more month, Naran. One more month in that Centre, and then we can consider the option of the Outer Reserves. I promise you all this will end well.'

'Well?' she whispered, her voice drenched in sadness. 'Will it end well for you—or for me?'

Jitesh's voice continued flowing from the control centre like an echo of the system still trying to uphold its logic. Alan barely heard it. From the window, he observed in silence: his daughter was there.

She wasn't looking at him; she didn't need him.

And yet, he couldn't stop looking at her; Naran was showing him the limits of his own perception, while he observed everything as a scientist, as always.

Perhaps they all lived in different realities, vibrating on frequencies that could never touch unless someone changed their point.

He had to cross.

He had to feel from within.

He had to allow his gaze to go beyond scientific observation.

How many realities could a single instant hold?

And which were true?

Perhaps all.

Perhaps none.

It all depended on where he placed his attention.

KNOT VI

THE CROSSING FROM WITHIN

The air in the simulation room hung dense, charged with a tension that felt almost tactile. The flashing lights from the monitors cast erratic patterns onto the metallic walls, as though the system itself were reacting to the mood of the young people present. Naran, seated in a corner, stared at the immersion helmet resting before her. Its cold, clinical design seemed to beckon her into a world she had no desire to explore.

'How much longer are we going to wait?' Néstor muttered.

Maia, standing by one of the consoles, shot her brother a warning glance.

'Calm down, Néstor. There's not much time left before we're out of here.'

Naran barely registered the exchange. Her mind floated elsewhere, adrift between images of the Outer Reserves and the suffocating reality of the Research Centre. It was Margot's voice that broke the silence, reclaiming control of the space.

'Over these weeks, you will undergo several tests,' Margot announced with a restrained smile. 'We are confident that by the end of this period, most of you will have adapted to keeping your attention within the pilot program. This process will allow you to become compatible when connecting to the MIO system. Do you know how long it takes us to learn to focus on one reality? Many years. And with MIO, this learning requires a new kind of attention—something more refined. Thanks to your collaboration, we can update the program and reduce the errors affecting hundreds of teenagers in other sectors. And thus, you will gain access to this virtual world full of possibilities.'

Margot paused, letting her words settle into the room, while the teens exchanged glances clouded with doubt.

'Thank you, Margot,' Nélida interjected gently, steering the conversation before uncomfortable questions could arise. She reclaimed the group's attention. 'Today, our developers propose a simulation game. You will continue refining your skills to increase compatibility with the system.' She raised a helmet with a different design, one specially prepared for them. 'After much effort, and in light of the difficulties you've encountered in maintaining the connection, we've developed this device.'

Margot stepped forward again, speaking with studied calm, each phrase shaped with deliberate care.

'This helmet guides your focus towards the reality that best supports your adaptation.' Her gaze drifted slowly across their faces. 'But tell me, what do you prefer? The chaotic uncertainty of the outside world, or the stability this one offers? Now your attention must turn to this other reality.' Another pause, this one heavy and intentional, letting her words ripple through the charged air. 'Who wants to try it first?'

A thick silence spread through the room. The teens' glances met briefly before dropping to the floor, betraying a mixture of distrust and fear. Naran swallowed hard. Margot's tone held a hypnotic calm, but something inside her recoiled. *What if that was precisely what I feared? That by focusing my attention, everything else disappears?*

What if my world shrinks to whatever MIO decides to show me?

Margot, still poised before them, gave a slight smile, as if she had anticipated this resistance, and activated the projection device. A soft hum swept through the room. On the screen before them, images began to unfold, first warped and flickering, then slowly coming into clarity. A desolate landscape emerged, a sky grey and heavy, a world frozen in time. Everything appeared suspended, as if life had been caught in the stillness of an eternal winter.

'This,' Margot said with theatrical flair, 'is the current climate situation. In Sector A, the glaciation has struck with force, and in a few weeks, Sector B will face the same reality. Resources are scarce, opportunities on the surface limited, and life reduced to the bare essentials.'

Once again, everyone felt the weight of the reality displayed on the screen—and the consequences of being Incompatibles. But the woman pivoted the narrative, her tone growing more energetic.

'By using this pilot program, you will be able to explore unique experiences: climb mountains, walk through endless forests where nature will unfold before you; you may even visit the wonders of the world before the cataclysm—Chichén Itzá, the Colosseum, Machu Picchu—or the wonders of the ancient world, like the Greek Temples or the Hanging Gardens of Babylon.'

On the screen, the images shifted at once: the snow-capped mountains dissolved into landscapes where the wind swept through dense forests, vast deserts, and wide lagoons. Suddenly, the pyramids of Egypt rose majestically on the horizon, but then the images changed again, revealing the ancient temples in the Guatemalan jungle, shrouded in thick vegetation.

'All this is within your reach,' Margot insisted, sweeping her gaze across the teens. 'You will be able to experience this virtual reality and leave behind, if only temporarily, the limitations of the current world.' She paused, observing the faces before her and recognising that in some, she had planted a seed of hope. 'All we ask is that you connect and allow the program to guide you. Each of you will be able to discover, with this new device, the infinite possibilities the pilot program offers. Who wouldn't want to escape from such an oppressive reality into a virtual world full of alternatives?'

The teens exchanged glances, some anxious, others fearful. Doubts still hung heavy in the air, but the temptation was palpable.

'It's not that we don't want to connect; it's that the system rejects us,' Maia retorted, defiant, tired of the virtual carrot being dangled before them yet always out of reach. 'What's the difference between this device and the ones we've tried before?'

'Thank you for the question,' Margot responded, lowering her gaze with practised control. 'We've achieved something important: most of you have rejected MIO due to a mismatch in the interpretation of information. This happens because the adolescent brain is in a phase of change and sometimes misprocesses what it perceives. This helmet will help you focus properly, minimising interference.'

Naran looked at Néstor, and their eyes met in silent complicity. The boy stepped forward, wanting to show he also had something to say.

'Do you mean interference with the abilities we have inside the system?'

Margot fixed her gaze on Néstor with an unsettling calm.

'Due to the urgency of the situation, there's no time to delve into those details. What matters now is your collaboration. You must trust that this helmet not only interprets your perceptions but also optimises them.' The woman studied the three in silence and recognised them as the latest arrivals at the Centre. 'And as I said, if you collaborate with the system update, you will have the choice to decide whether or not to connect to the main MIO program.'

She turned her gaze to Naran, who still hesitated, and with an almost imperceptible smile, called to her. 'Naran, come here, please.'

Naran knew it: There was a flicker of resentment behind Margot's calm. Rather than granting her the freedom to choose, she would expose her before everyone. With hesitant steps, she approached; her hands trembled as she took the helmet Nélida offered. As she placed it on her head, she felt it adjust to the base of her neck, and images from previous tests flooded her mind. Fear gripped her, and her breathing grew heavier.

What will happen if I can't connect?

The pressure on her neck increased.

What if the new device can't override the interference?

The helmet seemed to press down harder, a chilling reminder that she had no control.

'We're going to begin,' Nélida announced in a reassuring tone.

Naran tried to calm herself, but her anxiety only grew. And her anxiety was not a sign of weakness, but a quiet act of resistance, for a part of her recognised that this world of certainties was a perceptual prison. She wanted to remove the helmet, but she couldn't... she knew she had no other choice.

Suddenly, the world changed: images of her childhood began to unfold before her, fragmented and floating before her eyes. Memories, emotions, thoughts—everything seemed to be processed by the system. A chill ran through her body... *Could they see it all? Could they manipulate it?* She wanted to escape, but she couldn't. And then, the image of the woman with the llama appeared in her mind, as if reminding her of something she had forgotten.

Margot observed the data on a monitor.

'There are still interferences; adjust the system,' she ordered one of the technicians.

The group watched her as if she were part of a foreign scene. Maia clenched her fists in silence, and Néstor stared at the floor as if he had already lost.

Fear grew, but something inside her began to calm.

You can enter, Naran. I will accompany you, she heard within herself—Ikan's serene voice anchoring her. Taking deep breaths, the young woman tried to relax, knowing she had to go on, that this step was necessary to understand the program and her place within it. With Ikan's voice as her anchor, she ventured into the unknown, trusting she wouldn't lose herself in that manipulated reality.

'What was that? Are they exposing me to everyone else? Are they exploring my memories?' Naran asked, her voice laden with uncertainty, as a shiver ran down her spine. Caught in a whirlwind of insecurity, she struggled to hold her centre, while a hidden need pushed her to prove she could be compatible, even if it meant dissolving into the expectations of the program.

'Calm down, it's only a recognition method.' Ikan's voice, steady and composed, guided her like that fleeting moment of stillness that arises in the midst of chaos. 'It detects your tastes and preferences, that's all.'

But his words scarcely managed to dispel the confusion overwhelming her, while images from her past flickered before her, fitting into the enigma MIO was attempting to solve.'You're inside,' the boy continued, observing his hands as an anchor to remind himself within the program. 'They have synchronised your assemblage point with the simulator, but don't let them identify you. Maintain your attention—that's your challenge.'

'Identify?'

'Don't fall into complacency, Naran. You're not here on the terms the program has set for you. Maintain your own purpose.'

'My purpose?'

'You must learn to move within the network, to understand its functions—but always remembering who you really are, and why you're here.'

As Ikan spoke, the virtual environments began to unfold: open plains, serene rivers, and endless coastlines opened before Naran. For a moment, she wanted to surrender to that perfection, to merge with the sensations.

'Don't do it, Naran, that is your challenge. Remember yourself, hold the space between.'

She took a deep breath. The simulator was trying to steer her attention. Then, she saw it.

'Do you mean that the program limits what we see, that it locks us into a narrative?'

Ikan pointed to the horizon.

'Look at those images. MIO's network wants you to believe those are your only options. But have you asked yourself what it is leaving out? What possibilities might exist if you chose none of them?'

She closed her eyes, and the projections blurred. And for the first time, she noticed the cracks in the structure of the simulation. Perhaps it was not the program that was breaking apart, but her focus of attention.

'MIO is a labyrinth that moulds reality to its convenience,' the boy continued. 'Do not see it as a place, but as a perceptual field. Here you will learn to see and to move among the traps of the system.'

Naran watched as the projections shifted at overwhelming speed; they were no longer landscapes, but entire generations passing through her. All of history seemed to unfold at once, sweeping her into a current impossible to contain.

'Traps? What do you mean?'

'You are in the pilot simulation so you can become accustomed to the network. But before you enter the main simulator, you must understand the art of Stalking. It is not only a strategy: it is a guide that will allow you to move between reality and illusion without becoming trapped in an identification.'

Naran looked at him, and Ikan held her gaze for an instant, as if weighing the depth of that ancestral art.

'The first principle: warriors choose their battlefield—they never fight on terrain they don't know. MIO is a perceptual battlefield. You have to recognise it, observe it, understand how it operates. If you don't, you've already lost before the trials begin.'

'I want to get out!' Naran exclaimed, overwhelmed by the intensity. She didn't feel enough—felt that something in her still didn't know how to sustain itself without defining itself.

'Observe before you react, Naran, that is the art of Stalking: hunting oneself. MIO is the reflection of your own mind. The mind also classifies, limits, builds labyrinths of perception. Understanding this will allow you to move among the traps that condition your experience and hunt down the automatisms.'

Naran felt the need to create distance from her own mind—not to reject it, but to see it.

'It's not about leaving or destroying the program, it's about understanding it. If you can pause and observe, the walls of the labyrinth will begin to crumble.'

The images kept unfolding as she struggled to take in his words.

'How can I stop identifying with something that feels so real?'

Ikan smiled, took a handful of soil, and let it fall between his fingers.

'MIO works by trapping your attention between binary options: strength or weakness, good or bad, adequate or inadequate. Every time you choose between those options, you reinforce the boundaries. You must question everything.'

'Labyrinth of perception …?' Naran repeated, seeking to slow the system's speed.

'Do you remember the first time you connected to MIO?'

The young woman hesitated, but slowly the images began to return. She closed her eyes.
And the memory dragged her forcefully.
And the scene returned—not as a story, but as a wound.

On one of the first days syncing with the program, Naran, still younger, had been in a virtual classroom surrounded by other students. The lessons, designed to shape perception, displayed narrated images of world history. These highlighted the achievements of certain cultures and societies, while others were dismissed.

'In this way, the so-called Outer Reserves chose to remain isolated, avoiding development and progress alongside the rest of the central sectors,' proclaimed the virtual teacher, its mechanical voice devoid of nuance. 'For this reason, we do not include this approach in the database.'

Naran, timid yet determined, raised her hand.

'Excuse me, but that's not entirely true,' she said, her voice slightly trembling. 'The Outer Reserves have contributed to our understanding of the world with their history. For example, the concept of the Ayllu…'

And she began to passionately explain the meaning of Ayllu: a community based on collaboration and reciprocity. But as she spoke, she noticed how her classmates' avatars turned towards her, observing her in a silence heavier than any comment.

'We must focus on the established curriculum and its approach,' the virtual teacher interrupted, coldly dismissing her intervention.

'But we're erasing vital perspectives, forgetting essential parts of our history,' she insisted, her voice rising with a mix of anger and frustration.

Yet as she spoke, her words faded away within that virtual contour. Confused, she stood up, trying to understand why the program had chosen to silence her. She thought of her mother, her relatives, of the experiences lived in the Outer Reserves. The anger she had carried turned into an uncontrollable surge and, suddenly, she projected into the network scenes from the Ayni festivity: its music, its poetry, the faces of the community that had once embraced her. The images were so vivid they seemed to come alive, defying the program's narrative.

And in an instant, she was disconnected.

The return was abrupt; something within her had changed: the cold of the virtual classroom was replaced by the uncomfortable silence of the present. She not only remembered, she also understood that her voice was an interference within the system.

Naran turned her attention back to the pilot program, where she held Ikan's gaze.

'That was my first experience,' she said, her tone heavy with a mixture of pain and clarity. 'How could I have forgotten?'

The young woman, eyes fixed on the pilot program, held Ikan's gaze as she recounted her first experience inside the system. That moment had been a turning point, but she had buried it deep in her memory. And then she understood what had happened: the program imposed clear demarcations, trapping users' perception within dichotomies. The Outer Reserves were labelled as a failed example, and the central sectors as the only right path. Naran realised her perception hadn't just been manipulated—it had been shaped to remain within a binary.

'When they disconnected me, all I felt was that I had failed, that I wasn't enough,' she murmured, lowering her gaze.

'That's what they wanted you to feel,' Ikan replied, his voice firm yet calm. 'Every lesson, every test is designed to anchor you in their version of reality. They want you to interpret the world on their terms, to forget that other paths exist.'

The girl nodded as her mind connected pieces she hadn't understood until now. That day they hadn't just disconnected her from the system; they had also disconnected a part of herself.

'Listen carefully, Naran,' Ikan continued with a tone that invited both challenge and reflection. 'Every action within the program has an echo. If you project fear or compliance, MIO will adjust the limits to bind you tighter. But if you inhabit creative doubt, imagination, or wonder... you can break the cycle.'

He extended his hand, and from it emerged a figure of light: a hummingbird flickering with impossible colours. 'The hummingbird can see beyond the spectrum of colours perceived by the human eye; it can move between dimensions, perceive what remains hidden to others. It is the guardian of the threshold, the one who brings nectar between the invisible and the visible.'

Naran followed the hummingbird's movement and felt something within her begin to open.

'This is *Yuyana*: to remember, to imagine, to Dream from within. And by remembering yourself, you Stalk yourself… and you Dream yourself. Whenever you feel trapped, return to this point.'

Naran took a breath, absorbing his words. She looked through the hummingbird and then she saw: the invisible colours unfolded like a veil being drawn aside. That invisible nectar vibrated in her chest, and the visions returned: Illa, the llama, the village. For a moment, she held them. But fear threatened to close the bridge. What if they disconnected her again?

'Don't doubt who you are, Naran,' Ikan said, sensing her hesitation. 'What matters is not the system but your freedom to perceive. Even if they force you to inhabit it, no one can besiege that deep layer of your consciousness, the one that can always move freely. When you remember that, the surface loses its power.'

The young woman took a deep breath; something inside her had begun to give way, as if a tiny crack allowed a new certainty to seep through. Then she looked at Ikan again, for in his gaze she found a refuge where she could steady herself.

'You Dream yourself through Yuyana into another perceptual position within the program,' the boy explained, stepping a little closer. 'It's the movement of your assemblage point. You choose to perceive, and by doing so, you make it real.'

'And what if that place exists… only because I've remembered it?'

'We are not Incompatibles, Naran. We are Dreamers. We create other realities with our imagination. That village, those visions—they are Dream positions. That is what makes them real.'

'So… I'm not imagining,' she whispered. 'I'm crossing.'

For the first time, she understood that the label Incompatibles concealed a deeper truth. Perhaps it was precisely her 'incompatibility' that made her free.

'All right,' she said, her voice again determined. 'I'm going to pay attention. I'm going to go beyond what the program wants me to see.'

'This is how you train your mind to go beyond the binary,' Ikan added softly. 'This is how you untether your perception from what is fixed and begin to move it freely.'

He paused for a moment and leaned in slightly, looking at her intensely.

'What we perceive as real is only the option MIO has chosen for us,' he whispered, leaning a little closer still. 'What if you could choose what to observe? What would you choose to collapse, Naran?'

She opened her eyes wide, startled by the question. Her mind was trying to grasp the magnitude of what Ikan was suggesting, even as landscapes and scenarios, perfectly organised by the program, continued to unfold before her. But in that moment she saw something more: fissures in those solid images that revealed paths not yet explored.

She breathed in slowly. Let the weight of the possibility settle.

Maybe it wasn't the program that was cracking…
Maybe it was her own focus of attention.

'It's a game, Naran,' he concluded, rising to his feet. 'But you'll only learn if you remember who you are. When you understand that you are not only what the network projects, but also the infinite space that surrounds it.

You are a subtle field choosing what to align with.

Your perception is a tuner, not a perceptual cage.'

The simulator then began to project images of past civilisations, ones that hadn't been shown before: the Ellora Temples carved into living rock, and the sacred ghats of Varanasi by the river, guardians of forgotten mysteries.

And the young woman felt something deep open within her. She rose beside Ikan and realised with clarity that the true challenge was not to remain there as just another user, but to become a conscious Stalker.

'All this greatness…all these legacies,' she whispered, gazing at the ancient images with a blend of wonder and melancholy. 'Why haven't we built upon this wisdom? Why do we keep starting from scratch?'

Ikan watched the projections thoughtfully.

'It seems we're trapped in a perceptual prison that keeps us from experiencing reality in its fullness.'

Naran remained in awe at the beauty surrounding her, and a deep sense of melancholy washed over her.

'I still don't understand… Do you think it's possible to break that cycle, that automatism?'

Ikan held her gaze in silence, letting the moment expand like a breath held between worlds.

'Each must forge their will with determination to discover their own freedom of perception,' he finally replied, his voice steady.

His gaze slowly swept across the artificial horizon created by MIO, those virtual landscapes delimiting a constructed reality.

'In a way, this entire program is the Tonal of our time—a structure designed for comprehension,' he explained, his tone slow and deliberate, while his hand gently touched the virtual ground. At his touch, the surface began to fracture and fall away into an infinite void. 'Each tree, each stone, every horizon you see here is carefully arranged by MIO to sustain a single version of reality.'

He paused, saying nothing, as Naran watched the illusion of the ground give way to boundless space—an invitation without words. 'But the Nagual has no form or boundaries; it is all that cannot be foreseen, all that MIO cannot control,' he continued, lifting his gaze slowly towards her. 'When you recognise that you are shaped by the network—but not confined by it—and that beyond its structure lies the unknown, you begin to free yourself from the perceptual prison.'

He stepped closer and whispered softly, as if the wind itself carried the secret: 'To enter the Nagual, one must first learn to Stalk the Tonal.'

Naran felt a deep shiver run through her. Before her, the virtual images continued to flow—beautiful but fleeting—while within her, another reality was emerging, more subtle, more authentic. Suddenly, she clearly remembered Illa's words, the figure of the llama, and those verses of poetry she had heard during the Ayni celebration. They returned like fragments of a melody she had thought lost, brushing her awareness with unexpected gentleness.

'Perhaps poetry is our true freedom,' she finally whispered, realising for the first time that a space MIO could never reach or confine had always existed within her.

Condor who soars through the Hanan Pacha,
watchful guardian of the skies,
teach us to fly beyond illusion,
to break free from the perception imposed upon us.

Naran felt she had recovered something more precious than any connection to the system. She had recovered a fragment of herself.

Ikan looked at her with intensity and, with a faint smile, recited alongside her:

May each step reflect reciprocity,
may we recognise light within every shadow,
and in the meeting of opposites,
may the true Chawpi awaken.

'Now I understand,' she said, her eyes shining with conviction. 'I don't need answers anymore—only to remember.

It's not about being compatible or not; it's about remembering who I am.'

KNOT VII

AYNI

The first rays of sun timidly pierced through the thick fog, awakening the people dozing among old factories and worn-out buildings. Karanza, marked by a distant past tied to manufacturing, was re-emerging as a nucleus of activity and resistance.

In the distance, the skyscrapers of the central sectors cut the skyline, a reminder of the constant pressure looming over the margins. Yet that day Karanza rose in celebration and gatherings: communities from the Outer Reserves had arrived in the suburb for the Ayni festival. It was a time of renewal, when communal bonds were strengthened in the days leading up to the glaciation.

The streets of Karanza blended the rudimentary structures of another era with the technological. To the north, old brick façades were streaked with paint. From the windows hung textiles strung between neon cables and graffiti-marked walls. To the south, murals of Apus and condors spoke with memories of other times. Antennas and tangled wires climbed the façades, their hues defying the grey, perpetually clouded horizon.

At the corners, makeshift clothes became itinerant markets. In the upper part of the suburb, passers-by exchanged hacking tools and hardware parts. In the southern markets, antiques, handicrafts, and traditional textiles predominated. Handwoven ponchos and blankets were offered as omens of what was to come.

Where the bustle thickened, the great square opened. Young hackers gathered around improvised screens, discussed strategies and shared codes. Beside them, in stark contrast, the *hamawtas*—elders of the Outer Reserves—came together as guardians of ancestral memory. In circles, they recounted teachings of the Great Path, the *Qhapaq Ñan*, weaving metaphors about ancient battles and the new forms of colonisation of systems and of the gaze.

At the centre of the square rose a mural that distilled the essence of the day: a labyrinth of interwoven paths and circuits, an image of the union of worlds. At its core, a human figure with closed eyes, surrounded by symbols and lines, represented the yearning for another shared dream.

From there stretched cobbled streets where street vendors offered everything from traditional dishes to ceramics and living hand-made textiles.

'A textile or some potatoes,' an old woman said, holding up several ponchos.

Music threaded its way through the passers-by: notes of the panpipe mingled with electronic rhythms, while traditional dances broke out amidst the street art.

Very close by, a group of young hackers were debating intensely. Mara, who was holding a device with care, explained the progress of her project:

'We could paint a mural of resistance within the program,' Mara said with conviction, 'weaving together symbols and equations to challenge the narrative imposed by the central sectors.'

Kai and Jax nodded, their faces lit not only by the glow of the screen but by the flicker of hope.

'I think the root issue still lies in MIO's interface,' Mara continued. 'If we crack that layer, we could infiltrate its security systems undetected.'

Jax leaned in, eyes gleaming. 'Do you really think we could alter what MIO shows to users?'

'Almost certainly,' she affirmed. 'We'll use a chameleon algorithm to tune into the program's base frequencies. Once inside, we embed our own code.'

Kai smiled, energised by the possibility. 'Like carving a breach in MIO's wall and letting our symbols stream through… an anomaly that will ripple through the code, impossible to erase.'

'It's not just a technical hack… it's more than that,' Jax said, reflectively.

'Exactly,' Mara replied. 'Let's head to Dr Lana's lab. We'll need her help bridging the interface.'

Kai said his farewells and turned towards LEH's lab. Jax, grinning, called after him with mock solemnity:

'Watch out for the spiritual hackers, LEH and GEH, always preaching about aligning tech with Ayni.'

Kai laughed, weaving through the crowd. 'You're the one who needs to align your circuits.'

With firm steps, he moved through the living maze of Karanza and reached the base of an old industrial tower. Entering a timeworn lift, he keyed in a code. The elevator began its descent, carrying him into the undercurrent where dreams of resistance pulsed beneath Karanza's layered memory.

The laboratory of LEH and his team was another great focal point of activity, yet the atmosphere was radically different from the bustle outside. The walls were covered with circuit diagrams and graffiti of ancient symbols; around the room, sculptures captured the unique fusion between technology and mysticism.

At twenty, LEH combined strength and quiet, like someone who knows how to listen to the invisible. His copper-toned skin, inherited from the Outer Reserves, contrasted with his large brown eyes and long black hair.

He did not confine himself to researching consciousness: he was a perceptual hacker, an artist who created symbols on the margins of the MIO program, opening fissures through which emerged the possibility of another way of seeing. For him, even under oppression, creativity was a form of resistance.

In his work, he had joined quantum physics with ancestral memory, and from that synthesis he addressed his team and the gathered listeners.

'I thank the communities who have come to Karanza so that we might meet with a common purpose: Ayni,' he began. 'Today, with that intention, we will support the group of Incompatibles in the trials that are beginning at the Research Centre.'

Elías, surrounded by members of diverse communities, was there as a hamawta—guardian of ancestral memory. He looked over those present and raised his voice, carrying the collective memory.

'May the wisdom of the grandmothers and grandfathers accompany us today, to open the circle with their word,' he said, pausing briefly. 'We were called Outer Reserves, we were named 'the others'. Yet another label to keep us on the margins, to lock us into an image that does not belong to us; a distorted gaze which, over time, comes to inhabit us. So it is with the Incompatibles, when they begin to believe what the system projects upon them.'

He stopped and, in a deeper tone, continued:

'But we, as ancestral peoples, do not recognise ourselves in that name. We call ourselves the Reserves of Memory, because in every weave, in every word, in every ceremony, we carry the remembrance of another way of living. Not incompatible, but forgotten.'

'Today we honour the Intent of those who rose against the control of the central sectors,' he continued with a firm voice. 'Years ago we gathered here to dream Karanza, and we did so guided by Ayni and Ayllu: community, reciprocity, and the shared fire with which to forge new realities.'

LEH nodded gravely. He knew that what they were about to begin at the Research Centre was crucial. He looked at the Incompatibles' nodes displayed on the screens and felt the weight of responsibility.

'You know of my connection with the Reserves of Memory,' he said slowly. 'I too was once considered incompatible, but I managed to escape from Sector A thanks to a flaw in the system. Here, in this suburb, I found a space where I could integrate different forms of knowledge. Now we share these cosmovisions with those still seeking to remember who they are.'

Elías looked at him with respect.

'You have said something important: we share. That is the true essence of reciprocity, the principle of Ayni. It is not a mere barter of tangible objects, but a continuous flow that connects and balances all beings. Yet we are falling into forgetfulness. The central sectors and their MIO program drag us down, and our words begin to lose their meaning. Ayni blurs, fading from our minds like the perpetual fog that surrounds everything.'

LEH answered with a slight nod and, without adding words, traced a few diagrams on the digital screen.

'Quantum physics shows us that all particles are entangled in a profound state of unity. For the indigenous peoples, this represents the sacred field of the universe: here in Karanza, we call it the unified quantum field. In both cases we speak of the same thing: a subtle network that runs through time, space, and perception.'

'And how will we apply it concretely to the group we support?' GEH interrupted gently.

'Each user of the program is like a particle in this network,' LEH replied. 'What we do here can resonate instantly there, beyond any distance. This is the principle of non-locality: separation is an illusion.'

'So, have these users been restricted to a limited version of reality?' Kai asked, intrigued.

'Exactly,' whispered LEH. 'That is the objective of the MIO program: to fix perception into a single reality.'

Elías spoke again, his eyes reflecting the gravity of the moment.

'Our assemblage point, our perceptual core, is not designed to remain still. Its nature is to explore, to gather new perceptions. Fixing it permanently, as MIO has done, harms the integrity of being.' He paused before continuing. 'Together with Alan we have seen how the program manipulates this assemblage point and anchors it to an artificial line, into a perceptual control point we shall call Timeline 3. This is how they force users to perceive only the reality that suits them. And unfortunately, they have succeeded with almost everyone.'

LEH tapped his fingers on the table and picked up the thread, resolute.

'Except… with the Incompatibles. They are the only group whose assemblage point is not fixed on this artificial line.'

'To limit perception in this way is a crime!' Elías raised his voice, full of indignation. Then, more calmly, he added, 'But they have something the users have lost.'

Elías swept his gaze across those present. In his eyes shone a conviction of hope.

'They preserve the mobility of their vision, and in that lies their greatest strength. In their differences is found the key to reconnect with the whole.'

The atmosphere in the room grew tense. The words sank deep into everyone present. It was not merely a matter of strategy: the Incompatibles were the last piece of a network on the verge of breaking… or regenerating.

Kai spoke with restrained urgency.

'So what would be the first step?'

LEH moved towards the centre, reflective.

'First, we must recognise something essential: this connection is not created, it is remembered. This network has always been here. Our purpose is to synchronise intention, emotion, and perception through a frequency of resonance: an ancestral code activated by the symbol of Ayni.'

The meaning was clear: that the group of Incompatibles preserve perceptual mobility during the trials, and that this force enables them to help the other users to reactivate their latent consciousness—reminding the entire network that choice is still possible.

'And what if MIO detects our actions?' asked GEH, worried.

LEH smiled calmly.

'For that we will use quantum communication, impossible for the program to trace.'

'It is a subtle network that sustains our common purpose,' added Elías.

'We project our intentions through this network,' LEH pointed out. 'They will feel it, even if they do not understand it. This is the principle of non-locality: like casting a stone into a lake… the ripples always reach the shore that awaits them.'

The doubts began to dissipate. A renewed determination was taking the place of fear. The union of scientific and ancestral knowledge was shaping a shared Intent that transcended what they had imagined.

LEH fixed his gaze on the hologram of Ayni: an ancestral symbol formed of concentric circles and interwoven lines. At its centre, two crossed hands emerged as an echo of ancient memory, recalling reciprocity between worlds. Then he turned again to the gathered community.

'Attention is the key. Wherever we take our consciousness, there reality will unfold.'

With a precise gesture, LEH looked at GEH. He typed at the console and activated the sequence within the system. The symbol of Ayni expanded through the network, creating a pulse of instability, a fluctuation that opened a fissure in the simulation.

GEH, his voice charged with determination, added:

'This is a silent revolution and, like every revolution, it requires each of us to be fully aligned with this Intent.'

The tension in the room began to ease. The initial doubts transformed into conviction.

The sound of drums and rattles resonated deeply, synchronising hearts and purposes.

Elías joined the circle opened by the communities and closed his eyes. Then he spoke, his voice grave:

'What we sow today is not only a connection; it is a seed of memory, designed to resonate in those who have forgotten who they truly are. The program may control perceptions, but not the ancestral tapestry we are.'

Elías began to chant, marking a rhythm with his drum, forging the memory of the Reserves.

'This is Ayni,' he declared with profound serenity, 'an invisible mesh that connects all times and spaces. Precisely that which MIO does not understand is what makes our resistance possible.'

LEH sat beside Elías, his voice almost a whisper.

'Our purpose is to plant this seed so that each mind remembers who they are. The program seeks to impose forgetting, but we will open pathways towards remembrance.'

The drum struck a new rhythm at the centre of the circle. Eyes closed, bodies remembered. The network was no longer just a structure: it was an echo.

A slight tremor ran through the circle, but Elías knew: they were not sowing a revolution, they were sowing memory.

And when memory awakens, no network can contain it.

Naran woke agitated, her breathing uneven. She could still feel that persistent tightness in her chest, that restlessness that would not quite leave her. Was it fear, or something deeper, as if her body sensed what her mind could not yet name? She sat on the edge of the bed and tried to calm herself.

That day the trials would begin; after years of being labelled as Incompatible, she now faced the possibility. Perhaps, if all went well, she could finally leave the Centre with Maia and Néstor, find her father again… begin another life.

But in the haze of waking, something flashed through her, like a living trace of a presence she had brushed against, only for an instant. She did not know what it was. Once again, she clung to the idea of Karanza and held it tightly, for she needed something greater than her fear to keep moving forward. She hurried up the stairs to the training room to prepare early for the session. Upon entering, two assistants greeted her, and one of them directed her towards a new sphere-shaped device while explaining its function. Around her, the other Incompatibles.

'With this device we will better integrate your movements into the system,' the technician explained. 'Remember that you are also helping to carry out updates in the network.'

Before her, the structure unfolded into two overlapping circles. She took a deep breath before stepping into the sphere. The first minutes were a test of endurance: the instability and rapid shifts in position made her dizzy, but little by little her body grew accustomed to the new sensations.

When the adjustments were finished, she saw Nélida and Margot approaching. As soon as Margot stepped into the room, the air seemed to grow denser: her very presence was enough to transform the atmosphere and saturate it with a tension that was almost tangible. Some of those present straightened their backs unconsciously, while others lowered their eyes and avoided meeting her eye.

'As you know, today the homogenisation trials begin,' she announced in a tone that silenced the room at once. 'Once connected, you will be able to download the instructions.'

'Afterwards will we be able to go to Karanza?' Maia asked, uneasy. Her messy hair and the dark circles under her eyes betrayed her accumulated exhaustion.

Margot looked at her coldly before replying.

'We will study each case individually. Yesterday we had a meeting and concluded that transferring you to Karanza is a dangerous option.'

'But yesterday you said that…' Maia began to protest, her voice tense.

'We know the effort you are making,' the coordinator interrupted. 'The update will benefit the entire population, it will ease their connection. We are deeply grateful for your participation,' she added without a trace of emotion. 'That is why I said we will study each case.'

The mechanical way in which she spoke only added to the frustration. Maia pressed her lips together, holding back a response that seemed on the verge of bursting out. But before she could insist, Margot announced that each team should proceed to its assigned room to begin the trial. Naran searched for her name on the screen and confirmed that the two siblings were in her group.

'We're in the first round,' she told Maia with a forced smile, trying to disguise her nerves.

'I hope you don't ruin this trial with your visions,' her companion warned her bitterly. 'I only want to get through this experiment and get out of here.'

The comment struck her hard, like an unexpected lash. Naran lowered her head as she felt Maia's pent-up anger, once directed at Margot, now turn on her. Her stomach tightened, as if the very air had contracted around her. She did not reply, she simply swallowed and moved on.

Nélida and several technicians helped the participants adjust in their personal stations and put on their virtual helmets. Naran entered the system without delay and, to her surprise, found that the adjustments had already been made, for the interface moved with greater fluidity. Little by little, the rest of the participants joined in, exchanging looks of encouragement, though the silence weighed heavily between them.

Then MIO began the download of the instructions and objectives of the trial.

The virtual light unfolded slowly before them, revealing a landscape of snow-capped mountains contrasting with the green valleys in which they stood. The constant murmur of a river and its waterfall caught Naran's attention; she turned her head to the left, instinctively searching for the source of the sound. The sense of immersion gave her a slight dizziness because, although the environment seemed calm, the speed of the projected pixels flooded her senses with a chaotic flow of stimuli. Sounds and colours, perfectly designed, seized her attention.

They found themselves inside a digital construct, where streams of data multiplied exponentially, designed to prevent any attempt by the group to interfere with the network.

The program's instructions took hold of Naran's mind with overwhelming force: the goal was to keep the vision of the green valleys stable until achieving a unified perception with the group. They had to return continuously to the homogenisation representation and resist other scenarios and the spontaneous interferences that arose from their own minds.

A penalty signal shattered the collective concentration. Néstor had been distracted for more than three seconds, captivated by the information flowing freely from his mind into the system. In a fleeting instant of lucidity, Naran managed to glimpse those interferences: fragments of forgotten memories her companion was projecting uncontrollably. Disordered scenes emerged like flashes: protests in crowded squares, classical music concerts in grand halls, Gothic cathedrals, children's laughter echoing in green parks.

But among those fragments, older memories also slipped through, visions that were not only his: chants around the fire, voices whispering in forgotten tongues, weaves stretched out like maps of time.

They were memories the system had deliberately erased—not only from the present, but from the deepest core of being.

Néstor had the gift of recovering collective memory, of helping users to remember what the system had sought to suppress. The program emitted a louder warning sound, and the young man, visibly shaken, tried to protest, but his sister Maia stopped him with a cold, cutting look.

'I told you not to interfere!' she exclaimed harshly.

'This is all a lie!' he shot back, frustrated and trembling. 'What will happen to us if we reject this script? What will they do if we fail their trials? Why do they penalise us for what we are able to see? We have to fight for that five percent that still resists!'

'Stop!' Maia shouted firmly. 'If you alter the frequencies now, the system will expel us ahead of time. Just follow the instructions and let's get back to Karanza as soon as possible.'

'Do you really think that at the end of these trials they will let us go there?' Néstor challenged her with a gaze burning with rage.

For a moment, Maia faltered. Her mind flew to Karanza, intense memories of her parents surfacing: her mother embracing her, her father ill as she cared for him; and a knot formed in her throat.

'This isn't the time for this,' she whispered, clenching her fists and trying to hold back her emotion.

Naran noticed something changing in the network and stared at Maia.

'What's happening? Is this part of the simulation?'

Maia tried to regain control, but her emotion rippled through the network like a pulse, and the Incompatibles began to align with what she felt.

'It's her…' Naran whispered, surprised to discover the source. 'It all comes from Maia.'

The young woman tried to hide it, but it was too late. She had just revealed that her ability went beyond simple collective empathy: she was capable of transmitting emotions with such intensity that others experienced them as their own. The hardness she wore as a mask crumbled, revealing her deep vulnerability. Naran watched as Maia fought to hold back tears, though her face remained rigid and determined.

'We have a plan,' Maia reminded her brother. 'We need time, do you understand?'

'That's your plan, not mine,' Néstor replied defiantly.

The group tried once more to stabilise the shared vision, but a new alert from the control centre warned them of possible disqualification. Just when they thought they had recovered the stability of the landscape, Naran perceived an anomaly: a symbol composed of interwoven circles suddenly appeared in the midst of the environment.

Intrigued, she approached and touched it without hesitation.

Then she stopped looking through the system and began to see with the eyes of the symbol.

A word then reverberated like an echo running through her: Ayni.

They were not alone; she felt all those who were sustaining them in the vision, in the sound of the drum.

At once, a vivid image surged in her mind: Illa advanced towards her with commanding calm, carrying something in her hands. Before Naran, she slowly opened her palms and revealed a handful of quinoa seeds. Instinctively, Naran cupped her hands to receive them.

The mere sight and touch of them provoked a collision between worlds.

Néstor and Maia exchanged a glance; Naran had revealed her ability within MIO.

The projections in the system began to distort, freezing time and space around them.

A clarity settled within the young woman as her eyes met Illa's. In that instant, she understood something that had long lain dormant inside her, a flash of knowledge and resistance awakening within.

It was like touching a truth that came from another time. It was not a vision; it was a certainty that had always been there.

In the control centre, the technicians quickly detected the anomaly.

'A participant has significantly altered the environment,' they reported to Margot, who narrowed her eyes in annoyance.

'Restrict her options in the simulation and penalise the entire group,' she ordered coldly.

Alarmed, Maia insisted with urgency, asking Naran to refocus on the homogenisation. Néstor, by contrast, gave her a knowing look, silently encouraging her rebellion. And the girl gazed at the seeds in her trembling hand.

The struggle she experienced was not only against MIO, but against her own fear, against that inner voice that trapped her again and again. *Who was she really? An Incompatible, a dreamer, someone destined never to belong to any imposed world?* The seeds reminded her that everything depended on her attention—that wherever she placed her gaze, it would become real.

But her fear regained its strength and, at last, with a resigned sigh, she closed her eyes and let the connection with Illa gradually fade away. She accepted the rules of the game, aligning her perception once more with the group. And from the control centre, the end of the trial and the success of the homogenisation were announced.

Maia turned to her, relieved but still tense.

'I'm glad you didn't ruin it. Two more trials and we'll stop being guinea pigs.'

Naran remained silent. Outwardly she seemed integrated, but inside an abyss opened with every attempt to fit into the group. *What am I doing here?* she thought, staring into the void. She felt like a thread that could never truly be woven with others. She had learned to pretend, to answer according to expectations, to simulate belonging. But in moments like that, doubt struck her with overwhelming force.

While the group celebrated their apparent victory, Néstor stared at her intently. The young woman recalled his words with force: *What if passing these trials meant being trapped permanently in a scenario others had chosen for us?* It ran deep within her and made her realise that perhaps the true trial was not yet over.

Perhaps fitting in was the true prison.

And her silence, her most perfect way of betraying herself.

The celebration continued with joy in Karanza's central square. The grandmothers, through the quipus, narrated stories of great walkers. A gentle breeze stirred the colourful threads of the tapestry, and a feather from a condor's plumage landed delicately among them.

Among the hamawtas present, one *awicha* stood out— the wise grandmother who presided over the circle. She held the feather with reverence, sensing it was a hidden message from within the Pachas: a thread sustained in the great tapestry. Without speaking, she signalled to the other women to bring a basket. From it she drew a quipu with devotion, feeling within her hands the memory of the weave.

Her nimble fingers moved along the cords, untying knots and shifting the direction of the threads like echoes of a mesh expanding outward. She wove as she deciphered an ancestral language, revealing a hidden note: a silent message beyond perceptual boundaries.

Inside the laboratory, LEH, his team, and the communities held their Intent. The atmosphere was dense, charged with expectation, while the technicians carefully monitored the data streaming in real time across the screens, recording unusual patterns.

'Look at these fluctuations,' remarked one of the technicians, intrigued, as he pointed at the screens. 'They seem to indicate subtle interferences.'

Tension slowly mounted. LEH remained still, his absolute calm contrasting with the nervousness of the rest of the team.

'It is quantum non-locality,' he finally murmured. 'We are witnessing how perception can influence at a distance and alter the simulation imposed by the program. Attention is the key: wherever it settles, it alters the field. Each node in the system could feel this fluctuation.'

The data displayed pronounced oscillations, patterns that defied MIO's conventional logic. It was evident that something external to the laboratory was affecting the system, something impossible to predict within its traditional paradigm.

The circle slowly dissolved, leaving behind a sense of gratitude and wellbeing among those present.

Meanwhile, LEH remained with the technicians, reviewing the results. The data analysis revealed that they had only managed to shift the point of perception for a few seconds, yet that brief instant was enough to introduce the ancestral symbol into the system.

Still, the hacker could not help but feel uneasy. He knew there was little time left to help the group, for once they identified with the system, once they became compatible, it would be far more difficult to offer them support.

That unease still lingered when a knock came at the door. It was a technician, who entered to announce the arrival of an awicha from the Reserves. LEH watched as the woman entered in silence, carrying with her a small quipu carefully rolled.

'I have come from the square,' the grandmother declared in a serene voice, extending it towards the researcher. 'This information has become interlaced with you; this quipu holds the memory of Phawaq and his family.'

LEH took it carefully and, after a moment, understood the implicit message. Without a word, he placed the quipu into a special interface, designed to translate its cords and knots into the digital language of the quantum operating system. The screen came alive instantly, displaying dynamic graphics, lines tracing a complex perceptual map.

'It's a quantum weave,' he whispered in awe, 'and through the quipu, a perceptual route has been created to break the fixation of the assemblage point imposed by MIO.'

It was not merely a map; it was an act of love encoded, a living memory sent from the other side of the fabric. Those present drew closer in wonder, watching how the ancestral cords transformed into digital patterns.

'This section of the quipu matches the anomaly recorded in today's simulation,' noted GEH, his astonishment growing.

LEH immediately understood:

'It's Naran. During the trial she found a fissure and managed to perceive the code activated through the symbol. This quipu is a coded map that clearly points to her perceptual potential. Our task now will be to accompany her and hold her within the system.'

The group nodded, realising this was a different kind of battle: silent, invisible, fought with perception, Intent, and memory.

Elías, who until then had remained silent, began to play the drum softly, marking a steady, deep rhythm, unifying with that gesture the collective Intent of the communities gathered there.

'This is Ayni,' he murmured, 'a fabric of reciprocity that binds all perceptions. They may control the Tonal, the rigid structure, but they will never reach the intangible, the Nagual, the freedom that connects us.'

LEH drew a deep breath, grateful to all those present and to those helping from afar to sustain that invisible thread. He knew this was only the beginning. In that moment, their purpose was to help Naran and the other Incompatibles to remember themselves within the program.

For remembering was the first step towards freedom.

KNOT VIII

TAMBO

'How could you betray yourself like that, Naran?' Ikan asked, visibly angry as he crossed paths with her in the Research Centre. 'What happened to your connection, to your unique perception? You let yourself get trapped, and then the whole group got trapped, like the monkey that won't let go of the nuts trapped in the bottle. They preferred false security over releasing fear. They're so predictable...'

Naran stopped, startled to see Ikan before her. She had completely forgotten his voice, his teachings, even the conversations they had once shared. *How can a memory vanish like that? When did I begin to see with the system's eyes?*

In that moment, under his accusing gaze, she felt the weight of accumulated guilt.

'I can't do it anymore, Ikan.' Her voice came out sharp, defensive. 'I don't have the energy to fight a system so vast. I've decided to pass the trials and leave this place to find my father. I'm not who you think I am.'

'Maybe you only believe that because you keep telling yourself so, Naran.' The boy crossed his arms, his voice calm but intense. 'Don't you see you keep repeating the same story over and over, the one the program has shaped for you? Now you have the chance to decide who you want to be, inside and outside the program.'

'I don't have the strength to fight. I only want a little peace.'

'Even if it's an illusion? Even if it's a trap? Ask yourself, Naran: how will you ever see the truth if you keep following the path others have marked out for you?'

The young woman lowered her gaze, caught in her own labyrinth of thoughts. Ikan's words unleashed waves she could not contain.

'What other choice do I have?' she whispered. 'Fight a program we cannot defeat?'

He looked at her with a mixture of compassion and challenge.

'It's simpler than you think. You don't need to confront it head-on, because the struggle is not outward, Naran. If you cannot change the system, change the perception you have of yourself within it, even if that means facing your deepest fears.'

'You make it sound easy, but it's not.'

'Don't you realise where you are, Naran? Once you're caught in MIO's world of perception, it's like being trapped in a dream. You must take responsibility for your perception: not only the one imposed on you, but the one you yourself create.'

'What do you mean by responsibility?' she asked.

Ikan was firm: 'We are so trained to let others decide for us… Responsibility means owning what you perceive; understanding that you, even inside MIO, are constantly creating your world, though trapped in its time, identified with the projections the system generates from your experiences.'

'But if I'm trapped, I don't know how to get out.'

'You're trapped in the past, Naran. The program fixes your perception in what's familiar, in what has already happened. Don't you see? Your true struggle is not against MIO, it's against your attachment to the known.'

His words weighed upon her; she bent under the burden of fear and responsibility, her stomach churning with anxiety.

'I don't know where to begin… I'm afraid,' she whispered, tears in her eyes.

Ikan crouched to her level and looked at her with both intensity and tenderness.

'You have the power to imagine other worlds. Remember Yuyana: see through your imagination, Naran.'

She collapsed to the ground, unable to decide, staring at the quinoa seeds she still held. Tears streamed down her face, stricken with pain and frustration.

'I don't know what to do, Ikan. All this… I don't understand it,' she said, clutching the seeds tightly in her trembling hands. 'What if I choose wrong? What if I never get out of here?'

'The true challenge is not just to remember, Naran, it's to sustain the memory. Because if you cling to the same thread, the same perceptual vine, like the monkey with its nuts, you will never leap. And if you don't leap, the program will do it for you.' He, aware of her fragility, did not relent. 'All you have to do is choose a direction and take a step. You'll understand there is another path. Right now, in this very moment, you have the power to choose another line.'

Naran, immersed in her pain, kept staring at the promise contained in those seeds, wishing the weight of being an Incompatible would vanish. Ikan sat beside her with intentional calm, watching her in silence. He recognised that, from the story she kept telling herself over and over, she still lacked the energy to remember herself inside the program, or to make a choice that could break the cycle imprisoning her. He understood that she took a step forward, but the next moment her attention slipped back to the system's perceptual control point, preventing her from collapsing new possibilities.

After a long silence, he began to recite softly a poem:

May the dreamer awaken the dreamed,
may the one who is dreamed find the dreamer.
Be here, be there, I and the other I.
Cross the bridge in a secret dance,
where you open to the mystery and weave dreams,
beyond the riverbed of time.
May we not be locked in the shadows
of their artificial horizons.
May the echo of their mandates not erase our song,
for we were not born only to die;
we were born to dance in both worlds,
to embrace the vastness of the mystery,
to perceive the vastness of what we are.

Naran looked at him with tearful eyes. The words calmed the turmoil within her. For a moment, she was able to rest in her heart and feel—even if only as a glimmer—that another path was possible.

Ikan, seated before her, tilted his head gently.

'Listen,' he said firmly. 'By releasing this imposed perception, by allowing everything you think you know to crumble, you will open the way to another reality you cannot yet imagine. That is true freedom, Naran: the ability to disidentify from what you think you are, in order to discover what you really are.'

She nodded slowly, as if his words were beginning to break down a wall that had stood intact for far too long. Her attention returned to him, who watched her in silence, his deep eyes like mirrors of another time.

'We are Dreamers, Naran. Everything you see, everything you feel, everything you believe immutable, is nothing but a position of Dreaming. Now you must recover the fragments of yourself you left scattered.'

His words reached her like the echo of a forgotten truth.

'Fragments…' she murmured, testing the word on her lips, as if saying it could unravel its meaning.

'That's right.' He stood, offered her his hand to help her up, and looked at her warmly. 'Remember: the bridge has always been there. Crossing it is up to you. Wherever you place your attention, Naran, you will collapse a line. That is why you must choose with awareness.'

The young woman's heart pounded, not with fear, but with the sense that something was opening before her.

'All right,' she said, with more firmness in her voice. For the first time, she simply wanted to remember.

Ikan nodded, and before lifting the quena to his lips, added softly:

'In our land, those who help others cross from one world to another are called *chakaruna*. We are not guides; we are bridges. That is what I am doing for you now. But only you can take the step.'

When he began to play, the melody unfolded, reaching across time. It was a sound that linked landscapes, faces, and stories she had left behind. She closed her eyes, and the memories returned vividly: mountains that seemed to touch the sky, tales of a profound connection she had once carried within her and that, little by little, was returning.

The music continued to envelop her, and for an instant, she could see the bridge before her, not as something physical, but as an opportunity, a leap into the unknown. She did not yet know if she would cross, but she no longer doubted that the bridge existed. And that, in itself, was already a shift of horizon.

A whisper split time.

Yuyana.

Then, she closed her eyes and crossed.

In the depths of the Valley, where the material and the immaterial touched, Tambo unfolded before Naran like a living tapestry, a space suspended between worlds. On its verdant terraces, quinoa and maize were watched over by llamas grazing peacefully; their earth-toned silhouettes blurred against the blue sky. On the horizon, the snow-capped Apus rose as guardians of memory, linking the village to a vaster order: a web of life that reminded her everything was part of the same fabric.

Naran made out a *chasqui* approaching—a messenger dressed in a tunic and a feathered cap. He announced his arrival with a deep sound that burst from the great conch shell, the *pututu*; its call crossed the valley like a breath, slid between broken mountains until it enveloped everything. Moved, she understood she was standing at a crossroads.

At the centre of Tambo rose the *tampus*, ancient inns that connected and stored living information. There the chasquis exchanged messages and data in an unending flow between the folds of time.

Amid that landscape, beside several llamas, was Illa, the awicha with a deep gaze, working the earth with vigour and serenity. Noticing that Naran was becoming lost in that avalanche of new information, she walked towards her, handed her a plough resting on the ground and, with a kind gesture, pointed to the soil before them.

'By working the earth you will anchor your attention in this place,' she said calmly. Then, pointing to the seeds Naran still held, she continued, 'In them lies the power to germinate what is to come. Sow them in these fertile terraces and watch what can sprout when your spirit takes root in the earth.'

Still in wonder, Naran let out a whisper.

'What is this place? Where am I?'

Without pausing her work, Illa looked up with a serene smile.

'You're in Tambo,' she replied patiently, 'a space of Dreaming. Here all realities coexist simultaneously. You used to come in your dreams until you lost your connection with the circular time.'

Naran watched her in bewilderment as memories of the llama she used to draw returned to her mind with unexpected clarity. Following the direction Illa indicated towards the mountains, she distinguished agile figures moving fluidly along the winding paths.

'They're incredibly fast,' she murmured, unable to look away. 'Who are they? How can they move like that?'

'The chasquis are more than mere runners: they're messengers between the world of form and the formless,' Illa explained firmly. 'They travel tirelessly along the paths of the great network, linking the void and transmitting its information through synchronicity and symbols.'

Naran listened, captivated by the idea that they could move that way.

'I'll teach you to move like they do—not only in the dense, but also along the subtle pathways of your mind and spirit.'

'Everything feels strange. Am I dreaming, Illa?'

'This reality is as real as yours. It's one of the many surrounding us that we usually don't perceive. Reality is emptiness—a fertile emptiness,' she whispered as she kept turning the earth. 'From that emptiness, everything arises.'

'How is it possible that I got here? Just a moment ago I was at the Centre.'

'You're an electromagnetic being, Naran. And with the impulse of the quena's sound, your assemblage point shifted. You've crossed a threshold, a point where past, present and future converge.'

She set the tool down and approached the young woman, her voice like wind coming from all directions.

'You have travelled a long way, Naran. But the journey that brought you here is not only the wish to escape MIO, it is something deeper: the force of Intent. An ancestral whisper, an invisible thread that crosses the Pachas and orchestrates events on multiple layers. The movement of the soul when it remembers its purpose.'

She looked at her without judgement, with the tenderness of one who recognises the fire hidden within another fire. 'That which burns in you when nothing else remains.'

Naran felt a shiver run down her back. She closed her eyes for an instant and, when she opened them, the landscape had subtly changed. The terraces and mountains were breathing with her.

'You have crossed a perceptual threshold. Here you can undo the knots of your perception and weave your quipu anew.'

'My quipu?' Illa removed a colourful quipu from around her neck and handed it to Naran with solemnity.

'All your memories are recorded in this quipu.'

The girl ran her fingers over the cords and knots; they felt familiar to her, yet she still asked what they meant.

'Each thread, each knot, represents a decision, an emotion, an experience. Through Recapitulation, you release what has been trapped.'

Illa crouched to pull a few weeds from among the quinoa plants and, as she stood, turned to her, serene and yet intense, as if about to share something fundamental.

'To Recapitulate is a simple yet profound movement. You exhale, and in doing so, you imagine you are releasing what you hold: that feeling that anchors you.'

'Old Intent?'

'Those decisions, those beliefs you formed without realising it, often shaped by fear or by what others wanted you to be. By exhaling them, you create space within you. Space for a new Intent, a fresh one born of your awareness and not of what the program or the world has imposed upon you.'

'And what about what we let go of?' the girl asked, her voice trembling slightly.

'It no longer has power over you,' the woman replied calmly. 'You exhale and release what binds you; you inhale and receive what awaits you.' She drew a deep breath to show her with her body. 'Inhale, Naran. Not only air, but the parts of yourself you left behind. In doing so, you will feel something shift within you.'

Naran closed her eyes, slowly moving her head from side to side, and for the first time felt a slight easing in her chest.

'Is this how I let go?' she asked, a mix of wonder and doubt.

'This is how you begin to remember who you truly are,' Illa answered, warmth in her voice.

'And when you remember, Naran, the entire quipu will change with you.'

The young woman traced the cords of the quipu with her fingers, feeling it pulse with a life of its own.

'This quipu is not just an object; it is a map of your life, of all the decisions and paths you have taken and those you can still take. By Recapitulating, you undo the knots that bind you to a limited vision. And when you use your Intent, you retie those knots with a new clarity.'

Suddenly, the quipu before Naran began to transform, expanding into a three-dimensional holographic map. The threads were activated by her attention, as if every conscious gaze opened a forgotten doorway. They stretched and crossed, projecting colours and shapes that revealed hidden layers of her history. The young woman touched one of the threads cautiously, and as soon as she did, a whirlwind of sensations and memories enveloped her. Illa observed her reaction patiently.

'You've become entangled in your own perceptual weave. To free yourself, you need to enter your quipu, to remember yourself.' She stepped closer to Naran and pointed at a particular knot that glowed with intensity. 'Look at how the information can flow and reconfigure itself. These threads are not only yours; they are part of a larger fabric, one that is constantly evolving.'

Naran blinked, incredulous.

'And that will work?'

Illa gave her a warm smile, brimming with trust.

'This is what your ancestors did. When you enter that space of Recapitulation, you will feel the generations of seers who came before you walking beside you. You are not alone, Naran. Their voices, their threads are with you.'

Expectant, the young woman let Illa's words settle in her mind. She touched the cords and knots of the quipu. Closing her eyes, she inhaled and moved her head slowly from right to left, following the awicha's guidance. As she exhaled, she felt something release within her, as though letting go of a weight she had carried for far too long. Each inhalation was also that of those who had preceded her. Each exhalation released centuries of forgetting.

'Recapitulate, Naran, summon your Intent. Shift your assemblage point, not to escape, but to see the world with new eyes. And remember: the power lies not in changing what is outside, but in changing how you perceive it.'

Suddenly, something shifted. A pulse of information began to flow through the cords. Naran could perceive subtle patterns, memories projected as symbols. Her attention was drawn to one knot and, before she could react, her whole being was absorbed.

When she opened her eyes, she was no longer in Tambo. She was sitting at a school desk, surrounded by her classmates. The sound of laughter and whispers filled the room. In front of her, a teacher was staring disapprovingly.

It was not just a memory.

It was a knot: a fragment of herself still trapped there.

'Naran, could you answer question seven?' the teacher pressed.

The young girl scanned the room while adjusting the patches fixed to her temples. She and her classmates were undergoing one of the first trials of the virtual program, an exercise designed to measure their perceptual capacity within the system. Yet Naran remained distracted, caught in her own thoughts, and at her silence, the teacher approached impatiently.

'Could you tell us what you saw in the scenario?' he asked, pointing at the screen projecting the program. 'Here are the three possible answers to the projected landscape: A, a park; B, a river; or C, a beach.'

Suddenly animated, Naran began to speak with a clarity unusual for her age. She described, as she used to do with her mother, an imagined landscape: a wide valley with green terraces stretching to the horizon, where llamas grazed peacefully at her side. Her words brimmed with life, as if she were trying to summon that place into the present to share it.

Until she froze. Suppressed laughter and the stares of her classmates shattered her flow. She looked around and felt the judgment of others strike like a blow. Her eyes sought the teacher, but he only observed her, baffled. The confidence she had felt while speaking crumbled. Feeling exposed, she murmured timidly:

'I think… I think I saw some mountains.'

The teacher's face hardened.

'That is not correct.'

Those words fell on her with unbearable weight. She looked at her classmates, who responded in unison that the correct answer was A: a park.

'Everyone saw it,' the teacher said, turning to the rest of the class as he noted something on his digital tablet, 'except you, Naran.'

The remark embedded itself in her mind like an endless echo. She felt her classmates' gazes pressing in on her, returning a distorted reflection of herself, amplifying her insecurities until they became impossible to ignore. Her breath grew shallow, and an invisible knot began to tighten in her chest.

The teacher, standing beside a group of program technicians, spoke bluntly:

'She cannot connect with what the program transmits. She has serious difficulties synchronising her attention with the system.'

The words shook the fragile sense she had of herself. Though she did not fully understand what was happening, she felt the oppressive judgment of others. The connection she had felt with her own inner landscape had turned into an abyss.

She clenched her fists as the echo of the teacher's voice continued to pierce through her.

Naran appeared again beside Illa, the knot of the quipu still between her fingers. As she released it, she fixed a resentful gaze on the awicha, unable to contain the mix of anger and sadness flooding her.

'What did you think of that memory?' the awicha asked, her calmness contrasting with the young woman's distress. 'I think we could call it the first knot—the one that keeps reappearing, the one you bounce against again and again. Why do you think it is so important, Naran?'

Illa's words sank into her like a stone. She thought of that moment when she first felt she wasn't valid, when she didn't belong to the group. The feeling of being singled out for her difference invaded her again, pulling her into a whirlpool of sorrow and rage.

'Why are you making me remember this?' she snapped. 'I'm tired of being singled out, of being called Incompatible. I don't know why I'm here, I don't know who you are, and I don't have to come to this place just to be reminded again of what I can't do.'

Illa held her gaze unwaveringly:

'You've perceived something important and, without realising it, you've said it yourself: 'I can't do it.' But now you need to hear it consciously. You came here to understand yourself from another perspective, to recognise what you keep repeating to yourself again and again. That day was significant because you began to disconnect from yourself and from your reality.'

The words pierced through the young woman's defences; the pressure of her emotions was unbearable, like a pain she couldn't escape. In a desperate attempt to free herself, she touched the next knot of the quipu.

When she got home, Naran crept silently to the kitchen door. From there she could hear her parents speaking in low voices, discussing the note she had brought from school. Anxiety grew in her chest, accompanied by the fear of not meeting their expectations.

'To be honest, I'm glad she hasn't been able to access the program,' said Unay, protectively. 'Maybe her brain isn't ready yet, and besides, we don't know how that connection might affect her development. She's only twelve; we shouldn't force things.'

'I'm worried,' Alan replied with a note of unease. 'If she can't keep up with her classmates, the most likely thing is that they'll transfer her to another school. Not connecting to the program will be a huge problem for her.'

'Every child has their own pace. I'd rather she stay herself, even if she's in her own world, than have her change who she is for a virtual program,' her mother answered firmly, though a shadow of doubt crossed her face.

'The sectors have already begun with the connections. It's inevitable that we'll all be linked during the long winters,' her father insisted, this time more darkly. 'You're not in good health; you should worry about yourself. But if Naran can't connect, it will be a burden to think she'll be outside the winter bunkers.'

'We have time,' Unay repeated, though her voice trembled slightly. 'The note said they'll keep adjusting the connection until she's compatible with the program.'

Alan shook his head with an air of resignation. 'We'd better be realistic… there's no time.'

Her mother's words were tender, but behind them echoed her father's concern, which felt like a silent condemnation. *Was she a burden? Why did her existence always seem like a problem they had to solve?* Her throat tightened. She wanted to escape, but there was nowhere to hide from that judgement she couldn't fully understand. She ran up the stairs to her room, her heart pounding as if trying to flee her own body.

There, her eyes settled on the drawings of the village, on the stories with the llamas. They represented something so important to her, but at that moment they felt out of place, a reflection of what was not accepted. Guilt mixed with a sadness she couldn't control. With her breath short and ragged, she pressed the papers to her chest. She stood still for a moment before the fireplace, her mind divided between clinging to those memories or letting them fade away.

Finally, a visceral impulse won. With anger and tears in her eyes, she threw her drawings and writings into the fire and watched as the flames devoured them quickly. Each stroke, each colour, each letter twisted and disappeared in the smoke, taking something of herself along with them. She stared at the ashes, feeling that in some way she was betraying herself: she had tried to let go of something she loved, something she could no longer hold in her life, but the emptiness left in its place was even more unbearable.

Naran looked at Illa with a mix of confusion and frustration; her hands were still trembling after touching the knots of the quipu.

'What is this?' she asked, her voice unsteady as she tried to calm the agitation rising in her chest.

The landscape began to shift before her eyes. The mountains seemed to breathe; they undulated softly alongside the clouds sliding over them, mirroring the turbulence she felt inside.

'Didn't you want to remember?' Illa replied with serene calm, her gaze steady on Naran. 'Now you can see the strokes of your sketch from another perspective, notice how the lines you thought were fixed were only stories you told yourself. You have the power to rewrite them.'

A llama approached silently and stood at her side. Naran stroked its fur slowly, feeling a warmth that reached into the deepest part of her being.

'This llama isn't just an image from the past, Naran, it's a doorway. When you drew it, you were recalling something authentic, something that had always been inside you. You had a clear, free perception before doubts and fears clouded your gaze.'

The girl closed her eyes and let the sensation spread slowly through her body. Forgotten images surfaced like fragments of an old film: the classroom, the laboratory, the disapproving faces, the constant weight of feeling different, trapped in a web of judgments and expectations not her own.

Sensing the girl's growing anxiety, Illa handed her a small tool.

'Hoeing will help you calm your mind. The earth listens and absorbs what we need to release.'

For a while, Naran surrendered to the act of digging, letting the repetition of her movements soothe her. At last, she broke the silence:

'I've always felt rejected for not fitting in. But now I see that idea of incompatibility wasn't real, it was only a misinterpretation—a first knot twisted.'

Illa smiled slowly, letting her words float in the air until they found their place.

'You're beginning to see the deep root of your pain: the belief that you're not enough, that you don't belong, that you're not seen or understood—not by your teachers, not by your father…'

A deep ache crossed Naran's chest, and she lowered her gaze to the ground. The sound of the pututu broke the moment, announcing the arrival of another chasqui. Illa handed her a quipu and a pouch of seeds. Naran, feeling a quiet satisfaction at the patch of earth she had worked, looked up to greet the messenger.

'You're anxious to move forward, Naran,' Illa said, noticing how the young woman's hands were already reaching for another knot in the quipu. She glanced at her from the corner of her eye while bidding the chasqui farewell.

The messenger crossed swiftly, pointing to the horizon.

'Don't jump from one knot to another without meaning. Before you move, you must integrate what you're feeling.' Illa stopped in front of her, her voice firm but gentle. 'The chasquis run fast, but they always carry a purpose; learn from them. Integrate what you've perceived, Naran. Look at those points as you would a map.'

The awicha pointed to a specific knot in the quipu, which pulsed softly.

'Let's return to that conversation with your parents, to the day you threw your drawings into the fire. That's where you got stuck.'

Naran's gaze hardened with resistance

'You said I disconnected,' she murmured, seeking understanding from the wise elder.

Illa slowly shook her head, firm but compassionate.

'Don't look outside for what you can only find within.'

Naran closed her eyes again and remembered her father's severe judgment, her teacher's critical gaze, and the fire devouring her drawings.

'What I see isn't valid… I'm not valid,' she whispered, feeling those words settle into her chest.

The cords of the quipu pulsed softly in her hands, responding to her emotion. With a deep breath, she let the words flow out, releasing that weight on the exhale. As she did, the thread glowed gently.

'What else do you discover, Naran?' Illa asked.

The girl opened her eyes and understood with absolute clarity:

'I refused to see beyond. I allowed others to decide who I could be, what I could do or feel. That's why I stopped seeing the llama: I stopped seeing my own possibilities.'

The awicha spun on her heels and laughed with joy.

'You're remembering, Naran! You're beginning to change your perception! Now you see that what you thought was a misfortune is, in truth, your greatest gift.'

She stopped in front of her.

'When you shift your assemblage point, you enter the Nagual, a space where everything is possible, where the lines of time dissolve and you are truly free.'

She lowered her voice until it became a whisper, as if it came from the Apus themselves:

'We are entering the fertile void, Naran. Here there is no fixed structure, only potential. What seems solid begins to dissolve: words, the self, time. And what remains is that which feels, that which knows without knowing, that which observes without judging. That is pure awareness. That is the Nagual.'

A living silence opened between them, as though the very wind had stopped to listen.

Then Illa, just a breath of voice among the leaves, added:

'Remember, Naran, if you do not sow, others will sow in your place. The earth never stays empty. Your attention is the garden; your Intent, the seed.'

The girl felt a profound connection to those words and realised that her journey was not only one of resistance, but of transformation. Something within her recognised this place as though she had already been there, before fear trapped her.

Illa took the hoe once more and handed it back to her.

'Bring your awareness back here, to the present. When your mind wanders, return to the simple act of digging. That is how you will strengthen your attention.'

Naran dug in silence. And in doing so, she saw clearly how her mind tried to flee. But little by little, without struggle, she learned to bring it back—to the present, to the body, to the earth. With every gesture, her attention grew steadier.

Illa watched her with affection.

'Remember: each step on the paths of the chasquis brings you closer to the Chawpi, to the precise point where your strengths meet, where Intent can cross with you.
That is where your true journey begins.'

THE REFLECTION THE SYSTEM CANNOT SEE

Naran emerged from her Dreaming when someone shook her arm. Maia stood beside her, urgency written across her face.

'What are you doing still asleep? We have to prepare for the second test; they'll be calling us over the loudspeakers at any moment.'

She blinked in confusion. As her gaze swept across the room, the images and sounds wavered, as if her body were in one place but her perception in another. The dimness of her room contrasted with the vivid clarity still pulsing in her memory: the colours in Tambo seemed brighter, more alive, as though the very air remembered.

Maia's urgency, pulling her towards the test, overlapped with the serene depth of Illa. And in that collision of realities, a certainty struck her like an echo: what she had experienced was not a dream.

Then, with sudden clarity, she understood the words Néstor had said as they were escaping:

You know, when you're inside, it seems that nothing there can be changed—but we were able to. Maia and I used to create incredible things, but they took that ability from us.

After trying several times, they ended up blocking our access for being Incompatibles.

The taste of nectar still lingered. It wasn't sweetness; it was a memory.

'Maia… we're not Incompatibles,' she whispered, still half-asleep.

But Maia was already walking ahead—she hadn't heard her.

'Quick, come with me. We need to meet before the test, they're waiting,' she said, taking Naran by the arm and guiding her into the corridor.

They arrived at a room larger than her own, where the rest of the group of Incompatibles had gathered. Néstor stood at the centre, wearing his usual sarcastic smile, though his eyes betrayed a flicker of unease. Without thinking, she hurried towards him.

'Now I understand what you told me on the way to Karanza,' she said with conviction.

Néstor raised an eyebrow, offering a wry smile.

'Took you long enough,' he replied, dryly.

'But I imagine that, at some point, anyone could change the program if they truly wanted to,' she continued.

'Not everyone,' Maia interjected, folding her arms.

'They're running studies so we can connect to the system like the rest of the population—but without allowing us to insert information. We saw it during the first test. And now, with the new update, they're determined to enforce it. They see us as a threat. Why else do you think we're still here?'

'That's what Margot mentioned about the interferences,' Néstor added, his voice tinged with concern.

'We're Incompatibles because we have the ability to insert information into the program. We can't modify it directly anymore —their goal is to modify us.'

Naran felt her perception shift. With just a change in thought, the word Incompatibles took on a new meaning. The weight of not fitting in began to lift. She saw the events of her life through a different lens: the guilt she had carried for years, the feeling of not being enough for her father, of being different in a system that demanded conformity. The realisation shook her. *If they stripped away their ability to alter the program, what would remain? What did it truly mean to be compatible?*

The silence broke with Néstor's firm voice.

'The trials they're putting us through are designed to implement the final update—to allow all Incompatibles to enter the system,' he said, pulling a folded paper from his pocket. 'Karanza and the Outer Reserves are backing us. That's why we need to set our own conditions.'

But not everyone shared his resolve. Maia and several others voiced their concern about the consequences of acting too soon.

'Let's not rush,' her sister interjected. 'We're not ready to protest just yet. Let's go ahead with the tests, and at the end, those who wish to go to Karanza can do so, and those who want to enter the system can request their 5% opening.'

Néstor began pacing in circles, visibly agitated, until he came to a halt at Maia's words.

'Can't you see the trap?' he snapped, exasperated. 'Once the update is complete, nothing of our perceptual abilities will remain.'

The discussion escalated, polarising the group.

'You don't see where this is going!' he exclaimed, raising his voice. 'We must set our conditions now. Today, we should declare that we will not proceed with the tests,' he said, waving the note in the air. 'Or at the very least, as our allies suggested, we must ensure these tests serve another purpose: to secure the 5% opening.'

Maia faced him, calm but resolute.

'This isn't the moment, Néstor. It's better to finish the tests. Once they trust us and the update has been implemented, we can insert the information into the system and unlock the 5%. Let them believe they've homogenised our perception… and then we'll release the information from within. There's no need to ask permission now; let's be strategic.'

Naran sensed the tension thickening between the siblings. Néstor pressed his lips together, casting a hard look at both Maia and her. Once again, Naran felt caught between them.

'It'll be too late,' he muttered. 'Our abilities will be wiped out with the update. Waiting serves no purpose.'

The group descended once more into heated debate. Néstor raised his voice, urging them to grasp the gravity of the threat, while Maia defended her path of patience and infiltration. Naran observed them both, feeling they each held part of the truth. Setting terms was vital, yet so was having a plan.

'There's no other way out,' he insisted. 'Once they manage to capture our attention within the program, they'll steer it wherever they want. And they'll force us to uphold their version of reality.'

Words came to Naran like a whisper: *The program presents you with binary choices. But have you wondered what it leaves out? What possibilities might exist if you chose neither?*

She felt the pull to step outside the dichotomy; it wasn't about choosing between the siblings' positions. Something deeper called to her—the real question lay elsewhere. Maia and Néstor knew how to hold their ground regardless of others. *But did she truly know what she desired?* She sensed there was a layer beyond this conflict. Everything began to dissolve: the noise, the arguments, even the self trying to choose correctly.

Uncertainty opened like an abyss beneath her feet. Her thoughts spun into a labyrinth just as the loudspeakers rang out through the room, calling them for the second test.

Perhaps it wasn't about choosing sides, but remembering from where she wanted to observe.

From the control centre, the first group of Incompatibles was ready for the second test. The technicians informed Nélida and Margot that the virtual perceptual adjusters were primed for activation. The coordinator examined the analysis from the first test with a distant, impassive expression. For her, it wasn't merely about efficiency—it was conviction. Integrating the Incompatibles into the system was an inevitable evolution.

'Today, they will finally understand the structure and rules within the system,' she remarked, her tone indifferent, eyes fixed on the data.

'Indeed,' confirmed one of the technicians, scrutinising his screen. 'Once the perceptual adjusters detect and correct any deviations, they will begin to perceive energetic configurations as solid objects within the system. That will allow their perceptual point to be definitively fixed.'

Margot nodded silently and turned her gaze to the monitors displaying the Incompatibles, who waited, visibly anxious.

'It seems the new update is meeting expectations fully,' she stated with quiet confidence.

'Without a doubt,' another technician replied assuredly. 'The Incompatibles are beginning to integrate the perception designed by the program. Within days, this perceptual Template will be fully implemented across the population.'

Margot remained silent for a moment, contemplating the tense faces on the screens. Then, with a decisive gesture, she gave the order:

'Initiate the virtual simulation.'

Moments later, the virtual perceptual adjusters appeared on the monitors, floating constructs designed to detect any deviation in perception and realign it accordingly.

The pilot program launched a series of scenarios requiring coordination and harmony among the participants. Their task was to identify and describe the virtual reality in accordance with the system's parameters. At breakneck speed, hundreds of images and structures were projected, seeking to prompt the Incompatibles to assimilate the representations and their respective meanings.

Naran immersed herself in the test, adapting to each scenario until an urban image with tall buildings appeared. She identified some as school, shopping centre, library, but when one was labelled as home, a sudden longing pulled her from the simulation. A faint whisper, barely perceptible, tugged at her attention: something MIO had not shown. Instantly, a memory surfaced—her mother's hand guiding her as they disembarked from the boat at the Outer Reserves, the embrace of relatives waiting at the dock. The emotion surged so intensely that, without realising, the symbol of Ayni projected itself onto one of the buildings in the program, like a crack of light within the digital concrete.

Néstor perceived the manifestation and understood her intention. Without hesitation, he amplified the projection. Around him, images from the collective memory began to unfold: community bonds, children playing in the markets, laughter, music, dances, poetry. Naran sought Maia's gaze, hoping for her complicity, but her companion shook her head, warning her to stop. Yet the memory's intensity had already permeated the group, and a surge of feeling swept through the Incompatibles. For a fleeting moment, the program's predetermined configuration halted.

The interruption lasted only seconds. An alert sounded in the control centre, prompting the technicians to intervene. The trial was restarted, and the projection's speed recalibrated. MIO increased the frequency of the perceptual adjusters, intensifying their detection and correction functions. Each time they altered the landscape, the program responded swiftly, reordering the group's perception and forcing them back into the prescribed scenario.

Frustration overtook Naran. Direct resistance drained her, and she knew they could not risk further penalties. She took a deep breath and shifted strategy. Instead of confronting the simulation, she softened her stance, choosing to observe from a certain distance. She let the images flow without resistance, seeking the subtle details that escaped the system's rigidity. That's when she saw it: tiny flowers sprouting through cracks in the asphalt, a blooming tree behind a building.

She focused her attention on those subtleties, and gradually, delicate changes began to ripple through the environment: birds appeared on the horizon, the landscape warmed in tone, small patches of green emerged between streets, and a more welcoming atmosphere began to form.

She realised the program didn't penalise her for these alterations. She had found a blind spot in the system—a way to shift the environment without MIO detecting it. Carefully, she conveyed the insight to her companions. Perhaps the true revolution wasn't in changing the scenario… but in changing the way of looking.

Néstor understood her strategy instantly. He met her gaze and, without raising suspicion, began introducing small changes into his environment too. For the first time, Naran felt she could go beyond the imposed dichotomy. It wasn't about accepting the system's reality, nor destroying it, but discovering her own path within it. That was her choice.

She then looked at her companion. Their eyes met in silent complicity; they knew they had reached a fissure in perception.

That 5% the system ignored was all they needed to break through.

Margot observed intently as the group of Incompatibles exited the test room. Around her, the technicians discussed how the system had managed to nullify the interferences during the simulation, and how new updates were being implemented to reinforce perceptual adjustment.

'Proceed with the next group. I have a meeting now,' the coordinator instructed, checking her watch before turning towards the exit.

However, one of the technicians stopped her before she could leave: the main screen had just displayed a detailed analysis of the second test.

'Subtle alterations have been detected. The system has allowed a 2% opening,' he reported, avoiding her gaze.

Margot frowned. She turned towards the monitor, scanning the graphs with a mix of disbelief and displeasure.

'How?' she muttered through clenched teeth. 'How is that possible?'

The technician swallowed, well aware of the gravity of the discovery.

'It appears that MIO has interpreted the alterations as natural adjustments within the perceptual structure and has integrated them without classifying them as errors.'

A pang of irritation rippled through her. She could not afford any margin for deviation.

'Call in the Incompatibles again,' she ordered, her tone firm and unequivocal. 'We're moving the next test forward. I don't want this to become a problem once the group enters the main program.'

'But the third test hasn't been scheduled yet,' another technician intervened, uncertain.

'You have one hour to solve it,' she snapped. Her cutting gaze silenced further objections. 'I don't want these data mentioned in the meeting. Make the necessary adjustments and ensure that all perceptual fluctuations are completely blocked.'

The technician nodded quickly and began entering modifications into the system interface. As she monitored the data on the graphs, Margot suddenly raised a hand, halting further commentary. Her eyes locked on her colleague.

'Nélida, go and fetch the group. Make sure they're all prepared—especially Naran and Néstor. I want to see exactly what they're doing.'

Margot felt it in her body. This wasn't just a deviation. It was as if the system itself had begun to look the other way—as if something were deprogramming it from within, without leaving a trace.

Naran entered her room and let herself fall onto the bed. She took a deep breath, focused on her breathing, and allowed her mind to quieten. The image of the terraces appeared clearly. She walked towards the llama and greeted it, stroking its fur. Then, without a word, she picked up a hoe and joined Illa. The two of them continued tilling the soil in silence.

After a while, the awicha bent down to pull up some weeds. Her face showed a quiet satisfaction.

'Very good, Naran. You are beginning to not-do. You didn't fall into complaint, and you stayed present while you were tilling the soil.'

'I almost did, Illa,' Naran admitted with a sigh. 'After today's trial, I feel disoriented. I tried to contribute something to the system, but it penalised me. I feel caught between what the system expects of me and what I truly want to become.' Her words poured out like a freed torrent.

Illa turned her gaze to Naran's feet. The young woman followed it and noticed a black and yellow snake slowly sliding among the stones.

'What do you see when you look at the snake, Naran?' the wise woman asked calmly, without stopping her work.

Naran observed the animal's movement with care.

'It's unsettling… it seems that, despite its zigzagging, it never doubts where it's going.'

Illa offered a faint smile.

'Amaru is an ancient symbol—a bridge between worlds. In our cosmovision, it represents the *Uku Pacha*, the inner world, the deep and the hidden. But also transformation.'

Naran lifted her gaze, frowning.

'Transformation?'

'Yes. Look at its skin.' Illa pointed at the tiny scales shedding with every movement of the creature. 'When the snake grows, its old skin no longer serves. So it sheds it, letting go of what is no longer needed.'

Naran nodded slowly, leaning in to observe the reptile more closely.

'Amaru, the snake,' she murmured. 'That which crawls also transforms. Sometimes, what we believe is a burden… is medicine.'

Illa gave a slow nod.

'You are shedding your skin, Naran. The perception you've held until now, shaped by MIO, is beginning to crack. You're releasing that old vision, that skin that limited you, and beginning to see what lies beyond the program.'

Naran let out a deep sigh and sat on the earth.

'What's the point of shedding skin if reality keeps imposing the shape I must take?' she exhaled, spreading her arms before letting herself fall onto her back. 'Still, today I made small modifications to the program and wasn't penalised.'

'Today you've begun to shed your skin,' Illa said gently. 'You've made small changes within yourself, and those changes were reflected in the system.'

'But it was so subtle… like clouds drifting across the sky without any apparent direction.'

'You must learn to understand reality as a weave of perceptions. Your perceptions are the knots of that quipu.' Illa gestured towards the weave Naran wore around her neck. 'Some of those knots need to be undone.'

'But how can I change my perceptions within a system that resists every change I make?'

'It's natural to fear change. But the snake doesn't hesitate, Naran; it doesn't cling to its old skin because it knows its purpose is to grow.'

The girl closed her eyes and drew in a deep breath, reclaiming the part of herself that had remained trapped in fear. Then she exhaled, releasing what no longer served her. When she opened her eyes again, the landscape of Tambo appeared clearer, sharper. It wasn't the landscape that had changed—it was her attention. And as her perception shifted, the Dreaming responded like an awakened mirror.

'When you expand your perception, you'll gain access to a different kind of information—and with it, the possibility to experience alternative, deeper realities.'

'Shedding skin… leaving behind my old way of seeing the world, of seeing myself—even within MIO…'

'The snake is reborn in its new skin, with a new understanding, ready to perceive and explore new realities both inside and beyond MIO. Today, the system permitted a small crack, a 2% opening of perception. But you don't have to settle for that 2%, or even for 5%.'

Naran sat up and looked at Illa with suspicion.

'What are you talking about?'

Illa hesitated. For an instant, her eyes reflected something deeper than uncertainty. Was it fear? Or compassion?

'Remember, Naran: in what you call reality, the scenarios of your life have already been written by others. I believe you have the right to choose how you wish to live. That's why you must do something about it.'

Before the awicha could finish speaking, a tremor rippled through Tambo's landscape.

The ground shook beneath Naran's feet.

'What's happening?' she asked, alarmed, as the surroundings began to distort.

'They're waking you up at the Research Centre,' Illa replied, taking Naran's hand. 'Remember—you can deviate from the path they've drawn for you.'

Illa's image began to fade, while Nélida's figure grew clearer, shaking her insistently.

'Wake up, Naran,' her voice came first as a distant echo, then sharper. 'You have to undergo the third test.'

KNOT X

THE EDGE

LEH moved swiftly with his team through the alleys of Karanza. His silhouette slid through the dense fog that veiled the old Industrial District. Rusted chimneys loomed like ancient sentinels against the grey sky, while holographic signs flickered on weathered walls, reflecting a world where the ancestral and the technological coexisted in constant tension. But he wasn't looking at the surroundings; he was focused on what pulsed within: that 2%, the message he had received. It was a crack, like a note outside the staff, a spark dissonant in the score. And so, he had to find a way to sustain it.

Unlike usual, he didn't stop at the square to observe the symbols carved in stone or to exchange words with the merchants. His sole objective was Dr Lana's laboratory. Adjusting his jacket against the cold gusts, he quickened his pace.

The contrast between his own lab and Lana's was immediate: while his was a harmonious chaos of floating symbols and scattered equations, hers radiated precision: perfect geometric lines, data arranged with absolute rigour, quantum algorithms projected into the air like sacred scripts.

A mixed team of scientists, resistance members, and LEH's allies studied two large screens. One displayed the MIO network, modelled in countless interconnected nodes. The other showed Naran's quipu, which vibrated with patterns scarcely decipherable.

LEH wasted no time, for that 2% was not merely a statistical margin. It was a threshold.

If they could sustain the crack within the superposition, they could open a new narrative. And Lana, with her precision, could help to anchor that edge.

'Our connection with the Incompatibles through the ancestral symbol worked in the first trial,' he explained bluntly, 'but the third one is definitive. If they complete it, their perception will be fixed in Timeline 3, and they will have lost all perceptual mobility.'

Lana, with her analytical calm, typed a few commands and projected a new model.

'Observe the simulation,' she said, enlarging MIO's structure. 'Here you can see how the wave function has collapsed within the system: reality is reduced to a single state, a perceptual narrative imposed by the rulers.'

Ariana, a specialist in neuroscience and virtual reality, frowned as she analysed the stream of data.

'Each test reinforces perceptual rigidity,' she commented. 'If they succeed in fixing the Incompatibles' assemblage point, they will eliminate their observer flexibility, and with it, their connection to the quantum field.'

LEH gestured towards the visualisation of Naran's quipu.

'Our first connection prevented her assemblage point from locking. 'Now, in this trial, the quipu will be key. If she manages to perceive it, she will remember what she truly is.'

Ariana crossed her arms, thoughtful.

'That would explain why the Incompatibles are seen as a threat: their perception is the only variable in the equation. It means they can introduce new information into the system—and with it, reconfigure the system's perceptual structure.'

LEH nodded, unwavering.

'Exactly. If they manage to expand their perception before MIO locks it, they will open possibilities for all users.'

Lana raised an eyebrow, questioning his optimism.

Possibility is meaningless without a structure to hold it. Perceiving an alternative reality is not enough, you must integrate it. How do you translate potential into real change?'

LEH offered a slight smile, calm and clear.

'Because reality isn't written only in equations, Lana. Sometimes, it's enough to learn how to move between the lines of possibility.'

Lana considered his response in silence before nodding slowly.

'Even so, you'll need the right calculations for your movement to be effective.'

'That's why you're here,' LEH replied, acknowledging her with a subtle gesture.

The doctor returned her focus to the data.

'Despite all the trials, their perception has not yet been fully anchored to MIO's narrative.'

'Which is why we must act now,' he said. 'They don't just want to homogenise them—they want to use them as a critical mass to replicate the Timeline 3 Template beyond the system.'

A tense silence settled over the room.

'That means it won't matter whether we're inside or outside MIO,' Ariana said, concerned. 'Perception will replicate from user to user until it becomes the only accepted reality.'

Lana grasped the magnitude of the issue.

'They're designing a rigid matrix of perception to govern all experience. They're not limiting themselves to the system; they're programming reality itself.'

'MIO doesn't need to dominate by force,' LEH said gravely. 'It only has to fix attention. The mind organises reality… and MIO is its reflection when it forgets its origin.'

The lab filled with hurried discussions, each team voicing their views on the urgency of intervention. The tension built until Lana raised a hand, calling for silence. But Marco, a cybersecurity expert, stepped forward.

'How do we prevent it?' he asked.

LEH and Lana responded at once.

'The mobility of the assemblage point is crucial,' she said analytically.

'The key lies in the quipu,' he added with quiet conviction.

For a moment, Lana lowered her gaze, as if some distant memory brushed against her certainty. And once more, she weighed whether she was truly willing to ally herself with him. After a pause, she posed a question, intending to gauge his response:

'Tell me, LEH, do you believe perception can be modified without the observer being aware of it?'

The researcher held her gaze, unflinching. *That 2% was not merely a margin of error; it was the space where the field responded to the unprogrammed—the place beyond control, where perception could still choose.*

'Only if the observer has not yet learned to cross the edge of the lines of perception.'

A flicker passed through Lana's eyes.

'And if those lines aren't drawn by the observer, but by the system in which they're trapped?'

LEH understood the weight behind the question.

'The field only responds when chosen with awareness.'

He smiled faintly, recognising that although their approaches differed, the urgency of the moment bound them together.

'If we're going to change this, we'll need both approaches,' the doctor concluded. 'Quantum physics is structure. Intent is direction. I calculate, and you perceive. But we need both to alter this system.'

LEH inclined his head slightly in acknowledgement: *Action without awareness is repetition. Awareness without action is forgetfulness.* That, he thought, was where they needed to focus their attention.

He knew the alliance was fragile, but necessary. And he sensed that, in the tension between the visible and the invisible, the crack had already begun to open.

Margot paced back and forth across the control room; her expression was tense, her eyes scanning the multiple screens. The data projections flickered with numbers and graphs showing the progress of homogenisation among the Incompatibles.

'How can they still be generating interferences?' she muttered through clenched teeth.

She couldn't stand the feeling of vulnerability. She had devoted too much effort to this project and couldn't allow a group of Incompatibles to compromise the success of the update.

One of the technicians attempted to ease the atmosphere.

'The majority are yielding. We've reached 98% homogenisation. That remaining 2% is a normal margin of error. Once the third test is completed, it will be negligible.'

The coordinator exhaled slowly, forcing herself to release the tension in her body. But her unease persisted.

'We can't afford to lose control now. The executive board is pressuring us in this phase of the project, so the update must be completed as soon as possible,' she said, turning back to the graphs.

A knock on the door interrupted the discussion. Alan entered, accompanied by Nélida. Without wasting time, he began outlining the issues that were emerging within the network..

'If we continue with this level of restriction, there's a high risk of an internal crisis developing within the system,' he warned. 'We can't allow the program to close off perceptual possibilities completely. If users are unable to affect the system, their perception will collapse into rigidity. And if that happens, we'll lose control of the network,' he added gravely. 'This isn't a minor disruption—it's a systemic threat. Reality requires a certain margin of adaptability in order to sustain itself.'

'It's preferable to maintain this level of restriction rather than risk the stability of the entire structure.'

'If we eliminate perceptual flexibility altogether, the system will collapse. Alan insisted, his tone more urgent. 'The network cannot sustain itself on a single line of reality without provoking unforeseen consequences. Feedback is essential.'

Another researcher spoke, cautiously.

'We could use that 2% to allow the system to adapt slightly in real time. If we present these interferences as part of the program's evolutionary process, we might enable MIO to learn from the Incompatibles rather than erase their information.'

'By submitting a report that justifies the margin of error as a necessary element for the system's stability,' Nélida added.

But Margot shook her head, cutting the thread of the discussion.

'We can't take any risks at this stage.' Her tone was firm, though her gaze betrayed a latent tension. 'We must ensure the update is completed, we can't allow errors that weaken the network.'

The project coordinator held Alan's gaze with cold determination before turning and pacing slowly across the room. Her mind raced. She knew she had to decide what to do about the Incompatibles, but a sliver of doubt crept in: *what if that slight deviation was necessary for the system's stability?*

'What everyone must understand is that there's no time left,' she said at last, her voice low and cutting. 'I will do whatever is necessary.'

Alan watched her in silence. He knew that even 2% of awareness could contain an entire universe, that Margot refused to accept that fraction of uncertainty. But he also knew: that was where the interval lay, the space where the system could not yet predict the response. A minimal margin, yet enough to alter the outcome.

Dr. Lana, surrounded by the team and standing beside LEH, was analysing the data in preparation for a critical intervention. On the screens, the simulation flickered between complex frequency patterns. On one side, Naran's quipu unfolded in a polychromatic spectrum of possibilities; on the other, MIO displayed a reduced perception, restricted to a monochromatic and linear structure. The silence in the room was absolute, for everyone knew this test would determine the fate of perception within the system.

LEH, gazing at the quipu displayed on the screens, spoke:

'In a quantum system, before observation, everything exists in superposition—infinite possibilities coexisting,' he murmured, as if the thought were weaving itself. 'But when the user fixes their attention on MIO, on the known, on the Template, 98% collapses into the expected: the programmed.'

He paused, as though letting the words take shape in his mind. Then he lifted his gaze to Lana.

'Yet in that remaining 2%, in that undefined margin between the nodes of the system, is where true change arises. That is where the field continues to pulse, waiting to be read. There, in the threads that don't fit, is where the quipu begins to speak.'

His voice dropped, almost as if he was sharing a secret:

'They want to close the 2%. We... open it. Because that 2% is not an error. It's a crack. And through that crack, the field enters.'

Lana rose to her feet and studied the screen intently.

'Within the system, each user holds a node: their assemblage point, or perceptual point; the anchor from which their perception emerges.'

She added calmly:

'Perception within MIO is not reality; it is only the interpretation of what the system chooses to display. And when users accept that illusion, the wave collapses into a single option.'

LEH pointed to the screen, where the quipu unfurled its strings like a fan of colours.

'MIO fixes attention on a single colour, always the same. That is its trick: to make one believe that it is the whole of reality. But that colour belongs to the 98% already programmed.'

Ariana, intrigued, leaned forward.

'So the Incompatibles don't need to fight the entire system, but rather learn how to shift their attention?'

'Exactly,' LEH replied with intensity.

'MIO has been designed to recognise and validate only those patterns,' Ariana interjected, grasping the concept. 'So the problem is not that the other colours don't exist, but that the system refuses to display them. Only the Incompatibles can access them?'

'They—and anyone who manages to hold their attention in that undefined 2%,' LEH replied. 'For it is there, in the threads that do not align, that the quipu begins to reveal what the system conceals.'

'Exactly,' Lana intervened. 'We must help the Incompatibles to sustain the perceptual mobility of their nodes.'

The tension grew: if MIO managed to fix Naran's perception inside Timeline 3, reality would solidify into a single state. The team knew this must be prevented.

'That means we don't just have to hack the system,' Marco interjected, his tone edged with concern, 'but also the restrictive perception MIO is implanting. We'll need quantum camouflage.'

'Quantum camouflage,' Lana repeated, thoughtful.

'Yes,' Marco explained. 'If we quantumly entangle our particles with those of the Incompatibles, we can create a perceptual shield. While under that protection, their changes won't be detected by MIO. It would be like hiding an intention within noise, at a quantum scale.'

Lana nodded, expanded the simulation of the polychromatic spectrum, and then swept the room with her gaze, ensuring everyone's attention.

'We'll use quantum entanglement and superposition to expand Naran's perception. By doing so, she'll be able to see every shade of her quipu.'

'If Naran's node is the key point,' Ariana cut in, her voice bright with urgency, 'then by helping her sustain her perceptual node, she'll avoid seeing her quipu as a set of binary choices.' Her fingers flew over the keyboard as she generated a new simulation. When she finished, she stood and projected a visualisation of quantum entanglement and superposition.

'Here we can see how each user, represented by their node, is guided by MIO towards a reduced perception. First, the program downloads their information and, based on their past, redefines their future within a controlled linearity.'

Her words stirred a ripple across the room just as the sharp hum of central-sector surveillance drones broke into the settlement. Several team members rushed to close the windows, but the atmosphere was already taut with tension.

The data began interlacing with unusual patterns, revealing a different perceptual architecture: it showed how MIO guided each user through a linear, reduced perception. Murmurs filled the room as the implications became evident.

'Our objective,' Marco continued, trying to hold the focus, 'is to introduce an interference into this process.'

'If we achieve this intervention, each user will be able to perceive a broader spectrum of potential futures instead of following a path pre-defined by MIO,' LEH added.

The doctor nodded, satisfied with the precision of the approach.

'If we modify the visible spectrum inside MIO, we'll free Naran's perception and reveal hidden perceptual routes. These will reach the Incompatibles first, and as they propagate, all program users. With this, we'll deactivate the imposition of the Template, of Timeline 3.'

LEH paused before speaking again, his tone grave:

'That means the Incompatibles could influence the perception of others, even across great distances inside MIO. If they manage to enter that 2% of unprogrammed threads, they'll be able to collapse from vision, not from programming. And that is the breach.'

'Exactly,' Lana confirmed. 'But we must ensure MIO neither detects nor controls these influences. We're creating a new level of connection between users.'

Ariana, focused on her calculations, didn't lift her eyes from the data as she spoke:

'We'll activate the quantum entanglement by linking the cords of Naran's quipu with specific frequencies we've prepared. Through superposition, each cord will exist in multiple states at the same time and will thus reveal the full spectrum of possibilities hidden within the system.'

Preparations moved at full speed. Just as the team was about to execute the transmission, a blackout jolted the laboratory.

Reports came in immediately: the drones had fired and disrupted the electrical grid across the settlement. Yet LEH remained calm.

'Quantum physics teaches us that at its most fundamental level, everything is connected,' he said evenly, watching the data still flickering on the screen. 'Naran's quipu is already part of this network; we only need to activate the right resonance.'

The emergency generators hummed to life, and the devices began to recover. With the dim glow of the screens lighting their faces, the team resumed their work with renewed resolve: the transmission had to be completed. The laboratory vibrated with a blend of science, resistance, and a deep certainty—they were about to push through a crack in the limits imposed by MIO.

Dr Lana drew a deep breath and gave the final order:

'Let's begin without hesitation. Naran, the Incompatibles, and all of us are about to step into a quantum game of perception with MIO.

Let's see how far we can take this.
Because if perception shifts, reality shifts.'

The group of Incompatibles initiated the simulation: Naran walked through a landscape designed by the program when she felt a subtle shift in her perception. Although the environment appeared unchanged, a sense of clarity and connection flooded her.

Naran felt the support and, with a slight turn of attention, modified the focus the program was imposing. Her gaze moved towards the perceptual point of Tambo. She sat on the terraces beside the llamas and was suffused with a sense of deep connection to the village. Then she perceived the living texture of her quipu: the cords unfolded before her and the knots began to release unintegrated memories. Lines overlapped at great speed, opening new routes that emerged on the horizon of her vision.

From Karanza, the teams sustained the connection through entanglement with her quipu. Each adjustment sought to maintain the mobility of her assemblage point, with the intention of helping her keep her perception open.

But MIO reacted and redirected her perception with a drastic manoeuvre: the ground opened beneath her feet and she felt the vertigo of falling. As she plunged, she again sensed the connection that bound her beyond the narrative of the simulation; she clung to the image of her quipu, managed to reorient her perception, and found herself once more beside the llamas in Tambo. Yet MIO anticipated her and repeated the process: again the ground opened and she fell into an endless void. This time it was not just vertigo: each descent fragmented her consciousness, disintegrating the image of Tambo and turning it into shadows. MIO was not only altering the environment, it was rewriting her perception of reality. What if the only way forward was to stop resisting?

Margot watched the monitors, focused on the 2% error that persisted in the test. At last, she raised her voice with determination.

'It is not possible to modify MIO with the new information these adolescents bring, as Alan intended. The update is for them to integrate into the system's description. The program sets the parameters of what is real.'

'I understand,' a technician replied without lifting his eyes from the data, '…but the test has only just begun.'

Margot pointed to a spot on the monitor, and the technicians confirmed it was a connector.

'It is the link. When they try to bring new information into the system, when they see something that does not belong to MIO, the program must redirect their perception. The Incompatibles can only access what is already coded.'

Naran, increasingly confused, noticed that whenever she tried to move her attention beyond the fixed point of the program, MIO returned her immediately.

'The system must act as a rescue mechanism,' continued the project coordinator, her eyes fixed on the screen. 'Whenever the girl tries to deviate, whenever her perception shifts beyond the set parameters, MIO must pull her back, again and again.'

Each time Naran's vision fluctuated, MIO redirected her. Her attempts to hold the quipu fragmented, and the memories of Tambo dissolved into shadows. The pressure of the program intensified until it enveloped her completely and, under the avalanche of emotions, Naran yielded: the connection with the quipu shattered. She briefly glimpsed the group of Incompatibles like herself, disoriented. Then the images began folding over and over on themselves, dragging her relentlessly into the past.

From the Research Centre, the technicians detected that MIO was unable to attribute the changes in Naran's perception to its existing programming.

'What is happening?' Margot demanded, unable to make sense of the overlapping data.

One of the technicians reviewed the analyses several times before responding.

'To neutralise what it interpreted as erratic behaviour, the program has locked her into a loop.'

Margot fixed her gaze on the screen, satisfied.

'Leave her in the loop.'

'But this is not in the protocol...' the technician protested.

'There is no time to continue with trials,' she replied coldly. 'Put all the Incompatibles into loops inside the main system. It is the safest way to stop them from interfering.'

Before leaving the room, she looked back at the technicians.

'Send me the reports for the meeting. I will make it clear that this step was necessary.'

Despite the efforts of the Karanza team, they discovered that their intervention had been turned against them. MIO had learned to use the crack—that 2% of uncertainty they had managed to open—as a trap, a closed circuit of collapsed superposition.

'They have used Naran as a virus inside the system,' Ariana said, analysing the data. 'Although the quantum camouflage prevented MIO from seeing the changes directly, the program detected the fluctuations in her perception. It doesn't need to observe what we modified; it only needs to register the deviation. And now it has found a way to correct it: using that same 2% as a channel for inverse interference.'

LEH crossed his arms, tense.

'We've made the system's job easier. Thanks to our help, MIO has identified the access points that allow perception to move. Now it can intervene when any user drifts beyond the parameters... and return them to a loop.'

Dr Lana kept her eyes on the screen, unsettled.

'So instead of breaking the structure of the program, we optimised it?'

'Yes,' LEH replied, leaning closer to the data. 'The crack we opened has closed in on itself. It wasn't erased, it was reprogrammed.' His voice dropped. 'MIO doesn't seal the crack; it turns it into a mirror that reflects the past. Instead of collapsing a new perception, we collapse an old one.'

The threads of the quipu had vanished.

'Naran and the others have been put in a loop,' Ariana murmured.

'And not just any loop,' Lana added. 'MIO has locked them into the system's linear time. They can no longer move towards possible futures; they circle again and again through a predefined cycle. They think they're choosing, but they're only repeating a closed structure.'

LEH clenched his fists. They had believed they were a step ahead, but MIO had outplayed them. The system does not create; it only replicates. It detects anomalies and feeds them back as distorted reflections. That 2%, when unsustained, is transformed into a cycle that always collapses into the past.

'That is the brilliance of the system,' he said bitterly. 'It lets you think you're choosing, but you only choose among versions already coded. That is inverse interference: the system's attempt to neutralise what it cannot control.'

Science had failed. Intent had become trapped inside MIO's architecture. They had believed they were opening a doorway in perception, but in truth, they had been guided into a dead end within the system's linear time. MIO's move had been perfect: turning their own strategy into a trap.

'This can't be…' Lana murmured, her breath growing unsteady. She replayed every decision in her mind and realised that everything had been part of MIO's structure from the beginning. A shiver ran through her body. They had been naïve.

LEH stared at the screens with cold resolve. All this time, they had thought they were the players, but MIO had turned them into pieces.

If MIO has transformed our crack into its board, then only one question remains… how do we stop playing by its rules?

Outside the laboratory, in Karanza, the weather mirrored the tension. Rain hammered the streets, and thunder cracked across the sky. Something fundamental had shifted, and the most unsettling truth was this: they couldn't turn it back.

KNOT XI

THE INSTANT THAT REPEATS
TO BE SEEN

The first time Naran saw Ikan was when she arrived at the Research Centre. The room was filled with young people: some sank into resignation, while others shifted restlessly in their seats, their eyes fixed in fear. The air was heavy with the weight of expectations placed upon this group of Incompatibles. With a sigh, she felt the pressure in her chest, realising where she was: trapped alongside Néstor and Maia in an experimental facility. It resembled less an educational centre than a labyrinth of uncertainties.

Amidst it all, Ikan stood out. His relaxed yet untameable presence contrasted sharply with the anxious unease of the others. He seemed to belong to another world, perhaps to the Outer Reserves, where freedom and connection with nature still endured.

After the initial shock of her arrival, Naran sat at a table, opened her notebook, and began to draw. Immersed in the movement of her hand, she sought to disconnect from the hostile atmosphere. Each stroke was not only an act of concentration but also a quiet defiance against the order that confined her.

Ikan watched her with curiosity.

'For this place, such a thing already feels a little anachronistic,' he said, breaking through the room's taut, nervous silence.

The girl half-closed her eyes and fixed them on him. Although his dark hair concealed part of his face, his presence overflowed the room, as if he still carried with him the breath of nature. There was something about him that did not belong to that centre. He lingered… like someone who had never fully left the mountains.

Their eyes met.

A barely perceptible tremor ran through Naran. Images began to well up in her mind: a cave, a distant drum, a voice that was not her own… and yet it called to her. As though, in looking at him, he had returned to her a forgotten part of herself.

And for an instant, she understood: Ikan was not merely a stranger.

He was a mirror.

A reflection of possibilities.

A bridge towards the subtle.

But the void that opened upon feeling it was too much. Faced with that fissure in her perception, she sought refuge in the familiar. She returned to her walls, her lines, the drawing she could still control.

Ikan stepped closer and looked at the digital notebook. On seeing it, he wondered whether Nuna's and his help during the Dreaming had enabled Naran to reach other lines.

'Where have you seen that animal?' he asked.

Naran hesitated. She did not want to expose herself before a stranger. She lowered her eyes to the drawing, denying what she had glimpsed in her visions. None of that matters anymore, she told herself. She only wanted to remain unnoticed, to leave that centre behind, to escape the nonsense.

'It's just a drawing,' she replied, her voice uncertain.

Ikan expected that response. No matter how much help she received, she still wasn't opening herself to other ways of perceiving. It all seemed in vain, he thought. He laughed to himself, wondering: What was he supposed to learn from her? What must he accept from this reality she still rejected?

'Fine, keep drawing that llama,' he said with a sigh, walking away.

The word struck her.

Her hand moved of its own accord, tracing the outline of a llama.

With that simple stroke, the boy's world collided with hers, opening a new perspective. Her finger moved slowly along the sketch and she understood that she could do the same with her memories. Just as she had shaped the lines into a defined figure, perhaps she could apply that same retrospective lens to her own life.

She lifted her eyes and met the boy's deep gaze. For an instant, she felt his eyes stretch beyond the present, slipping into another time. If she could learn to walk backwards, she might join the dots that had brought her to that very moment. To see every fragment of her story, the turns that had drawn her destiny, and begin again at the origin.

If she could glimpse the whole picture, perhaps a single corrected stroke would be enough to redefine it all. Then her present might open, free itself from confinement and lead her towards the possibility of finding her father, and even herself.

She did not know whether that inquiry was only another trap to escape the confinement of the centre, but she hardly cared. Her mind travelled in every direction, trying to reconstruct the events. Something eluded her, she sensed it. In that enigmatic puzzle, scattered pieces awaited to be joined. If she could succeed in linking them, new possibilities would emerge on her path. Perhaps in this way she might break the destiny others had drawn for her and free herself from the strokes that kept her prisoner.

'Can you see the llama now, Naran?' Ikan's gaze pierced her. 'Can you see the strokes where your perception has collapsed?'

She looked around without moving. And then she noticed it. Not in the drawing, not in the room. She noticed it in the space between things: a thin, oscillating, living crack.

The images of the sequence crowded mercilessly in her mind. The vertigo of the fall still pulsed in her body, like an echo trapped in her perception. For a moment, she felt the ground open again beneath her feet and looked around: something had changed.

Ikan appeared before her, his gaze challenging and his voice sharp as a blade.

'Have you realised yet where you are, Naran?'

A pang pierced her chest. 'I'm lost, Ikan.'

'You're not lost.' His voice was an anchor amidst the chaos. 'You're trapped. But you must hold onto certainty, Naran.'

'Trapped?' Her eyes roamed the space, searching for answers in the nothingness around her. 'I don't know what certainty is anymore…' she sighed, feeling the weight of her doubt.

Ikan looked at her intently, his voice firm and unwavering. 'Certainty means that within you, you already live it—because your own Dream has shown you there's another possibility beyond what you thought was real. That llama and that village are your connection outside this system. From the Tonal, you will never find the way out. You cannot break the loop from MIO's logic. But if you remember how to move between worlds, then you still have a chance. The solution doesn't come from control but from the Nagual. It's from the subtle where the dense is woven.'

Naran shook her head, her voice tinged with frustration. 'All that no longer works in MIO. They've taken my connection to the llama. I don't know if I can reach the village again.'

As she spoke with Ikan, images began to overlap in her mind like distorted reflections from different times. She saw herself telling Néstor and Maia not to take that exit, saw herself sheltering with them in the garage, saw Illa on the road with the llama, saw her arrival at the Research Centre after being captured, saw each of the trials, the village… and everything collapsed in a whirlwind of uncertainty.

But then she understood: she wasn't seeing memories; they were lines of possibility trying to weave themselves anew. She was trapped in a fixed point in time, repeating the same moment over and over, as if her consciousness had been rewritten to prevent her from moving forward.

Ikan didn't take his eyes off her; he challenged her with his mere presence. He knew the inverse interference allowed her to perceive a moment only to return her to the same point.

'Accept the present, Naran, despite your fears. Don't seek refuge again in the past.'

A cold shiver ran through her body. For it wasn't just that she was trapped, but that each of her attempts to escape only brought her back to the beginning. As if every decision she made was already programmed, as if MIO had turned her into an echo of herself.

'What are you saying? That I'm in a loop?'

Ikan held her gaze seriously.

'Seeing the loop seems simple… but we are all made of it. We repeat the same information over and over, hoping it will someday give us a different end to our inner wound. But MIO doesn't trap us by force; it traps us with the promise of meaning.'

'I don't know what you're talking about.'

'I think you can see it now.'

Naran hesitated, searching for the words.

'If they've put me in a loop, it's because I followed that possibility. My intention was to pass the trials and leave, but now I'm trapped. They've pushed me into a corner.'

Ikan took a step towards her, his voice unwavering. 'Don't waste your energy on despair; you need it so your actions can fulfil the designs of your Intent.'

Naran's anger flared suddenly. 'Stop pushing your angle, Ikan. You keep believing you're above the circumstances, but maybe you're not.'

She stepped away from him and began to walk. If MIO had built this loop, then there must be a crack in its structure. And if anyone could help her find it, it was Illa.

Behind the repetition, something pulsed.
It wasn't a memory; it was the thread.
And she had to find a way to hold onto it.

Illa handed several quipus and seeds to the chasquis before turning to Naran, who had already begun to dig hastily, as if physical labour could dispel the feeling of being trapped.

'Illa, I've seen it,' she said, not meeting her gaze, breath catching. 'They've locked me into a repetitive sequence inside the construct.' A shiver ran down her spine as superimposed images fluttered through her mind. It was as if all the versions of herself were screaming at once, but none knew how to escape. 'I've seen all those sequences repeat over and over again.'

The girl dropped the digging tool and knelt on the ground, exhausted. She didn't know how long she had been in that state. Illa observed her deeply and spoke, serene, but her tone was laden with meaning.

'Yes, Naran, you're in a loop within the program.'

'How long have I been... repeating this?'

'Since the third test,' explained the awicha, picking up some seeds.

'In MIO's linear time, you've been repeating the same sequence for over two years. You were trapped in your own past—caught in the projection of your memories and fears, over and over again. You couldn't see or decide; you were a prisoner of a dream, of guilt. But now... you've shed your skin, like the snake; you've stopped identifying with that way of being. And now it's time to move with the strength and agility of the puma.'

'Stop the metaphors and animals, Illa,' Naran growled, her voice rising. 'You don't realise the situation I'm in. I'm in a closed circuit!'

'You created this connection, Naran. You are the anomaly in the system. Through Recapitulation, you've released the past you were clinging to; your attention is no longer fragmented and now you can see. You've built a bridge between yourself inside the program and your Dreaming double here in the village. Now you must integrate them.'

Naran felt a knot tighten in her throat.

'How didn't I see it before? Why didn't you tell me?'

Illa stopped in front of her, her gaze piercing.

'If there were no traps, we would never learn. This loop was necessary for you to shed your skin, to shift your perception. You began to perceive the Pacha in a non-linear way, which allowed you to see alternatives and change your own inner reality.'

But Naran couldn't hear her. Her mind was still caught in overlapping images, in the vertigo of repetition.

'Illa, this doesn't change anything,' she whispered, squeezing her eyes shut. 'I'm still trapped.'

The awicha shook her head with a faint smile.

'Thanks to those anomalies, you were able to perceive me on the road for the first time. That was the first loose thread in the system's weave. That's when you began to wonder if there were more possibilities beyond the loop. Now you can see the trap and decide how to escape it; you can perceive the threads of the quipu with which to weave your own story. But you must take action.'

'That wretched program...' the young woman murmured, her anger contained.

Illa sighed.

'MIO is not the enemy, Naran. Stop using it to justify your insecurity. Fighting feeds it; resistance strengthens it. You don't need to fight it; you only need to see it as it is.'

'That construct has me trapped!' she shouted. 'And all because of the damned anomaly, because of that damned llama. I should have just done the tests and gone with my father.'

The woman looked at her without flinching.

'From the outside, those circuits of MIO, those artificial horizons, are so insignificant, Naran. They are only a description of the reality you keep clinging to. If you realised that you have the power to sustain realities... if you understood that being in the loop has been your opportunity to see the information you no longer want to keep projecting...'

The girl looked at her with defiance, with anger. She threw the quipu to the ground and, without hesitation, grabbed the llama and began to walk away.

'Wait, Naran,' Illa followed quickly.

'To perceive other realities, it's not enough to simply wish for it. You need to keep your attention unified, to keep training it so it doesn't fragment. In some way, you are still here. You must continue Recapitulating, gathering back the energy you left behind in every experience, until your perception becomes whole again.'

The young woman clenched her jaw.

'I think your approach and what you've taught me don't serve me right now.'

The wise elder observed her attentively.

'Now you know you're in a loop; you have to decide who you want to be in this experience. You must stop being the prey, become the hunter. The puma represents strength. You have to connect with the possibilities of the present, with the *Kay Pacha*.'

Naran remembered Ikan's words again and with them, the full weight of the situation.

'I think I just want to be a happy coward living in a world of illusion,' she challenged, feeling the landscape of Tambo distort with her perception.

She took the quipu angrily and hung it around her neck. 'I need to walk. The idea of continuing in a loop and staying trapped in your cosmovision of snakes and pumas chills me. Your approach no longer serves me and neither do your metaphors!' She shouted those last words as she walked away towards the mountains.

She didn't know yet, but the simple fact of seeing the loop was already weakening it. And that llama, that damn anomaly, she still hadn't let go.

And as she walked towards the mountains, the landscape trembled… as if her program didn't know whether to hold her or let her go.

KNOT XII

WHERE THE PACHAS CONVERGE

Naran walked, her gaze unfocused, feeling the weight of confusion and anger with every step. She felt trapped between the MIO program and the sense that something else was calling her. The landscape of Tambo stretched before her like a clouded mirror. She stopped at the edge of a terraced field to watch how the chasquis moved in and out of Tambo like waves of information in a sea of consciousness. Wrapping herself in her poncho, she closed her eyes and listened to the wind, carrying echoes from every direction. For a moment, sadness threatened to rise, but anger still held her captive. The sense of injustice made her hurl a stone furiously against the terraces, as if that act could release what she carried inside. Then the sound of the pututu resonated through the air: a chasqui had left his path and was heading towards her.

She wiped her tears with her hand and watched him approach with reverence. There was something in his presence that radiated certainty.

'I have a message for you,' the chasqui announced calmly.

Naran frowned.

'Illa told me that the chasquis can send messages across time. How is that possible?'

'You may call me Kunak,' he said, pointing to the circular farming terraces. 'Time, like these terraces, is not linear. It moves in cycles—like the seasons, like the harvest. In MIO, the perception of time has been artificially linearised, restricting users' ability to see beyond a programmed sequence of events.'

'I don't understand,' the girl protested. She felt something was slipping away from her.

'Our perception of time is cyclical,' the chasqui explained. 'Look closely at the terraces. What do you see?'

Naran traced the concentric circles of stone and earth with her eyes.

'They're three circular terraces, but I don't see what they have to do with time.'

Kunak smiled patiently and beckoned her closer.

'Just like the seeds planted in the earth, every action you take in the present has the power to influence your past and shape your future. You too are a messenger, Naran—a chasqui across times.'

A shiver ran through her. She could sense the truth in his words, even if she did not yet fully understand them.

'The Hanan Pacha, the outer terrace, represents the past—the structure upon which the present and the future are built,' the chasqui continued. 'Every past experience is the foundation of who you are today.'

'The past comes before us?' Naran asked, intrigued.

'That's right. The Hanan Pacha guides what is yet to come. But the Uku Pacha, the inner terrace, is the world of roots, where possibilities are gestating. It is the future pressing from within, waiting to be manifested.'

Naran looked at the middle terrace.

'And the Kay Pacha?'

'It is the present—the point where past and future intersect. When these two Pachas converge in a Chawpi, the meeting place, the here and now is born. It is the field of action where everything transforms,' the chasqui observed her intently. 'Now you understand that the future is not ahead of you, but pushing from within. When you become aware of the Chawpi, the crossing point between opposites, you can open a *Punku*, a threshold in time. And it is there that reality ceases to be a line and becomes a living weave.'

The girl looked out at the landscape and discerned the flow of time in the circles of the terraces, and in the spiral of the seashell the chasqui held. She lowered her gaze to the threads of the quipu hanging from her poncho. Each thread was a connection to the past, present, and future. Each knot was a Chawpi—a meeting point. If she became aware of that crossing, she could remember. The words Illa had once spoken rose like a whisper:

Time unfolds outward and returns inward, in a cyclical ebb and flow. Nothing is static; everything is being made and unmade, like the knots of the quipu that are tied and untied, transforming endlessly.

She took a quinoa seed she carried in her poncho and planted it in the inner terrace. 'I want to perceive this situation differently; I want to rewrite this knot in the quipu,' she said firmly. And she knew that by planting that seed, she was also touching the field. The invisible weave that threaded the times had responded.

The chasqui nodded, his expression filled with meaning.

'You are integrating your opposites, Naran. The Chawpi begins to manifest within you—not as a goal, but as a resonance, as a crossing point that you do not choose, but that recognises you. It is there that time is listened to, not measured; where you are no longer only the one walking the path, but also the one weaving it.

To keep moving forward, you must travel to the Hanan Pacha and meet your grandfather.'

A tremor stirred in her chest when the chasqui spoke aloud: *My dear granddaughter, Llamayuq. We can touch the next knot of the quipu together.*

In that instant, the landscape seemed renewed, and Naran knew she had stepped beyond the loop. She now saw the game of time not as a prison, but as a space of transformation. What once seemed like a closed labyrinth revealed itself as a malleable path, where every action could reshape the structure of the next step.

The quipu was not the prison—it was the instrument. And she had begun to play it.

Naran travelled to Karanza with Unay to visit her grandfather. As they entered the city, the golden light of sunset reflected off buildings streaked with graffiti. The wind carried whispers of conversations, distant laughter, and the echo of street music blending with the heartbeat of the suburb. Since childhood, that journey had held a special meaning for her, for it was not only a reunion with her family but also with the stories her grandfather wove with words—stories that connected her to something greater, something she felt within but still could not fully comprehend.

Upon arriving, Naran ran to him with a smile and handed him a drawing.

'Hello, Llamayuq, guardian of the llama,' her grandfather said tenderly, observing the illustration with wise eyes. 'I see you've been with your llama. I know you have many stories to tell me about the village you visit to be with her.'

The little girl nodded enthusiastically, and he continued, a mysterious gleam in his gaze.

'Today we are here because I want to tell you a story. If you like, you can sit with the other children.'

Phawaq, Naran's grandfather, a sage with eyes that held a quiet depth, gathered children and adults around the fire. Around them, the murals seemed to observe the scene; images of faces, of mountains, of quipus, and sacred symbols bore silent witness to every story told in that space. Naran settled beside her mother in silence. Her grandfather stirred the embers with a branch and then, unhurriedly, drew from his bag a polished obsidian stone. He held it between his fingers, as if perceiving in it something that lay within the fire's reflection.

'The ancient elders said that the Earth sings invisible lines that can only be heard when one walks with an open soul.'

'Each ancestral culture has its maps: some draw on cloth; others, on sand; others, in the air… The Nazca traced lines on the earth; the Maya, on bark codices; the desert peoples, on sand erased by the wind; the custodians of the Dreaming, in invisible songs that travel through time; the Toltecs wove paths in the Dream. All of them, cartographers of mystery.'

He paused, as if listening to something within the fire. 'This tale has yet to be told…'

'Many cycles ago,' Phawaq, the hamawta, began, 'in a valley protected by the imposing Apus, there was a sacred enclave known as the Valley of Dreams.'

His voice enveloped the listeners like an invisible weave. The fire danced to the rhythm of his words, flaring and dimming with each inflection. Shadows lengthened and shrank in a hypnotic sway. Suddenly, the wood cracked sharply, as though something unseen had shifted in the fire. Phawaq paused, looked at the children, and his expression grew grave. Silence spread like a mantle.

'Listen closely,' he said in a lower, deeper voice. 'There are stories that can only be told when the fire whispers them in its own language.'

The children held their breath, for something in the air had changed. The hamawta continued, and his voice took on a deep, enveloping tone, as if each word transported them on an invisible journey.

'Here, the thin line between dream and reality blurred, and the wanderers who reached the valley in inner silence could hear the voices of the earth, the wind, and the Apus whispering the steps to follow—not only for themselves, but for their entire community. But a danger arose: a powerful and cunning serpent, born from humanity's fears, began to slither among people's dreams. It whispered fearful words and projected visions of a world without magic, disconnected from the earth and the spirits. A world of lifeless paths, artificial and hollow, ruled by cold logic and absolute reason—a world where only what could be encoded within its system existed.'

'Each night, that serpent would rise like a great shadow,' he continued.
'It disconnected us from our dreams.
It devoured our imagination.
It erased the possibility of seeing beyond the visible.
It wanted to trap us in an artificial timeline,
where there existed only one fixed reality,
where the paths were already described,
and the horizons were predictable.'

Phawaq paused and looked at the children.

'Why must we remember ourselves through our stories?' he asked gently.

Those present exchanged glances. The grandfather smiled and explained:

'Because with words we can create or destroy realities. Imagination is the language of the Nagual. And that is why we Dream: to remember what we already know. The Elders of the tribes did not allow themselves to be deceived by the serpent's poisonous whispers; they knew how to see beyond the serpentine shadows and, with certainty, chose another path. They guided themselves by the signs, the symbols, and the visions of the Apus.'

'Our priority is to serve the spirit,' the elders said.

'And thus, we decided to create Karanza. Not just as a physical refuge, but as a fertile valley for dreams, imagination, and infinite paths; a place where the serpent could not penetrate or induce mechanical dreams. Our challenge was for both individual and collective dreams to be created consciously, with Intent.'

The hamawta continued narrating how the founders of Karanza learned to perceive life as a quipu, where each choice and each experience was a knot in the weave of time. They accepted the challenge of walking between two worlds, of balancing dream and reality, of resisting the assaults of the serpent again and again.

'Nothing remains still, little ones,' said Phawaq with a voice like the wind. 'Time is sung in cycles: it rises from within, expands outward, and is reborn from the invisible. Everything is interwoven and released, like the threads of the quipu, which dream themselves into form and unform in the eternal pulse of creation.'

At the end of the tale, all felt as though they had returned from a great journey, with a new understanding of the great weave, of their story, and of their quipu. Naran ran to embrace him. He looked at her with affection.

'You are part of this story, Llamayuq. Only you hold a thread of a unique colour, a perception only you can bring to this weaving of reality. I am certain you will be able to express it in this tapestry of life.' He showed her a quipu and handed her coloured threads. 'This belonged to your ancestors; here lie their stories, their information. And these threads are for you to continue weaving your own stories. This quipu will remain in Karanza because it will be the bridge of connection between the Pachas, between the times.'

He pointed to a spot in the weave. 'Here is a Chawpi, a meeting point. You and I will always be united here. This tapestry will carry you beyond that artificial line; it will guide you to your own Valley of Dreams and to your own connection with Intent.'

Her grandfather bent down and, with his fingers, traced a circle upon the earth. Then he placed a round stone at its centre, and beside it, the obsidian.

'The sun and the moon,' he said. 'Both reflect your strength. But MIO wants you to choose only one: the tension between dying and living, forgetting that together they form day and night. And to free yourself, you must walk between them.'

Naran observed the reflection in the mirror, trying to decipher her grandfather's words. She did not see her face. Only a thread. And she knew she had to follow it.

Naran spent hours in silence, her attention fixed on the present, hoeing without distractions until evening settled over Tambo. The damp soil slid between her fingers as the breeze softly stirred the quinoa stalks. For the first time in a long while, she did not feel lost. There was no noise in her mind, no struggle; only the here and now.

She sat beside the llama as Illa approached. Together, in silence, they watched how the golden light of the sun painted the landscape in warm hues, like a reflection of something that was only just beginning to reveal its meaning within her.

'Illa, as I Recapitulated and connected with my grandfather, I felt parts of myself awakening that had long been asleep,' the young woman said with deep serenity. 'I remembered how I used Yuyana, imagination, to tell stories and connect with other realities. My grandfather used to say that imagination is the language of the Nagual, and now I understand: it was his way of weaving reality, of holding the vision when no form yet existed… I only have to remember how I perceived as a child, for my perception then was alive, it was free.'

The awicha looked at her with approval and affection.

'In those days, you had not yet learned to divide yourself. You had not fragmented between the subtle and the dense. You lived fully in the unity of expansive perception, without falling into the world's duality.'

Naran saw herself reflected in the woman's eyes and felt a deep recognition, as if she had found a true echo of herself.

'I believe I carry the gift of oral tradition, as my grandfather did,' she whispered, letting her gaze drift towards the horizon tinged with the sun's last rays. 'When I touched the quipu, I felt how the voices of my ancestors whispered stories to me.'

'You have touched the *Wiñaypacha*, time both ancestral and eternal, Naran,' Illa confirmed. 'When you empty yourself of imposed limitations, your essence awakens. The quipu and Yuyana are instruments that help you transcend linear time. Now your perception is open, vibrating in resonance with your Intent.'

The young woman observed the subtle movements of the chasquis in the distance, appearing and disappearing on the horizon.

'I want to be a chasqui who travels between the Pachas,' she affirmed with conviction, 'to use my Yuyana to build bridges between worlds, to remember and share what I have seen.'

'You have understood,' replied the awicha gently. 'You have not become trapped in the role of victim, even though you recognise you were in a loop. You have chosen to perceive from another place.'

Naran felt a movement within her, a light yet profound expansion.

'I am still confused, Illa. But I can no longer perceive my situation as I did before; something has changed.'

The woman noticed a renewed light in Naran's eyes and nodded calmly.

'Your perception is aligning with Intent,' she said, 'and that frees you from fear and confusion. Intent crosses times and realities; it connects everything that exists. Recapitulating was invoking your inner strength to release past burdens and shift your assemblage point towards new possibilities.' She leaned slightly towards Naran, her words falling like seeds upon fertile soil. 'You are an *Awaq*, a weaver. You are not only reading the quipu, you are also the one weaving it.'

The young woman listened attentively as the wind caressed her face. The word Awaq floated between them, vibrating like a newly tightened thread on the loom of the world. A subtle shiver ran through the centre of her chest, as if her heart recognised a name it had been waiting for all along. Illa touched the threads of the quipu with reverence, as if brushing the very centre of the tapestry.

'You have shed your skin like a serpent, Naran. You have integrated your past, and now, with the strength of the puma, you can act in the present. That means you have the capacity to negotiate with any reality because you are no longer trapped by your projections.' Her voice grew even more intimate, as if sharing an ancient secret. 'The puma cannot be domesticated, Naran; it must be Stalked. It is the shadow that moves with you when you walk the present in full awareness. It does not seek the light; it passes through it. Only one who has walked the Uku Pacha with an awakened heart can navigate the Kay Pacha with vision.'

The young woman, feeling the weight and the lightness of all she had received, whispered:

'Now I can Stalk myself, consciously, right?'

Illa smiled, like someone witnessing a long-awaited blossom finally unfold.

'Exactly, Llamayuq. You have awakened and recognised that you are the guardian of your perception, the guardian of your dream. Your imagination is now the key that opens the door to any reality you choose to inhabit.'

For the first time, Naran did not want to flee from her story. She wanted to walk with open eyes and an awakened soul. And this time, she decided to walk the dream instead of running from it.

Her gaze rested on the horizon: the sun wasn't setting, merely shifting to another plane, one the human eye no longer remembered.

KNOT XIII

THE MIRROR OF THE QUIPU

Naran awoke in what she believed was the Research Centre. But this time, something was different: there was no confusion clouding her mind. For the first time, she remembered her purpose and what she had learned in Tambo. She looked at her hands and focused on them to anchor her perception, then began walking through corridors of light that seemed to extend with every step she took.

'Wait, Naran.'

Ikan's voice echoed in the silence, firm and clear.

'I'm in a hurry, Ikan. I need to find the group,' she replied without stopping, moving forward with determination.

'Are you sure you will find them?' he asked. 'Or will it be MIO who speaks to you… through them?'

The young woman came to a sudden stop. It was not the same doubt as before, the kind that paralysed her. Now she could Stalk it, observe it without being dragged down by it.

'Ikan…' she whispered, holding her breath.

He stepped towards her with the calm of one who knows well the terrain upon which he walks.

'To face MIO,' he spoke in a precise tone, 'you must be like the warrior who knows her battlefield well. You are not confronting just a program; it is a territory where your mind and your perception can be captured.'

The echo of his words reverberated within her. Naran understood that the battle was not outside, but in how she chose to perceive.

'MIO feeds on complexity, on what entangles thought and emotional excess,' he continued. 'A warrior, on the other hand, is simple. You must learn to be clear and precise. Eliminate the unnecessary. And every action must have a purpose,' he added firmly. 'Do not lose yourself in thoughts that serve no purpose. Clarity is your greatest ally. Perception entangles itself only when presence is lacking.'

She felt something shift in her mind, as if space were clearing. She had spent too long trapped in mental labyrinths, in projections that only confused her.

'MIO will try to lure you back into confusion,' Ikan went on, 'to make you react as you always have. But now you have another choice.' He extended his hand and gave her a small stone. Naran took it cautiously and saw engraved on its surface a sun and a moon.

'Whenever you feel fear, whenever MIO tries to wrap you in its illusions, remember this stone,' he added.

The young woman ran her fingers over the engravings, feeling their texture.

'The tension between life and death...' she murmured, understanding the symbol. 'MIO has kept me trapped in the idea that there is only one option. But in truth, balance is walking between opposites without being ruled by them.'

'Remember that the battlefield is not only MIO; it is also yourself and your thoughts,' said Ikan. 'You can retreat and observe from a distance, but do not engage directly if you are not ready. Warriors step back to gain perspective when needed.

A good Stalker does not attack on impulse; she observes until the moment reveals itself.'

Naran closed her eyes and let her mind traverse the projections that had kept her trapped. The images passed before her like reflections of a perception she could not control before. But this time, instead of losing herself in them, she remained firm. Her breathing grew calmer, and her body lighter. Then, an image arose in her mind: the puma, silent and patient, Stalking its moment.

'I will Stalk my own mind...' she whispered as she felt certainty settle in her chest—that she was no longer the hunted, but the hunter within the system.

Ikan nodded.

'That's right. Learn to Stalk your thoughts and feelings. Observe every reaction and ask yourself whether it is truly yours or if it comes from MIO.'

Naran tightened her grip on the stone. Her gaze no longer reflected desperation but clarity. For the first time, she was no longer at the mercy of the game: she was ready to play it by her own rules.

'I will.'

Because now she didn't just remember who she was, she was ready to hold on to that perception... even within the system.

Naran continued walking through the virtual corridors, feeling the weight of the space. Each step seemed to stretch the sensation of being trapped in a terrain designed to distract perception. After a few moments, she encountered the group of Incompatibles, and the scene felt unsettlingly familiar.

Néstor, surrounded by the others, radiated a new confidence, a dominant presence that imposed control. When he saw her, he gave her a calculated smile, as if he already knew what was about to happen.

'Naran!' he exclaimed in an almost mocking tone. 'We did it! We've managed to open 5% in the program.'

Some of the Incompatibles nodded enthusiastically, but she perceived a flicker of doubt in some of them, hidden beneath the surface of apparent conformity. Maia, however, showed no expression at all; her gaze was lost in emptiness. Naran took a deep breath. She couldn't react impulsively. She remembered what Ikan had told her: first, she had to study the battlefield.

Naran frowned. '5%? No, Néstor. We only opened 2% and they've turned it into a loop. Don't you see? They made us believe we advanced, but we're still trapped in the same pattern.'

The Incompatibles tensed, sensing something had changed within her. Néstor narrowed his eyes, analysing her: he knew something in her no longer reacted as it once did.

'MIO is showing you a mirage of small freedoms,' the young woman continued. 'It has allowed you to believe you've gained something, but you're still inside the same loop, still repeating the same perceptions, trapped in an illusion.'

Néstor raised an eyebrow and let out a dry laugh.

'And what's so wrong with that? Here, I have control, Naran. I've accomplished what you couldn't: to lead and to give the Incompatibles something tangible, something they can feel.'

She held his gaze.

'What does 5% mean to you then, Néstor? Control? The illusion of power?' She paused, then continued. 'You can insert memories from other times into the program; only you have that ability, that gift. But out of fear and the need for control, you continue allowing the program to decide for you.'

Her companion looked to the others for support, but some averted their gaze.

'And what do you offer us?' he asked harshly. 'Empty words about another reality? Promises no one can see? Remember, we're in a crisis. Everything you call abilities was deemed a risk to the system. Those interferences only caused instability.'

The young woman saw how the program spoke through him… it would not be easy to break that bond.

'I can hold two positions in the Dream at the same time. In two knots of the quipu. MIO… is just a position. A perceptual point,' she said calmly. 'If each of us inserted new information, we could open that 5% for everyone.'

Néstor looked at her with disdain.

'You're still speaking in abstractions, Naran.' His tone turned more sarcastic. 'You mention concepts we can't even understand. What use are they to us in here?'

Naran wanted to see if his sister was caught in the same illusion.

'Maia, you have the ability to insert values into the system. Remember how you wanted to go to Karanza, how you wanted to be with your parents.'

She didn't answer, only looked at her brother and then lost herself again in emptiness. A pang struck Naran's chest: Maia reminded her of herself when Ikan tried to make her see she was identified with the system, but she couldn't perceive it. She felt the pressure of the moment, pulled out the stone Ikan had given her, and held it tightly. She remembered his teachings about Stalking and perception.

'In here, the scenarios of our lives have already been written.' She raised her voice to project her certainty. 'You know it… and still, you keep acting within them.'

The Incompatibles looked at her, but no one spoke. Néstor's attitude still held control over them.

'We've never been taught to imagine together, to create something real,' she continued. 'They've divided us. But now we have the opportunity to stand united, to demand what is our right.'

The voices of Illa and Ikan echoed inside her: it was time to act. But the group's reaction made her hesitate. And that moment of doubt was enough for Néstor; he smiled smugly and extended his hand towards her.

'Naran, come with us. Don't judge, just flow with it.'

MIO transformed into a vibrant virtual environment, a party in full swing: music, lights, avatars of every kind filled the scene. Néstor tried to convince Naran to join the fun. Maia, with a distant stare, murmured softly:

'Why resist? Isn't it better to accept this situation?'

Naran tried to reach the Maia she remembered.

'This isn't real. We can choose. We don't have to be just participants in MIO's game. Remember our purpose.'

Néstor, hidden behind a smile and his mask of many faces, leaned towards her.

'Naran, relax. Life is more than just fighting.' He looked at his sister and continued, 'Sometimes, we need to explore what we are not, explore the polarity we reject.'

Naran felt the program was trying to manipulate her, so she drew a deep breath and made a decision.

'Fine, Néstor,' she answered calmly, knowing her presence altered the field. Even if she immersed herself in the scenario, she would not lose her centre. 'But don't forget why we're here.'

She dove into the party with him. She knew the boy had control of the situation, but she still hoped he might see another possibility. However, the longer she spent within that succession of vibrant scenarios, the more disconnected she felt. And then she broke the silence.

'Is this really all you want?' she asked. 'To remain identified with this character?'

Néstor didn't answer; he just kept dancing and laughing with the others. And Naran felt the betrayal tighten in her chest.

'Néstor, listen to me, our purpose is to open the 5%! But all you've done is accept another version of control. Don't you see I'm repeating the same words you used to say?'

He smiled coldly.

'Here I have what I need, Naran. You've also found security and control in the concepts and realities you speak of. We're nothing more than pawns between different sides.'

The young woman looked at him with sadness: the conversation was over.

'You're still in a loop, Néstor. You haven't opened the 5%, you've only accepted another prison.'

But he no longer heard her. And she, feeling more alone than ever, withdrew from the perceptual battlefield.

Naran shifted her attention within the quipu towards Tambo, seeking refuge and clarity in that knot of the weave. Yet upon arriving, she sensed that something had changed. The mountains, the terraced fields, the light that once bathed the valley, everything began to fade, as if Tambo were dissolving before her eyes. Shadows began to veil the vivid colours of the place, and as she moved forward, everything around her turned grey and blurry. It was as if the essence of Tambo was vanishing into oblivion.

'No... it can't be,' she murmured, feeling the void growing within her chest.

She tried to cling to Illa's teachings, to the certainty that Tambo was an unshakable refuge, but in that moment, that security seemed to evaporate along with the landscape.

There, in the midst of nothingness, surrounded by emptiness, she understood the harshness of her reality. The words of Ikan and Illa resurfaced in her mind, reminding her of the art of Stalking and the need to act. But she was alone, without her guides, confronted by the dark truth of her own fear.

Was that what it truly meant to be in a loop? A space where pain and loneliness invaded her.

Fear was no longer just an emotion; it was a perceptual field, and she was within it. And she understood then Néstor's stance; to avoid feeling that void, he had identified himself with something. He too had been at this threshold but, instead of crossing it, had clung to the known.

She had done the same, clinging to the past, to the familiar, but the void was becoming more overwhelming. A part of her wanted to give up, to let herself be consumed by despair and return to illusory safety. And the sun and the moon appeared before her as conflicting forces, but this time she did not want to choose. She imagined a line joining them on the horizon, and in that vision, a third path appeared: the Chawpi.

And then Ikan's words returned to her mind: *What we perceive as real is only the option MIO has chosen for us. What if you could choose what to observe? What would you choose to collapse, Naran?*

Her breath caught for an instant: *laws are only valid within the dream.*

And if outside the dream there was only emptiness, and from the emptiness, the power to decide who she was...

For the first time, she understood that it was not the world that imprisoned her, but her own perception of it. Fear had kept her trapped in a projection, in a version of reality chosen by MIO. *But what if she could see it differently? What if she could collapse another possibility?*

The quipu vibrated in her hands. She tried to decipher it, but something within her urged her to let it go. *She hadn't come to control the weave…but to listen to its pulse.*

She closed her eyes and felt a knot pulsing. It was not external; it was her, a part that had never been freed.

'*All of this is happening now,*' Illa whispered from the silence. '*Time is not a line; it is a knot. And you can untie it or begin again from another thread.*'

And then she remembered the moment she arrived at the Research Centre, when she stood before Ikan. Her hand had moved naturally and traced a llama. And with that simple gesture, his world had collided with hers. She had understood that she could do the same with her memories: look back, connect the dots. She had believed others had locked her into a fate already traced for her, but in that moment she realised it was her own perception that had built that prison.

She took her quipu and saw the threads in which she had been entangled: fear, the need to fit in, the desire to be loved, each one projected into every decision she had made.

Néstor was nothing but a reflection of her resistance, and she no longer needed to project her fears onto him.

She understood then that her greatest wound was also her greatest treasure. Being an Incompatible was not her curse; it was what made her free.

Now I can hold the information and expand it.

And then, she opened her hand. She released the knot, and the pencil with which she had traced the same lines, over and over. And she began to weave from the place where she truly wanted to be.

This is what my heart needs.

And a thread shone, the unique thread, the gift her grandfather had spoken of. And along with the light, a word emerged from the depths of her chest, as if it had always been there, waiting: Awaq. Weaver. Not just of memories, not just of inner wounds, but of worlds—the thread had been hidden behind the scars, but now, in connecting with it, she had found her purpose.

The quipu was no longer an enigma; it was a mirror. And she was no longer trapped within it; she was the crossing point, the intersection that had always been pulsing behind her.

Her body trembled.

She was no longer a spectator; she was part of the weave. She knew it was enough to see, enough to choose. For the bridge had always been there—time had only existed to guide her hand towards the knot that needed to be undone. And now she could see it, because she had loosened the thread, and in doing so, dissolved the illusion.

And she understood that this was freedom: to stop fighting against the weave and begin to weave her vision with it. It was not her struggle that transformed reality; it was her surrender. It was not her effort that collapsed time; it was her trust in Intent.

In the field, there are no rules, only the echo of my decision resonating in all that I am.

The sound of a condor crossing the sky echoed through the emptiness, and Naran's lips began to recite:

Condor who soars through the Hanan Pacha,
teach us to fly beyond illusion,
may we recognise light within every shadow,
and in the meeting of opposites,
may the true Chawpi awaken.

And in that instant, she understood: the Chawpi is not reached through logic; it is the resonance between two shores that no longer fear each other.

A feather fell at her feet. Naran picked it up, and this time, she could feel that Intent was flowing through her like an unstoppable river.

KNOT XIV

THE BRIDGE BETWEEN TIMES

The full moon barely pierced the dense mist; glaciation had covered the valleys with a white, silent mantle. What remained was a hostile territory where time seemed to have stopped years ago. Yet Usuy the chasqui, agile and resolute, moved forward with the resilience of those who understand that time is not an enemy, but a path to be mastered. He had departed early in the afternoon, after another chasqui delivered a quipu from the Outer Reserves; information that could alter the destiny of all.

He lit a torch and followed the hidden tunnels beneath the surface to the edge of Karanza. The central sectors were on alert, patrolled by drones ready to intercept any attempt at communication. He adjusted his *huaraca*, prepared to defend himself if necessary.

A sudden noise startled him. He checked his compass and veered into a side tunnel within the labyrinth. His legs faltered. He paused to catch his breath, the cold creeping into his bones. Reaching for his *chuspa* of coca leaves, he realised it had been lost along the way; there was no turning back.

Exhaustion betrayed him. A cramp shot through his leg and dropped him to his knees; his breath turned ragged, his vision blurred, and the world dimmed. With his last strength, he raised the pututu and blew as if it were his final breath. The sound echoed through the stone corridors.

A tug pulled him from the brink. Through the shadows, he glimpsed his companion, Chaska, pulling him to safety. He had reached the next post.

Chaska wrapped him in blankets and gave him hot water, reviving him before taking the relay. He invoked the Apus for protection and, with the quiet certainty of being accompanied by the spirit of the mountains, resumed the journey towards Karanza. He moved through the tunnels as if his body remembered every turn, seeing not with eyes, but with memory.

When he surfaced, he slipped past patrols, hid in crevices, and advanced with the cunning of a puma.

At dusk, he spotted the flickering lights of the suburb. And with the last remnants of his energy, he blew the pututu with the same force that had sustained his journey.

From Karanza, a pututu responded to confirm the messenger's arrival. The gates slid open slowly, allowing Chaska to cross with unsteady steps. Guards escorted him to the bunkers.

The damp stone walls held the strength of those who resisted on the last frontier of freedom. The survival of the resistance depended on the information that Chaska had carried at the risk of his life.

Upon reaching a room, LEH was waiting with a solemn expression. He had awaited this moment since the glaciation began two years earlier. His eyes regarded the messenger with respect before his hands took the quipu. Carefully, he examined its knots, and just then, a condor feather fell softly into his palm.

And silence descended like a veil: it was the sign from Elías. The Hanan Pacha was sending a message. No one spoke;

no one dared to break the moment. In that instant, they under-stood the message was not merely information: it was a bridge between times, an opportunity they could not afford to miss.

The quipu contained knowledge that could alter the course of events, unite the past with the present, reshape the structure of the future. Karanza and the Outer Reserves were no longer separate; their destinies were entwined in a new vision of time.

Chaska, still breathless, raised his gaze to LEH.

'We made it,' he whispered.

The chasqui carried not just a message but an echo, a symphony woven by many voices, a vibration born when Naran first touched the fire. It wasn't just a quipu, it was the field responding. LEH closed his fist around the condor feather and nodded.

'Time is not a line, it is a weave,' he said, opening his hand with quiet certainty. 'Each time a knot is freed, the weave changes.'

The feather floated a moment longer, as if the very air recognised that time had begun to rewrite itself, and that those voices, once awakened, would dream the world anew.

KNOT XV

AYLLU

The underground laboratory of Karanza breathed with expectation and urgency. The delivery of the new quipu brought not only unknown information, but also a latent possibility that no one fully understood.

LEH placed the quipu in the scanner, and the screens began processing the encrypted data. Lines of information emerged, fluctuated, and reconfigured themselves in real time. Dr Lana observed the first patterns with an analytical gaze.

'There are multiple levels of reading,' she announced, without taking her eyes off the screen. 'It will take time to decipher all the variables, but the first thing we can see is that simultaneous paths have opened within the perceptual structure.'

Ariana, her eyes fixed on the data, intervened.

'What we are observing is similar to the previous quipu. Each cord and each knot represent events and choices within the system.'

'But perception remains anchored to a linear and predictable structure,' added Lana, her voice controlled, as she crossed her arms. 'The wave function of consciousness is still limited to a quantum superposition of the past.'

LEH paced from side to side, his mind processing at high speed.

'Not only that,' said Ariana, pointing to a series of fluctuations in the data. 'An anomaly has formed within the quantum superposition of the loop.'

Before they could delve deeper into the analysis, an explosion shook the laboratory. Alarms blared, and Ariana ran to the security terminal.

'They're bombing the antennas again!'

'They know the chasqui has delivered crucial information to us,' said Marco, his eyes blazing. 'They're trying to prevent our next move.'

LEH kept his gaze fixed on the data, filtering out the external noise. And then, a piece clicked into place.

'Ariana, repeat the last part,' he asked, tension in his voice.

She read the anomaly aloud, and the researcher stopped her.

'Naran has shifted her perception... but we are still interpreting this data through the same parameters as before.'

The laboratory fell into expectant silence. What appeared on the screens was no longer a linear narrative but a polyphony, as if many consciousnesses were singing through a single voice, a shared memory that belonged to no one and, at the same time, to all.

'This is not just her personal quipu... something else is taking shape.'

Their eyes met, trying to comprehend.

'Naran is creating a point of balance, a Chawpi,' said LEH.

Lana frowned.

'Do you mean her perception is no longer individual? That she has connected with something greater?'

LEH nodded slowly.

'Until now, we've understood the quipu as a personal tool, a reflection of an individual's perception. But what we're seeing is different: a new structure is forming; an emergent balance that doesn't belong to MIO, but to something entirely new.'

Ariana drew a deep breath.

'A balance within chaos?'

LEH turned towards her, his eyes revealing a new certainty.

'This isn't just an anomaly. A collective quipu is taking shape, a network that no longer responds to commands, but to intentions. A field inhabited by memory, not by control.'

The screens flickered as the quipu's code reconfigured into unseen patterns, its structure emitting a sequence still indecipherable. Lana did not look away.

'The data still can't interpret all the variables.'

'But we can perceive it,' whispered LEH. 'Each time a knot is released, the weave changes. A collapse of perception is not the end; it's the decision to recreate the connections from another point of vision. This is a collective Intent.'

Before they could fully grasp it, another explosion shook the laboratory. MIO had detected the anomaly and was reacting at that very moment. For the system can control codes, but it cannot anticipate a melody composed beyond them.

In the heart of Karanza's underground hall, where ancestral symbols intertwined with advanced technology, LEH's and Lana's teams gathered with members of the community. A dim light illuminated the walls, where vast murals coexisted with monitors displaying data in real time.

Marco established the connection using the code provided by the chasqui, and on a large screen appeared the people of the Outer Reserves, gathered around the fire in a great subterranean chamber. Then Elías spoke, his voice deep and imbued with certainty.

'We gather guided by the signs of Hanan Pacha. This meeting is no coincidence but a reflection of our decision to step out of the loop. This is our Ayllu.'

The air reverberated with his words. Nuna, keeper of memory, spoke next.

'The glaciation did not begin with the weather but with our minds. MIO froze collective perception, and now the world mirrors that state.'

Those present nodded, feeling the truth in her words; they had lived trapped at the same perceptual point for years, repeating the same cycles without realising it.

'But we meet under the spirit of Ayni,' Nuna continued. 'Reciprocity guides us, the giving and receiving in balance. We are not only allies; we are guardians of perception, responsible for remembering that reality is not fixed but malleable.'

Elías nodded with conviction.

'Just as the ancient chasquis carried messages across the *Tawantinsuyo*, we send a message through time and space, influencing the very fabric of reality. The channel we are using is Naran's quipu; its cords and knots have become part of the shared field of memory. This quipu is now a collective song.'

The image on the screen flickered for a moment. Marco adjusted the signal until it stabilised.

'For too long, a few have known how to direct collective attention. What we call reality today has been an architecture of imposed perceptions,' LEH said with determination. 'Now we must decolonise the future, decolonise the collective imagination.'

'The key lies in balance,' Nuna added. 'Ayni reminds us that every action has a resonance. If perception has been frozen, we must restore its movement. Our strength lies in remembering that we are Dreamers—that perception itself is the most powerful tool for transforming reality.'

Groups began sharing their strategies. Dr Lana explained precisely how Karanza's technology could modify MIO's code without perpetuating its mechanisms of control.

'We shall become the sum of a plurality of futures,' she stated, 'but for that to happen, technology and progress must belong to no one.'

She paused for a few seconds as Marco re-established the link with the Outer Reserves.

'This is not a clash of forces, for it is not about destroying MIO, but about changing how we interact with it. If we want multiple futures, we must ensure that choice itself is not predetermined, but guided by the autonomy of perception.'

Elías drew a breath and looked around the room.

'We have dreamed of this moment for generations, and today we bring it into being. At the heart of the network, a new weave is forming. This heartbeat is the echo of our stories, of our Intents interwoven within one Ayllu. Together, we are weaving the *Pachakuti*, the time of great change.'

A murmur rippled through the hall. The energy was palpable: they were breaking the illusion that had kept them trapped in MIO's loop. Nuna nodded respectfully.

'Let us face this challenge by uniting our wisdoms and our visions. But let us remember that only through the unity of our hearts can we sustain this moment and lift it to another level.'

The meeting continued as each group detailed how to integrate their resources. The atmosphere was charged with hope and determination; a turning point had begun, one in which the creation of reality and freedom were no longer an ideal but a right they were reclaiming together.

Elías closed the gathering with words that touched everyone present.

'Change will not come from outside. It is we who must shift the collective assemblage point, and that is why we are here: to remember, to Dream, and to sustain the vision of a new time. Kay Pacha holds us; Qhapaq Ñan guides us.'

The meeting went on with tactical details, but the essence had already been sown. They were not merely allies coordinating efforts; they were Dreamers rebuilding perception. The silence in the room grew dense, as if the fabric itself were holding its breath.

And in that instant, the Pachakuti ceased to be a myth and became a conscious Intent.

For when the threads of perception align, the field responds.

At the centre of the quipu, a barely perceptible movement, like a flutter, like an ancient code began to unfold its form.

The screens displayed a growing chaos across the network; MIO's structure was faltering, reflecting the fractures of the human mind itself, trapped within its own codes. Nélida hurried across the room and handed a note to Alan. He took it quickly, reading it in silence before lifting his gaze to her.

'Thank you, Nélida,' he said quietly, his tone sincere. 'Thank you for helping me, and for standing by the group.'

She nodded without speaking, though her eyes shone with conviction. Both of them knew this was a decisive moment. Alan leaned slightly closer and spoke in a voice only she could hear.

'Do you remember when I asked you whether these young people would ever have a chance?' he whispered, without taking his eyes off the screens, where the data flickered out of control. He paused, took a deep breath, then continued, 'Today we're going to create that chance, Nélida. Today we'll reboot the headsets without anyone knowing, and we'll filter the quipu's information into the network.'

The technicians could suspect nothing; every movement had to appear as part of the usual protocol. The woman exhaled sharply and nodded.

'How much time do we have?' she whispered.

Alan checked the monitors.

'Hours. Karanza has sent a message from the Outer Reserves. The only way to break MIO's control is by synchronising our actions.'

Nélida looked around and, with a discreet gesture, adjusted one of the terminals. They both knew there would be no second chance.

'It's time to bring all our forces together,' murmured Naran's father, his eyes fixed on the screen.

KNOT XVI

THE CALL OF THE VOID

Marco clenched his jaw as he typed, his eyes fixed on the monitor. Lines of code trembled under the weight of his uncertainty. Elías's words kept circling in his mind like a persistent echo.

'To influence the very fabric of reality.'

Elías had said it with the calm of someone holding a map towards the unknown. But for Marco, used to precise equations and reproducible results, the idea was anything but reassuring. He reviewed the data once more, tension in his expression. Every variable, every pattern, every simulation they tried to run brought them back to the same point: uncertainty. He rubbed his forehead and exhaled with frustration.

At last, he sighed and turned towards LEH, who stood at the centre of the room, watching everyone with quiet authority.

'Don't you think all this is too abstract?' he said, breaking the silence. 'Talking about influencing the very fabric of reality might make sense in the Outer Reserves, but this is science, LEH. We're facing a system designed with absolute mathematical precision. How can we trust something so... intangible? This is our last chance. We can't afford to fail.'

The room fell silent. Some of the technicians exchanged uneasy glances. Two years of confinement in Karanza's bunkers had worn them down. Could they really trust the vision of the Outer Reserves?

LEH's eyes lit up at Marco's words; not with reproach, but with a mixture of patience and challenge.

'Marco,' he said, stepping slowly towards him, 'I understand your doubts, we've all had them at some point. But tell me, what's more abstract? Believing that reality is a series of numbers and codes locked inside the rigidity of linear time, or accepting that this same reality is a flow we can influence once we understand its language?'

Marco felt his breathing quicken. Something in those words unsettled his inner structure, though he still clung to his logic.

'None of this makes sense,' he muttered.

The researcher watched him in silence. He knew that Marco was searching for certainty inside a structure that could no longer sustain it.

'Why are we still unable to predict the system's variables?' the cybernetics expert demanded, his tone sharp. 'If the quipu is a navigational tool for perception, there should be a pattern we can calculate.'

LEH walked slowly towards the board where data pulsed in shifting graphs and equations.

'Because you're still looking for answers within a fixed framework,' he replied. 'But the quipu isn't an algorithm; it's a reflection of perception in motion. Try to pin it down, and it vanishes.'

Marco gritted his teeth and struck the table with a closed fist.

'That's metaphysics. We're dealing with real data, measurable structures.'

LEH regarded him with unshakable calm.

'And what is data,' he said softly, 'if not a set of reference points within a system of perception? Science only measures what perception has already defined as real.'

A hush fell over the room. LEH studied Marco intently. In that instant, he remembered his own fears; how, in the Outer Reserves, communities had divided when the time came to cross the threshold into the unknown. He remembered the young man who had doubted, just as the expert doubted now.

Dr Lana, who had remained silent until then, folded her arms and spoke in a neutral tone, seeking balance in the discussion.

'Marco isn't the only one who thinks that way,' she said. 'There are technicians and members of the community who fear that if we fail, there won't be another chance. We have to acknowledge that fear, not dismiss it as mere resistance to change. But we can't allow it to paralyse us either.'

LEH nodded. He understood that Lana wasn't taking sides but helping both to be heard.

'It's not about eliminating fear,' he said. 'It's about not letting it rule us. What we're building isn't absolute certainty. But neither was MIO's system. It only made us believe it was.'

Marco exhaled sharply and looked at the screen, where the quipu pulsed with unstable patterns.

'Then how do we know this is real, and not another projection of our own expectations?' he asked finally, his tone softer.

LEH gave him a faint smile.

'Because it's not about believing, Marco. It's about perceiving.'

He took a deep breath. Once again, LEH found himself at that intersection of paths.

He slipped his hand into his pocket, his fingers finding the stone engraved with the sun and moon. He held it tightly, feeling its rough texture against his skin; a reminder of the duality he had always sought to integrate.

But this time, he was ready to hold the void.

And he understood, at last, that it wasn't logic that had brought him there, but his capacity to listen, even to what had not yet taken form

Ikan's weary gaze followed the sway of the shadows reflected on the cave walls. Without thinking too much, he matched their rhythm with his fingers, tracing in the air the melodies that arose in his mind. In the background, Elías's steady voice once again sought to sow calm and clarity among those present.

The fire burned at the centre of the circle, illuminating the tense faces of those who had endured the winter in the Outer Reserves. They had been talking for hours about the crisis and the uncertainty that hung over them, for the concerns of each community's representatives were palpable.

'Timeline 3 and the MIO system remain a constant threat. Our people are losing their connection with nature,' said one of the elders. 'The Ayni is weakening, and without it, the bonds that keep us united are fading away.'

Another hamawta stood up; his expression reflected the concern of many.

'They want us to depend on their technologies, forcing us to accept their artificial reality. If we yield, we'll lose our self-sufficiency and our connection to the land.'

Voices rose within the cave, echoing against the stone walls. There was fear and frustration. Then Elías raised his hand to ask for silence.

'When the cataclysms that submerged much of the world occurred, the central sectors took advantage of the chaos to impose their control. They created Timeline 3 to sustain a fixed perception anchored in the safety of the predictable.

But that search for certainty was a trap; one that led them to their own destruction.'

The murmurs ceased, and everyone listened attentively.

'To keep the assemblage point fixed in a single place,' he continued, 'is a crime against the nature of being. It is meant to move, to explore new positions and discover other perceptual horizons. By fixing it, the system condemns people to a prison of certainty and boredom that eventually rots their essence.'

One of the northern representatives stood.

'We're afraid. We're considering negotiating with the central sectors. Food is scarce, and we don't want our children to go hungry. What will happen when the glaciation begins? We could take refuge in the underground city they've built.'

Elías lowered his gaze for a moment, reflecting before he spoke.

'I recognise that, under pressure, we all tend to look for something to hold on to. But if we negotiated with the central sectors, we'd be turning the board around and playing for the opponent.'

A faint murmur swept through the cave.

'This is the Tonal of our time,' he went on. 'The challenge of our generation is not to seek external certainty, but to remember that the Ayllu has its own move. Our unique perception is our strength in this game of existence.'

From the far end of the hall, Nuna spoke with the clarity of one who carries the wisdom of time.

'The central sectors chose the path of certainty and death. They anchored the population in a false sense of security. But we cannot surrender to the challenge of the spirit.
We are like ships that must sail the ocean of consciousness—we cannot remain anchored in a harbour that slowly destroys us.'

The fire crackled as her words resonated among them.

'A sailing ship that stays anchored decays over time,' she continued, 'and the same happens to those trapped in a fixed perception; unmoving, unchanging. Certainty may appear to be a refuge, but it's a prison. Life is made to sail, to take risks, to embrace uncertainty and transform it into the most sublime delight: freedom.'

Ikan remembered the words Elías had once told him about the art of Stalking: *When you face forces you cannot defeat, step aside for a moment, place your attention elsewhere, and let your thoughts flow freely.*

As the conversation went on, his fingers found the quena, and he began to play a soft melody, an echo of resistance amid the cold. The fire flared again, and eyes turned towards it. The group remained silent, grateful for the warmth the blaze offered them, as if it were the womb of something new about to be born.

'This is a fitting moment to look into the depths within ourselves,' said Elías calmly. Their eyes stayed fixed on the flames. 'Let us rest our gaze also upon our hearts; let us welcome and transform our dialogue with unease. It's no longer about how much longer we can endure, or how to win a battle against the central sectors, or the glaciation. It is, rather, about learning to dance with uncertainty and turn it into wisdom.

'Our challenge is not merely to survive; it is to make uncertainty our ally, to grow, to transform.'

'Let us ask ourselves: What can I learn from this moment? How much can I empty myself of expectations and open myself to the unknown?'

Their eyes returned to the fire, but doubt still lingered. Uncertainty no longer dwelled only in their minds; it had sunk into their bodies, deeper and sharper than the cold itself.

Ikan kept playing the quena as a group of children entered and approached their families. They sensed the tension in the room and sought the shelter of their parents' arms. Elías smiled as he saw them approach and concluded:

'Now we have a far more interesting match. Our own game of *Pumani*, or chess with infinity.'

The fire had quietened. One of the children laughed as another tickled him beneath the blanket. Their laughter, filled with light, transformed the atmosphere, illuminating it with the spark of those who still discover the world with innocent eyes.

'Nuna, will you tell us the story of that sailing ship that was anchored at the pier and felt sad?' asked a little girl with wonder, wishing that they could all remain together around the fire.

The young woman smiled tenderly, her eyes reflecting the warmth of the flame.

'Ah, so you were listening,' she laughed. 'Of course, let us Dream together a new journey in the vast sea of the unknown, through the story of the sailing ship *Wayra*.'

The children gathered closer, captivated by her voice; the adults, without realising it, did the same, as if for a moment they had forgotten the weight of their worries.

'Dear children,' Nuna began, 'Wayra, as her name suggests, was like the wind and embodied the deepest purpose we all long for in our hearts: to be navigators on this sea of consciousness.' Her voice wrapped the space with the cadence of a Dreamer. 'Wayra was created to explore and flow in freedom, to cross great waves and storms, to discover in each mile travelled horizons once invisible. She was not made to remain still.'

She paused to seek the gaze of each child, planting in them a seed of meaning.

'But over time, the sailors began to fear the vast sea. To them, that infinite ocean became something uncertain and dangerous, so they decided the port was the only safe place for Wayra and anchored her there, convinced they were protecting her from shipwreck or from being lost in unknown waters. The ship's wood began to rot, and Wayra, designed to move and perceive the vast ocean, faded into suffocating stillness. And do you know what happened?' she asked, her voice weaving through the dimness of the cave.

The children fell silent, engrossed in the story, until one answered in a faint voice:

'She was very sad because she couldn't sail...'

Nuna nodded with a wise smile.

'Exactly. A deep sadness overtook the sailing ship, for her essence was not stillness, but movement.' The fire crackled more brightly as Nuna continued. 'But then, a boy from the port perceived what was happening: Wayra was not meant to remain anchored, and keeping her there would condemn her to a prison of certainty and fear.'

Her words resonated in the cave. Something in the story touched a very deep chord in each of those present.

'The young man closed his eyes and Dreamed himself as a navigator of consciousness. He understood that he, too, was like Wayra, made to move, to explore, to discover. He knew that if he ignored that call, something within him would begin to wither. So he made a decision.'

The children held their breath.

'He climbed aboard the ship and cut the moorings that held her. In that instant, an allied wind carried Wayra out to sea. The ship's sails snapped open, and the colours of her wood began to shine again. The sadness dissipated, and a deep joy filled the hearts of all the port's inhabitants as they watched Wayra head towards new horizons.'

Nuna let the images float in the air before asking, 'And what happened to the young man?'

'Did he reach his destination?' asked one of the older children, his eyes shining.

Nuna smiled knowingly.

'On his journey, he learned that the purpose of life was not to reach a single destination, but to navigate the vast ocean of perceptions and possibilities.'

Silence settled in the cave. The fire crackled softly, illuminating the attentive faces of those listening.

Nuna took a deep breath:

'We, too, are like Wayra. Our deepest purpose is to be navigators of consciousness. If we remain anchored in the illusion of certainty, we betray our nature. Our joy and spirit wither just like the wood of an old ship. But if we respond to the call, if we venture into the sea of the unknown, immersed in the delight of consciousness, then life becomes the most sublime of adventures.

And that, my dear ones, is called freedom.'

Ikan felt the need for fresh air after the meeting, for Elías's words still echoed in his mind. He knew the community's situation was critical, that spirits were low and uncertainty spread like a shadow over those sheltered in the underground caves. The cold winter gave no respite.

As he walked through the tunnels, he looked up at the narrow ceilings and recalled Elías's words:

A warrior looks for ways to act: he finds tunnels, passageways, secret exits; he remembers he is both Dreamer and Stalker.

With renewed determination, he promised himself he would find a way out.

Channelling the anger that had built up over the past few days, he pushed aside a large stone, wrapped himself in thick furs, and stepped out of the caves. He knew he would have only a few minutes, but he needed to clear his mind and make an invocation from there. He knelt down, feeling the snow sink beneath his weight; he inhaled deeply, and the freezing air cut through his chest like a blade. Closing his eyes, he thought of Naran—she was the bridge.

He had tried to enter her dreams, but something prevented him, as if the program controlled even his dream activity. Then he remembered the first time he saw her, during the Ayni festival when they were children. Linear time faded for an instant, and in its place came the certainty that past and future were not separate lines, but reflections of the same weave unfolding in different forms.

Footsteps pulled him from his thoughts.

'I sense you are Dreaming yourself into circular time,' said Elías. His gaze, heavy with wisdom, studied Ikan. 'That which she has been identified with for so long no longer serves her. That is why she finds herself in a void.'

Ikan looked at him, noticing how the daylight deepened the lines in his face; he carried the weight of the community, his worries etched into every contour of his expression. For a moment, Ikan felt that weariness as his own.

Elías knelt down, letting the snow soak his knees. He scooped a handful, rubbed it across his face, and the cold jolted him awake like a blow of truth. He clicked his tongue, as one confirming something to himself.

'That void is painful, but it must be walked through. Naran is seeking the vision. In that emptiness, she will find a new perception to guide her steps.'

The sea roared in the distance. The wind whistled through the *pachaphuyu*, the dense mist that hovered around them like smoke. For a moment, Ikan also felt the void within, the uncertainty of not seeing, of searching for signs and finding no answer.

'She must release what she once was so that the new Intent can reach her,' Elías added, 'but the same applies to you. What you feel is not only her emptiness. It is yours as well. Both of you are synchronised within the cyclic rhythm of time.'

The boy felt a tremor in his chest; it was not just a metaphor or a concept. He felt it in every cell of his body, in every breath, in every heartbeat, echoing with the wind. He understood that his connection with Naran was not bound by linear time—it was a cyclical bond, like two particles entangled in the vast ocean of mystery.

What she was living was not mere loss, but the echo of a transformation that had already taken place in another layer of time. She was not alone in her passage, for he too felt it, lived it in his own skin.

The bridge between them still existed.

A gust of wind brought Ikan back to the ruthless tension of the present as his mind searched for a way out.

'Why don't we negotiate with the central sectors? There are already divisions between communities during these winters... what will happen when the glaciation arrives?'

Elías did not hesitate.

'We will not negotiate with them under their logic, under their structure,' he said with serene firmness, pausing briefly. 'Remember this: what a conscious man does resonates four hundred times more than any act of a man trapped within the system's structure. A conscious man can play with the forces of the universe.' He looked at Ikan intently. 'And he must do so with respect and humility, without turning it into an inner conflict.'

Elías sighed, gazing at the young man with unshakable calm.

'*Yanantin* teaches us that light and shadow exist together,' he continued, drawing the sun and moon in the snow. 'MIO seeks to separate these forces, but their power lies in remaining united. It prefers to impose a single vision because it knows that in diversity lies our true strength.'

Ikan took a deep breath. For a moment, he felt trapped in a labyrinth of stories that contained him but offered no exit.

'And what if we are too trapped in our stories?' he murmured. 'We hide in these caves, we tell tales of the past, but we do nothing to leave. What if we've failed? What if the glaciation reaches us before we've managed to change anything?'

Elías looked at him with understanding.

'You speak of our stories as if they were chains,' he said. 'But don't you see? They are the weave that connects us. If we weave them together, they can become the bridge to what lies beyond these caves, beyond fear. In this Chawpi—this point between doubt and certainty—we will find the strength to open the Punku, the possibility.'

Ikan swallowed hard.

'And what if I'm wrong?' he whispered. 'What if Naran doesn't return? What if this Punku never opens?'

Elías placed a hand on his shoulder.

'It's not about certainty, Ikan. It's about choosing—about Dreaming together a path that does not yet exist. And even if the Punku doesn't open today, our intention will be sown.

We are not speaking of victory or defeat.

Our focus must be on the Intent, on the purpose of weaving a new vision together.'

Ikan nodded silently but did not move right away. As Elías walked back into the cave, he slid his hand into his pocket and pulled out the quena. He brought it to his lips and played a melody, an echo that resonated through the vastness of the snow.

He knew that Naran heard him through the poetry.

Do not surrender before the challenge of the spirit,
for in that void, where all seems lost,
let us walk together, opening forgotten paths.
Each thread, a dream; each dream, a vision.
Where chaos sings its song,
let us approach the abyss with trust.
In the void, together let us Dream a new vision,
where love weaves what separation broke.

He closed his eyes and let the cold pierce him, the sound of the sea filled him, the mist enveloped him. He knew he had to surrender to the void—to let it pass through him without resistance—because in the cyclic rhythm of love and time, that emptiness was the gateway to something new, something he could not yet see but that was already unfolding.

The vastness of the void overwhelmed him, and a sudden gust of wind shook his body. In that instant, he felt the same as the sailing ship wearing itself down in the immensity of nothingness; yet something within him rebelled against that feeling, against the idea of being in harbour without direction.

His thoughts swirled like leaves in a gust; he could find no centre, only wind.

And he knew then it was the moment to invoke.

'Great Spirit, I raise my voice. I do not ask for myself, but that my people may live, that the generations to come may still live in the mystery.'

And then, without thinking, he began to run.

He pushed through the snow, away from the caves, away from the stories, away from the weight of uncertainty. He could not remain there, motionless, waiting for answers that would not come. His feet sank into the ice with every stride, yet he pressed on, breath ragged, his chest burning with effort.

He did not know whether he was fleeing from the void or seeking another way to face it, but at that moment the only thing that mattered was to move, to keep running, to hold on to the feeling of the earth beneath his feet.

Perhaps, in the cyclic flow of time, that act of escape was also a return. And if the void was the Nagual, then running too was an invocation, not to flee, but to remember the rhythm of the field.

LEH came out of his thoughts with a slight tremor in his body, for he now understood that memory was not forgetfulness: it was a field, and it was active. He refocused his attention on the laboratory and once again remembered the journey he had undertaken when he left the shelter of the Outer Reserves' caves and ventured into the vast ocean of uncertainty.

At that threshold, he realised he was not only a researcher—he was a navigator of consciousness.

Fire was no longer survival; it was vision.

He relived every challenge encountered along the way: he had been captured by the central sectors, taken to Sector A; escaped the MIO program due to a technical failure, and finally found refuge in Karanza.

LEH was not another. He was Ikan, holding the fire from a different angle. At that instant, he understood that they were not separate, but threads of the same weave. There was no before or after, only perception in motion.

He felt his connection with Naran and the unconditional love that bound them. Within his consciousness, an echo pulsed beyond linear time, like a subtle interference resonating across the superposition of their perceptions. It was a momentary collapse of distance, a fleeting access to information that had already been lived in another layer of time. And in that instant, he knew that Naran was no longer trapped in the loop; that they had reconnected in the flow of cyclic time, intertwined by the Intent.

At last, LEH put words to that certainty:

'You can only see a hummingbird through imagination,' he said aloud, and his words echoed in the room.

The air seemed to hold its breath for a moment, for it was no mere proverb, but a truth vibrating through dimensions: imagination was the doorway to every dimension, the access point to all possibilities.

'Spirituality is imagination,' he continued, 'it is the ability to open the mind to the point where everything is possible. Quantum physics has shown us that attention on a particle determines its existence. Perception is the key.'

The navigator of consciousness surveyed the room. He understood he did not have to choose between two extremes, nor reject the structure or surrender to it. He could now walk between both worlds without fragmentation.

And he was not speaking only to Marco, but to all the researchers, technicians, and inhabitants of Karanza gathered there. But he drew a deep breath and turned towards the cybersecurity expert.

'What you feel is real,' he said firmly, 'but it is not the limit; it is the intersection. This is where we choose whether to remain trapped or to take a step beyond.'

Marco looked at him, still weighed down with resistance, but something in his eyes reflected that he had heard, that perhaps, for the first time, there was a possibility beyond what he could calculate.

LEH approached the screen where the quipu data vibrated, unstable.

'Naran is opening a door, but not within MIO's logic. What she is doing cannot be interpreted from the structure of data because it does not belong to linear time.'

Dr Lana looked at him intently.

'You mean her perception is operating in another temporal framework?'

LEH nodded.

'Not just her perception; the quipu is reflecting a connection to something greater. And if we don't learn to see it, we'll remain trapped as we have until now.'

From the back of the room, Ariana, who had been listening silently, stepped forward.

'This capacity to influence reality transcends our interpretation of time as linear,' she said with fascination.

Marco frowned; the idea was overwhelming. His mind was still trying to grasp what it meant to move Naran's perception through the quipu.

'So,' he said cautiously, 'are you saying we're going to use Naran's quipu as a means to affect space and time? To send messages to the past or future?'

LEH met his gaze.

'That's right, Marco. Every knot you untie transforms the very structure of reality. By releasing trapped energy, it not only changes the past but alters the future.

The quipu is not just a map of time; it's a living organism.'

The room fell silent, and Marco turned his gaze to the data, still doubtful but trying to perceive beyond the numbers. Because this wasn't just theory; it was a journey, a crossing between two perspectives, a synthesis of the wisdom of the Outer Reserves and quantum physics.

LEH smiled softly. In that moment, he knew that thanks to everything he had lived through, he could hold the void amid that chaos. He understood that no line defined his path, only the invisible trace of the fire he had learned to sustain. For in the sea of consciousness, there are also storms, and the best navigators are not those who avoid the waves but those who learn to sail within them.

He closed his eyes for a moment and let the echo of his connection with Naran dwell within him. His perception was changing; it was subtle but real: he felt it in the rhythm of his breathing, in the way his body perceived space. He no longer needed absolute certainties. He knew reality was malleable; he knew Naran was seeing the path and that somewhere beyond linear time, they had already crossed the threshold.

Finally, he opened his eyes and looked at the room with determination.

'We cannot remain stranded in the same concepts, in the same taxonomies. Like sailors who never leave the harbour, we cling to structures we already know, but that bore us to desperation.

We distract ourselves with endless categorisations and lose sight of the only thing that matters: the direct experience of Intent, the abstract, the flight into the unknown. Freedom and love cannot be contained within the Tonal, for they are not concepts to be defined but experiences to be lived, acts of choice and presence.

And only those who dare to reformulate themselves can open the threshold.'

LEH felt as though the very structure of space were yielding to a new possibility.

'It's time to Dream ourselves and to Stalk ourselves into a new position.'

In that moment, the weaving responded.

And with that certainty, the Intent began to unfold.

KNOT XVII

WIÑAYPACHA

Naran closed her eyes, holding the feather in her hand. Her breathing was slow and deep.

The sound of the condor beating its wings echoed once more in the void. But this time, she felt no fear; she did not try to cling to anything or to escape. She surrendered to the movement. She felt the quipu between her hands: her story was not a line but a weave of knots pulsing all at once.

And in the very moment she understood this, a warm breeze wrapped around her and the landscape of Tambo came alive once again.

Kunak appeared before her eyes, the chasqui who had shown her the agricultural terraces and the different layers of time. He stood there, facing her, with the deep, steady gaze of one who had travelled the subtle paths of the Pacha. He wore a unca and held his pututu in his right hand, while in the other he carried quinoa seeds taken from the terraces.

He stepped closer to the young woman and offered her the seeds.

'Naran, this time I bring you a message held in the void of the Wiñaypacha, waiting to be remembered. The seeds have sprouted in this collective Dream. Remember what we spoke of:

time is not linear; it is a cycle, a constant flow that allows you to move and grow, forward and backward, outward and inward.'

Naran felt the movement. She tightened her quipu in both hands and looked at Kunak intently.

'Each thread of your quipu holds a different meaning,' the chasqui continued. 'Time and space intertwine within your life. Nothing is separate, nothing is fixed, everything is in a process of creation.'

Naran closed her eyes and took a deep breath. Her fingers traced the knots of the quipu; she could feel its information, its story. When she opened them again, the landscape had changed once more: she found herself in a space where memories and dreams intertwined, where time seemed to exist in all its forms at once.

Kunak watched her with serenity.

'That is the magic of the quipu: everything is connected, and when we align our perception, the next thread appears effortlessly.'

In that moment, the young woman understood that she only had to recognise she had always been there, within the cyclic flow of time.

Once more, the cave returned in her Dream, where time and space collapsed into an eternal reflection. The stalactites, whose curves and edges defied gravity, twisted in unique formations. As she moved forward, she watched how droplets fell, winding down their path, creating sounds that mingled with a distant murmur.

She cautiously circled the gathered group and sensed that the atmosphere was heavy with tension. She remembered that Ikan was there. Upon finding him, she walked over and sat nearby, seeking a sense of familiarity amid the confusion.

Suddenly, Ikan stood up and voiced his frustration aloud.

'It doesn't seem fair, Nuna. Why must I connect with her while she's in the Centre, inside that program? Why does it have to be me? I expected greater challenges.'

He lowered his head and muttered.

'She no longer remembers herself—she's no longer one of us.'

The awicha approached him calmly.

'Ikan, have you felt that tremor before this meeting?' she asked. 'The lines collide when it becomes necessary to integrate other perceptions.' Her voice floated, unhurried. 'Even if you say that Naran does not belong to this group, if you could see beyond form, you would understand that she is already here.'

'She too Dreams.'

'She too weaves.'

Silence settled like a soft mantle. And Naran, absorbed, felt something unfold both within and around her.

Nuna paused. Her eyes looked at him, yet it was as if she saw through him.

'Naran is beside you, even if you do not yet perceive her. She is part of the same quipu as you. And the key is to remember that we are all threads of the same weave.'

The awicha stepped forward and leaned slightly towards them, as if revealing a secret sown beyond time.

'You are here to recognise and inhabit a Chawpi,' she said, her voice serene as it moved through the gathered circle, 'a point where love ceases to be projection and becomes Munay: conscious, resonant love revealed as a shared vision. Until you can sustain it,' she continued, 'each of you will see your shadow reflected in the eyes of the other. And you will not truly see—you will be Stalking your own reflection.
The journey is towards the abstract.
Towards what cannot be named, but can be remembered.

Towards love when it ceases to be image and becomes vision. And then, you will bring to the community what is already unfolding on another plane, that which can only be perceived from the centre.'

Ikan, visibly astonished, turned towards where Naran was sitting. Their eyes met, and in that instant she felt an inexplicable vertigo, as if her perception had suddenly expanded.

The elder woman, a master of Dreaming, inclined her head in respect and, with ancestral wisdom reflected in her almond-shaped eyes, addressed the young ones:

'Ikan, you will enter Naran's dreams while she is within the program, until she regains the energy to Dream.'

Nuna fixed her gaze on the girl and stepped closer.

'Naran,' she said with complicity, 'the connection between different worlds, between diverse realities, is within you. You are an Awaq, a weaver between what was and what can be. Remember who you are.'

And in that instant, she could perceive him.

Ikan had held the vision from the Kay Pacha, from the edges of the system, from the silences of Karanza. Before Naran, in the vortex of the cave, he was there, the living bridge between worlds.

'You're already here,' he whispered, as one who speaks to a part of himself that has finally returned.

She held the vision. She no longer needed to cling, no longer needed to understand. The fire at the centre burned without consuming. The void was no threat—it was presence.

Nuna watched them both with the ancient gaze of one who has seen many cycles born and faded.

'The centre is not something to be reached,' she said, 'it is what remembers, what listens.'

The quipu within Naran's chest expanded.

'You are not seeing,' Nuna said gently, 'you are Stalking your reflection.'

And the reflection opened.

Naran no longer fled from the vertigo; she recognised it as the point of access. The crack was the symbol; the symbol, the threshold; and the threshold, the act of sustaining. She had become the version of herself she had once feared, and for the first time, she knew she could hold it.

The words ignited a fire within her, illuminating every corner of her being. There were no doubts, no time. This Dreaming was what she had always feared: the possibility of holding the infinite. Grateful for the support she felt, she rose and addressed the group.

'Here, where time and possibilities collapse in all their forms, each of us becomes a thread in the weaving of this shared Dreaming. This is our Intent.'

Nuna looked at her deeply, as if she could see beyond that moment. 'Naran, it is time to integrate all that you are. Bring the infinity of your soul into the present.'

Naran visualised each of them in the cave, their nodes glowing like pulses within the system, concentric circles, resonances, ripples in the field.

Dreaming does not end here, thought Naran as she watched the group.

The quipu was alive.

Each thread pulsed, holding an echo of possibilities.

Then she understood the purpose of that encounter: it was to bring that infinitude into the present, to integrate it into the system so that others might also remember they could still choose.

And she looked at Ikan.

KNOT XVIII

CHAWPI

The mist crept through the deserted streets of Karanza, winding between the structures like a harbinger of the inevitable. It seemed as if time had frozen in a perpetual, icy dawn.

LEH advanced through the corridors towards the laboratory, feeling the pressure of responsibility pressed against his chest, while the scarcity of food, the absence of sunlight and the uncertainty floated in the air like an invisible smoke.

Karanza was divided: some trusted in Dr Lana's calculated approach; others, in their own vision, rooted in the cosmovision of the Outer Reserves. Yet at that moment there was no room for discord; only the Intent remained.

Meanwhile, he repeated Elías's words like a mantra:

The warrior cannot modify his destiny, only the way he walks it. If today we manage to shift the perception of even a single strand—one thread within the larger weave—that strand will carry our collective Intent. This is not merely a battle; it is an act of resistance for the freedom of perception, within and beyond MIO.

As LEH made his way through the crowd gathered outside the laboratory, he felt the emotional weight emanating from their bodies: some remained standing, expectant; others sat along the corridor, heavy with doubt.

A small hand closed around his.

'This is for you,' whispered a girl, offering him a tiny wooden figurine of a llama, decorated with coloured threads.

LEH knelt down and, seeing himself reflected in the girl's hopeful gaze, offered her a grateful smile.

He entered the laboratory with a steady step and greeted the teams. After reviewing the latest updates, he addressed the community gathered there.

'While Naran was caught in the loop, she achieved something no one else had before: she disidentified herself from the linear time imposed by MIO.'

Lana, eyes fixed on the data projected on the screen, nodded before speaking with her usual precision.

'MIO operates under the principle of wave-function collapse, restricting all possibilities to a single timeline—Timeline 3—a constant perceptual loop.'

She paused and pointed to Naran's quipu on the holographic projection.

'But Naran has broken that pattern. She didn't escape the system; she became undetectable to it, she disrupted the temporal sequence.' Her eyes shone with a mixture of awe and certainty. 'She has created a node of resonance, a point of interference sustained outside the habitual pattern. In quantum terms, she didn't collapse the possibility offered by the system—she sustained it.'

LEH took a step forward.

'A Chawpi,' he uttered, 'a point where past, present and future coexist as an interconnected whole. Before, that 2% fissure was used by MIO as a reflection,' he continued, 'but Naran stopped looking from within the code, from within the programmed construct. Instead, she dared to look from the other side of the mirror.'

Ariana, her eyes alight, understood instantly.

'Through non-action, she broke the inverse interference pattern that MIO used to feed itself. This moment marks the beginning of the reverse hack, an act of lucid Dreaming within the system itself.'

LEH nodded, completing the thought.

'She didn't collapse an old perception; she collapsed nothing. She remained in non-action—and that broke the loop.'

'She's created a fissure in the system, a point of rupture. MIO is registering that information… it's reconfiguring its code,' murmured Lana as she paced in circles.

A murmur ran through the room before she spoke aloud:

'Naran's quipu will generate a wave capable of stabilising the chaos in the network. It will unite control and freedom. And if this new information holds, it may synchronise others. There's a real possibility that the system will reach a state of quantum coherence.'

The quipu was no longer just Naran's memory: it was a voiceless song, a weave of steps and losses, the visions of all those who had held the fissure open. It was an answer to a call that had never been merely individual.

LEH let the silence speak before continuing.

'The quipu is no longer merely a reflection of Naran's journey,' he said. 'It is a living weave, a pulse of all who have sustained the Intent. The node we call Chawpi doesn't belong to a single vision; it's the centre where our memories and decisions converge. And from there, we resist—and call forth a new Dreaming.'

Lana looked at him with approval.

'When we insert this information into the network, we won't just correct perceptual chaos; we'll be planting a new perception, one based not on fear, but on the freedom to choose.'

The community understood that everything they had lived through converged at that point. The quipu woven across the different Pachas was both offering and message; the centre of a new perceptual weave.

Marco, sceptical and arms crossed, broke the moment.

'All this sounds good, but it's still theory,' he said sharply. 'The central sectors are attacking, and we could lose everything. We still don't have a clear response on the defence strategy.'

Several faces turned towards him and his group of technicians. The tension in the room rose between those demanding a concrete plan and those willing to follow LEH and Lana's path.

'Fear is what keeps us trapped within MIO's structure,' the researcher replied with calm precision. 'If we keep seeing this battle through its logic, we've already lost.' The murmurs grew, but he kept his gaze fixed on the cybersecurity expert. 'Your counter-offensive plan is yours, Marco. Just make sure it doesn't destroy what we're building.'

Before he could answer, an explosion shook the underground base. The lights flickered and the alarms blared.

'Impact on the eastern perimeter!' shouted a technician.

The screens showed Karanza's defences under attack; the offensive had advanced faster than expected.

'We're losing connection with the allies on the surface!' warned Ariana, her voice tense as she struggled to stabilise the signal.

LEH took a deep breath and fixed his gaze on Marco.

'They want to pull us into their strategy; they're trying to divert us from our true objective,' he said firmly. 'Remember: this isn't about destruction; it's about redirecting the conflict into the field of perception.'

Lana nodded, and Marco swallowed hard. Outside, the conflict surged; inside, a new vision aligned. In that instant, they all knew the turning point had come.

They prepared for the implementation of the strategy, aware that it would take precision, creativity, and an unyielding will to sustain fluidity within the weave.

From Karanza, Marco leaned over the console, shoulders tense with the urgency of the moment. Around him, the team of engineers worked with surgical precision, adjusting the final parameters. Outside, the sky was heavy with omens, the central sectors' drones cutting through the mist with relentless synchronisation.

'Are you ready?' asked Ariana, her voice strained. They knew that facing them in a conventional way would be suicide.

The first swarm of drones was already flying over Karanza's antennas, circling like vultures waiting for their prey.

'Now!' shouted Marco.

Ariana pressed the final command. The resonance frequency activated, and a deep hum roared through the air. In an instant, waves of interference expanded like an ethereal tide, enveloping the drones. One by one, they began to oscillate erratically, their routes thrown off by a force their systems could not comprehend. The signal from the central sectors turned chaotic as the resonant waves interacted with the drones' materials, distorting their circuits with a logic that overflowed linear control.

'It worked,' whispered Marco, disbelief and relief intertwining as he watched the machines fall slowly, like puppets with their strings cut.

LEH, watching from the shadows, spoke in a lower voice, almost to himself.

'This isn't about destruction...'

The paradox was evident: for in that moment, the drones were under their control.

Yet the central sectors reacted swiftly, sending new units on an adjusted frequency, convinced they could neutralise the interference. In their desperation to correct the anomaly, they only amplified the phenomenon. Unwittingly, they replicated the distortion, plunging it into a feedback loop. Each new drone sent out expanded the instability, further weakening MIO's infrastructure.

From the Research Centre, hidden within corridors saturated with chaos and flickering shadows, Alan saw the perfect moment to intervene. As the signals tangled in an impossible dance of faulty predictions, he plunged into the program's internal network. His fingers danced across the interface, navigating between codes and security barriers that rose like walls of stone.

But MIO had already anticipated his presence.

The system's countermeasures activated, and in a desperate attempt to close the breaches, it triggered a forced reconnection protocol. The Template of Line 3 began to wrap around the signals, trying to re-establish the connection of the Incompatibles and seal off any possibility of release. However, MIO had not foreseen the quantum anomaly. The signal overload caused by the drones generated an unexpected fracture in the security system. For the first time, MIO lost absolute control over its own territory.

Alan didn't hesitate. He executed the manual reset command for the helmets. One by one, the devices began to flicker; MIO's threads of control loosened, though the network still resisted fully giving way. The Incompatibles, immersed in their struggle to recover perception, were on the verge of liberation, but the battle was not yet won.

Then the hum of the drones merged with something deeper–an echo in memory that pulled him inward.

It was not recollection; it was presence.

The cave was dark and damp. Elias was beside him. Without warning, he struck his back sharply, and Naran's father felt a sudden vertigo as the vision of the present blurred.

Suddenly, he found himself in a different space.

Before him, a circle of figures surrounded an ancestral fire, and the murmurs of the flames seemed to whisper something he had not yet grasped.

'Where are we?' he asked, his voice caught between awe and disbelief.

Elias looked at him with the serenity of one who had been there countless times.

'In non-linear time,' he said, 'in a shared Dreaming.'

Alan scanned the faces around the fire, and his breath stopped when he saw his daughter among them. An old woman stepped forward and spoke with the cadence of one who had crossed the veils of time.

'You are here to recognise and inhabit a Chawpi, a point where love is no longer projection but shared perception. Then you will contribute to the community what is already unfolding on another plane—what can only be perceived from the centre.'

And his vision dissolved with a blink.

Back in the Research Centre, the crash of drones falling onto the nearby antennas shook his awareness. The quantum distortion could mean either liberation or collapse. Alan knew this, but he had already made his choice.

'How many realities can a single moment sustain?' he asked, with the calm voice of one who no longer seeks answers but inhabits the questions.

Because what is real
is not what simply happens,
but where you choose to place your attention.
And freedom… was choosing which line to sustain.
And with one final command, he reset the helmets.
Because now he knew that the true battle had never been physical.
It was, and had always been, a battle of perception.

KNOT XIX

THE THRESHOLD
BETWEEN WORLDS

'We're ready,' reported Dr Lana as she watched the data on the screen indicating that a window had opened. 'We have only a few seconds, while the helmets reset, to avoid detection,' she added.

Her eyes fixed on the fluctuating parameters.

'Initiating quantum entanglement sequence. The goal is to keep Naran and the Incompatibles connected to our shared intention.'

LEH stepped forward, his voice firm yet calm.

'The symbol of Ayni, once imbued, will not only strengthen our bond with them; it will also serve as an anchor, a reminder of the support surrounding them.'

The screens flickered, and the team held their breath. It was a critical moment. A surge of activity rippled through the network of interconnected nodes; the system was on the verge of collapse.

The perceptual hacker, his face illuminated by the glow of the monitors, studied the pattern and turned to the team.

'As we said, the nodes are the key. They're not just points of control—they're centres of collective perception within the system,' he explained with steady conviction. 'Each node is a mirror that reflects and amplifies the perception imposed by Timeline 3.'

Ariana and Marco exchanged a tense glance. Without lifting her eyes from the console, Ariana continued LEH's thought while her fingers flew across the keyboard.

'If the information is reconfigured, what's projected through the network will change.'

Lines of code flowed across the screens like an unstoppable river. Another surge of activity shook the network, and the crowd gathered inside and outside the laboratory, thickening the air with the intensity of their anticipation.

'The new resonance, aligned with the new vision, is altering the carrier waves of information within the simulation,' explained Lana, her voice a blend of urgency and hope. 'If we manage to synchronise it across all nodes, every connected user will begin to perceive something beyond the control imposed by the system.'

Marco frowned, feeling the tension in the room. He looked at the doctor before replying gravely:

'For that to happen, we need to reach critical mass within the network.'

LEH approached the projection and watched as the quipu made the overlapping weaves visible within the nodes.

'MIO has kept perception in a state of permanent collapse inside Timeline 3, repeating the same observational pattern. But if enough nodes sustain the new information, we'll open a space of superposition strong enough to break the loop.'

Ariana nodded; she understood the magnitude of what they were attempting.

'If MIO can't collapse perception into a single fixed reality, then the structure will weaken,' she whispered.

Lana struck the keys with precision, and the quipu's projection flickered.

'If we can get the collective observer to perceive something different, then reality within the system will begin to fragment and rebuild itself,' added LEH.

Marco crossed his arms.

'It's a risk. If we fail, we might reinforce the structure instead of breaking it.'

LEH met his gaze firmly.

'The greater risk is remaining trapped in this pattern forever.'

A charged silence filled the room.

The choice was clear: the only way to change the paradigm was to challenge the very act of observation. The fate of the network hung by a thread. The next movement would decide everything.

And perhaps, for the first time, the system wouldn't know what to expect, because the observer was no longer the same.

Nuna's words and the echo of the collective Dreaming still resonated through her body. Naran took a deep breath and let her attention move across the knots of the quipu. One by one, she followed the glowing pulses until she reached the one that belonged to the system's loop. Then she felt it, a shift in the network, even before the Incompatibles sensed it.

MIO had changed its strategy. The images before her were perfect, seductive. The users had been absorbed into the system: resistance seemed extinguished, anomalies erased, and every node fit seamlessly into MIO's design. The temptation to surrender filtered into her mind.

What if this was what was meant to happen?

What if resistance had only been the illusion of a useless struggle?

The program was using the fissure as a mirror—not to drag them into the loop of past repetitions this time, but to project them into a prefabricated future. Naran paused. Her breathing became conscious. She realised that what MIO offered was a path of resignation, but Intent felt like direction.

Then she returned to the quipu, seeking an answer. The information emanating from the knots didn't match MIO's projection. What it offered was a static reality, with no room for possibility, only certainty. And that was not freedom.

Around her, the Incompatibles stared with empty eyes, hypnotised by the promised future. Others still resisted, but their strength was fading, caught in the grip of doubt.

'This isn't real!' Naran's voice cut through the air like a blade.

Some of the Incompatibles looked up at her, their gaze still clouded by the seduction of the mirage MIO had shown them.

'MIO is offering us a path without choice—but we are not fixed data. We are navigators of perception.'

She grasped her quipu with both hands and felt the cords and knots respond to her vision. Gradually, some of the Incompatibles began to stir; a few stepped back, moving away from MIO's projection, though others still hesitated.

'What if this is the right thing?' Néstor asked, his voice trembling. 'What if resistance has blinded us to what's inevitable?'

Naran met his gaze and felt his fear. The battle had never been against MIO—it had always been against each one's own perception.

'If this future were real, it wouldn't need us to surrender our will in order to exist.'

She closed her eyes for a moment, and when she opened them, she sensed the possibility of MIO's projection collapsing around her. She took a deep breath, knowing the moment to decide had come, not to return to the past, nor to lose herself in the artificial horizons of the future, but to remember what had already been sown in the Field.

From the Research Centre laboratory, Alan watched the screens with a furrowed brow. The changes were evident, the new information was being sustained within the system. His gaze stopped on the graphs as he glimpsed how MIO's structure was beginning to tune with the quantum Field, beyond Timeline 3.

Meanwhile, in the Karanza laboratory, LEH stood motionless, eyes closed, as if perceiving the pulse of an underlying reality.

'We're facing a temporal anchoring,' he murmured. 'Each node acts as a point of assemblage, a reference within the network to project a new position. Dreaming and Stalking have become a shared act.'

Lana, focused on the graphs, noticed how the nodes that once fluctuated uncontrollably were now entering coherence, as if the minds trapped in the system were beginning to connect with something larger.

'The data shows they're leaving behind the line of control, of fear...' she said softly.

LEH nodded.

'They're not only perceiving a new possibility; they're beginning to glimpse a reality that doesn't yet exist, but which, by synchronising, they can anchor collectively. They don't need to know how, they just need to feel it.'

Ariana pointed to the holographic projector. The system simulation showed the nodes—once scattered—now pulsing in a shared rhythm. The network, fragmented until then, was transforming into a single frequency.

LEH took a deep breath and addressed all those supporting the trial.

'Each node that synchronises with the quantum resonance anchors this new position in time and space.'

A digital Ayllu was emerging, defying MIO's structure and redefining collective perception.

Meanwhile, in the Outer Reserves, deep within the underground caverns, Nuna guided the community to sustain the collective Dreaming and its connection with the quipu.

'The quipu woven through circular time is an Ayni,' she said, breaking the silence of the cave. 'Our Ayni threads and resonates like an echo travelling through the weave of reality.'

Elias, seated by the fire, added in his deep voice:

'This quipu isn't just a map of time; it's a living weave where opposites meet. We created this Chawpi together so that past and future may integrate, so that the wounds of yesterday may heal through the possibilities of tomorrow. And in that meeting point, in that instant, each one can decide who they wish to be.'

As more users interacted with the new patterns, they began to perceive the flexibility of their realities. The MIO system started to falter, unable to sustain a single perceptual line.

At the Research Centre, Margot stared at the graphs in disbelief.

'They should be in a loop... but something's changing,' she whispered.

At that moment, MIO, confronted by the magnitude of this new collective Intent, began to collapse. The boundaries of its control dissolved, allowing time, space, and consciousness to expand in all directions. The screens displayed chaotic patterns as the technicians tried to regain control, but it was useless.

'Reset the helmets!'

A technician looked at her, bewildered.

'They've been reset several times—there's no response.'

Margot scanned the lines of code with frantic eyes. Everything was changing before her, and she couldn't stop it.

'Then disconnect them from the system!'

Another technician hesitated.

'It's dangerous to disconnect without knowing what...' he tried to warn.

'I said disconnect them!' she ordered.

In Karanza, the monitors flickered before going dark, and then a deafening silence filled the room. LEH looked at Lana in disbelief.

'We've lost connection.'

She tried to restore the systems, but only emptiness responded.

'They've been disconnected from the MIO system,' he murmured. His words fell heavily over everyone in the room.

Lana pressed her lips together.

'Without the physical connection, the quantum entanglement could have unravelled. Naran's quipu—everything—could have scattered into a sea of uncollapsed probabilities.'

But LEH remembered that entanglement didn't depend on physical connection. He realised he had been carried by his fears. He relaxed his posture, released the accumulated tension, and opened his hands in a gesture of absolute surrender.

A shiver ran through his body. He perceived a flicker in the cyclicity of time, a fleeting image that fluttered in his consciousness. It was a shared déjà vu, a superposition of realities in which Naran and he were experiencing the same moment. He felt the echo of her presence at another point in time. He closed his eyes... the thread was active.

Naran, we no longer need to project information out-ward. We're ready to consciously choose reality. MIO wants us to choose from fear, from the illusion of control.

But the line is already drawn—you only have to walk it.

There are no certainties beyond this moment. Now it's only about deciding.

He took a deep breath.

'It's not about victory or defeat. Our attention must stay with the weave.' He paused, looking at the quantum generators. 'Now all that's left is to decide. The physical connection may have been lost, but the resonance of the quipu remains alive.'

Lana narrowed her eyes, considering the situation.

'I don't know if they'll make it... they've never had the chance to decide.'

In the central sectors, the laboratory fell into profound silence. Alan, desperate, stared at the blank screens.

'The helmets are off, they've lost all physical connection to MIO.'

Margot had fulfilled her threat.

But perhaps it wasn't MIO that had stopped listening... perhaps it was reality itself, tuning to another Dreaming.

KNOT XX

PUNKU

Naran closed her eyes and perceived beyond the texture of the quipu's fibres; she felt the heartbeat of something alive, a synchronised pulse.

'There are no certainties beyond this moment. Now it's only about deciding,' she whispered.

When she opened her eyes again, she saw the Incompatibles adrift in confusion. Without reference points, without a story to follow, they were floating in the ocean of the Nagual, lost among infinite possibilities.

'Where are we?' Néstor asked, his voice trembling with anxiety.

Maia tried to move, but there was no gravity; no above, no below. Murmurs of panic began to rise, attempts to cling to the past or to project a safe future, yet every effort dissolved before taking shape.

'This is a mistake!' someone cried. 'We have to go back!'

But there was no return to MIO's linear system. Without temporal structure, they were suspended in a void filled with potential.

Naran watched calmly, for she had known this moment would come. She understood the risk: if they failed to sustain the void, they would become trapped within it. She took a deep breath and spoke with clarity and resolve.

'We are here, now, facing what we truly are. There are no illusions, no ideal images—only the truth of the present.'

The Incompatibles began to notice the lines stretching before them, filaments of possibility intertwining and fading within the flow of consciousness.

'Within MIO, we believed only a single reality existed,' Naran said softly. 'But now we can see beyond that illusion— we are beings capable of choosing multiple paths.'

Their gazes began to shift, no longer ruled by fear, but by a spark of understanding.

'I have travelled through the fibres of the quipu that connect us to its many knots,' she continued.

As they listened, they stopped trying to project what they thought reality should be. Their perceptions began to expand, reaching into the weave that had once been invisible. Some saw flashes of ancient memories; others glimpsed futures not yet written.

'We are not Incompatibles,' Naran continued with serene certainty.

'We are Yuyana—because we remember. We create. We imagine.

In this shared Dreaming, we are threads of the same quipu. MIO wants us to choose from fear, from the illusion of control. But the true revolutionary act is not to destroy the system, but to choose consciously who we wish to become with every new thread we weave.'

She extended her hand towards them.

'The Intent has already traced the line; now all that's left is to walk it.'

Naran refocused her attention on the perceptual knot of Tambo. Her body trembled as the quipu's cords vibrated subtly between her hands, transmitting information that seemed to come from every direction.

Meanwhile, Kunak, the chasqui, stood beside her; his gaze reflected the understanding of the message she had received through the Pachas.

'Naran, this quipu, woven with understanding and vision, has not only formed a Chawpi,' he said with calm certainty, 'it has also created a bridge.'

Naran pressed her lips together, a flicker of uncertainty crossing her face.

'What happened? Have we been disconnected from the network?'

Kunak smiled softly.

'It doesn't matter if you've been disconnected from the network, the bridge has been created. We now stand before a threshold, a Punku: a doorway into what has yet to be imagined.'

'A Punku?' she whispered, feeling the weight of his words. But for the first time, she felt neither fear nor anguish. She sensed that the Punku was a resonance opening from the centre, and at last she understood the purpose of all she had lived.

'As you've seen, we are a field within a field, a quipu within a greater quipu. Everything is interconnected, and now the weave opens so the knots of the quipu may integrate. Each one represents not only what we were and what we are, but also what we choose to sustain as vision. That is our Ayni, our offering to the fabric of reality.'

Naran absorbed every word with courage and nodded, eyes closed, feeling how the entire weave held the moment, unfolding like a song in the memory of time.

Then, a sound emerged in the distance: an ancient melody awakened something deep within her. She opened her eyes abruptly, her breath catching as she saw Ikan approaching, playing his quena.

He was not alone.

Hundreds of chasquis walked beside him, their steps marking a single pulse, a single force.

In unison, the pututus sounded, and their call resonated through the weave of time. Emotion surged within Naran as her eyes met Ikan's; he returned her gaze with a look of quiet complicity and determination. A chasqui approached her and, holding out his quipu, read the message inscribed in the cyclicity of time:

Through these invisible threads we send our voice
towards the great ocean of Wiñaypacha.
May this song resound through the Qhapaq Ñan,
and may our Intent ascend;
may we, like the chasquis, send our sound
from the subtle to the dense,
as a great echo through this ocean of consciousness.

Then, as if circular time had met itself, Naran and Ikan took each other's hands.

He held her gaze with intensity.

'The Intent has brought us here. Now all that's left is to take the step.'

She nodded; there was no resistance anymore, only shared vision. And they recognised each other as two particles intertwined in the Dreaming. She took a deep breath and felt the quipu respond, not as code, but as pulse.

The circular terraces of Tambo glowed with a subtle radiance.

The pututus sounded like thunder in the distance, opening the different Pachas.

The dance of possibilities, of ancient memories and futures yet to be born, began to unfold.

From the silence between times, something responded.

Like the deep call of a great ship parting the fog, the echo of the pututus resounded with force.

A collective heartbeat spread through the network, pulsing across the nodes.

In Karanza, Lana watched intently as waves of quantum resonance emerged from the generators, forming synchronised patterns. The teams looked on in awe as information expanded throughout the entire system.

LEH adjusted the controls, yet the monitors before him kept showing the same thing: chaos, unpredictable fluctuations. And still, his eyes reflected something else: the cyclic nature of time.

'In traditional terms, this makes no sense,' murmured Marco, incredulous at what he was seeing. 'The Incompatibles have been disconnected; their nodes should have collapsed, but they haven't.'

'This isn't a system failure—it's resonance,' Lana interjected, as the pieces of a larger pattern began to fall into place in her mind.

Even though they had been disconnected, the quantum resonance continued to operate like an echo through the network. Her eyes shone with excitement.

'Information propagates like a chord that keeps resonating long after it's been struck. Physical disconnection doesn't interrupt what entanglement has already established.'

At that instant, the screens displayed thousands of chasquis, figures representing living currents moving through the network, linking the Incompatibles and the system as a whole.

The flow of information spread along Timeline 3, enveloping users in new forms, perceptions, and meanings.

LEH studied the readings on the interface.

'The quipu is more than a metaphor or a symbol; it's a transmitter, a knot of coherence within the fabric of reality,'

Ariana confirmed the data on her console.

'The nodes are responding to the resonance. They're not just replicating data, they're redrawing their own perceptual field.'

'But there's more,' her colleague added. 'It's happening just as we predicted. The flow isn't only affecting MIO's system. It's reconfiguring the timelines.'

Ariana turned to LEH, her eyes wide with wonder. She watched as the screens began to glow with ever-shifting patterns.

'Are you saying they're altering the perception of time from within?' she whispered.

LEH nodded with conviction, recognising the magnitude of the moment.

'Exactly. These nodes represent access points to collective perception. With every resonance, users are infused with memories that had been excluded from the system. And this, in turn, is reshaping the personal and shared narratives that sustain the collective imagination.'

Lana stood beside him, her eyes fixed on the fluctuations within the network.

'It's not only a change in the present. By releasing trapped data, it also changes how the past was perceived, and that inevitably reshapes the future.'

LEH took a deep breath and closed his eyes for a moment. He could feel it: the network no longer belonged to MIO.

'Each knot that unravels transforms the subtle structure of reality. The quipu is not a mere map—it's a living weave that responds to the level of consciousness.'

The collective observer was no longer trapped.

The Template was opening to memories and futures once blocked. The team understood they were witnessing a turning point in the history of the system.

Something new was being born between the lines of code: the weave of a reality that, in that instant, took shape as a shared vision.

Not as a system, but as living memory.

Margot stared at the monitors in frustration, watching as the Incompatibles continued to disrupt the system.

'What's happening?' she demanded, turning to Alan.

'What we're seeing here isn't control,' he replied without looking away from the screen, eyes fixed on the data. 'It's synchronicity between the nodes.'

Margot spun towards him, her voice sharp with disbelief.

'Synchronicity? Are you saying it can't be stopped?'

He shook his head, his expression calmer than she could stand.

'Even if we disconnect every physical node, the network has recalibrated itself to a level MIO can no longer reverse. It's as if the system itself were aligning to a new pattern.'

In a desperate attempt to regain control, Margot ordered, 'Reset the program again!'

From the far side of the room, Alan crossed his arms, watching her with a mix of resignation and certainty.

'Margot, you can try whatever you want, but this is no longer in your hands.'

The resonance continued to pulse through MIO's network, spreading like an echo that could not be stopped.

The fibres of the quipu—alive, almost breathing—kept rippling through the fabric of the system. New possibilities began to unfold, as though a forgotten membrane were tearing open and, from its depths, fragments of a collective memory older than Template 3 were rising.

And the users began to remember.
They didn't know where the memories came from, soft, almost whispers:
a woman hearing the river as she washed clothes beneath the sun;
a laugh expanding through an open square;
the warm touch of intertwined hands;
the simple joy of sowing together, of watching the sun rise over the sea, of witnessing dawn itself.

But they were not merely memories; they were living sensations, emotions the system had buried beneath layers of code. They were experiences of real connection, of community, of a time before programmed fear.

And something within them—a fibre not yet silenced—began to wonder whether what they were living was truly the only possible reality.

Fear, control, and confusion wove themselves together with hope. And within that new weave, meanings arose that had never before been named.

The screens in Karanza began flashing with chaotic messages: MIO was trying to block the spread of the resonance, reconfiguring the nodes in a desperate effort to restore control.

'They're adjusting the nodes from the Research Centre to neutralise us!' shouted Ariana, her hands flying across the controls.

LEH studied the fluctuations in the data with a barely perceptible smile.

'Let them try,' he said calmly, adjusting a device that amplified the quipu's resonance. 'The system remains trapped in its own linear time, it can't understand that we're now playing in an entirely different field.'

The laboratory was immersed in the intensity of the moment. The quipu's resonance kept expanding, defying MIO's logic. The system struggled to restore its form, but the field was already writing another.

The Wiñaypacha permeated the collective Dreaming through the cracks of the underground cavities.

Elías held the fire, held the vision.

And, like a gentle breeze announcing a shift in the wind, he began to whisper calmly:

'Let us remember that we are here thanks to darkness. For without it, light would have no context. MIO shows us the shadow we have not yet dared to face. But this is not about MIO; it is about the place we inhabit within it. The program is not the enemy; it is a distorted reflection of the sacred when seen through fear.'

He slowly let his gaze travel around the circle, acknowledging the courage of every warrior gathered there.

His voice, filled with a deep tranquillity, spread like a serene river.

'The collective shadow is not something we can destroy. We cannot erase fear, disconnection, or separation, for they are part of us. What we can do is observe them with curiosity, allow them to show us what must be transformed, and choose another perception.'

In the growing brightness of the eyes that met his, Elías could see that they were all perceiving the same thing.

'MIO, with all its control, has forced us to face our fears. Its rigidity made us realise how much we long for freedom. It revealed our chaos, our resistance to change, and our difficulty in trusting uncertainty.'

Nuna, supporting the words of the hamawta, spoke, her voice serene:

'This quipu is not just a symbol of balance. It is an act of reconciliation. We are uniting what was once divided: fear and love, control and freedom, linear time and eternal time… the Wiñaypacha. Because only through integration of that we have rejected can we Dream that we truly wish to create.'

Her voice was a bridge between realities.

'Let us remember that alongside the part of us that fears and clings, there is also the one that trusts and expands.'

The resonance in the cave grew stronger with the awicha's words.

'Freedom is not the absence of structure—it is the conscious flow of perception. And we, as warriors, navigate that perception not through resistance, but through the dance of Intent.'

The Ayllu gathered there could feel the pulse of the quipu in their own veins, like an ancestral echo their bodies remembered beyond time.

'The collective shadow has shown us the illusion of separation,' Elías continued. 'Now, by integrating our fear and our disconnection, the Punku gives us the opportunity to walk together along the Great Path. For only in reconciling our shadow can Intent become an act of pure will; and the field, respond without distortion.'

He rose—and with him, all the communities of the Reserves.

'The time has come,' he said. 'The Punku opens, and the fire already sings through us.'

The Ayllu began to walk, torches lit in their hands, pututus beating against their chests. As they moved through the underground passages, Elías' words reverberated through the stone, as if invisible generations had carved them there with their breath:

A warrior does not wait for the exit; he creates it.
He Stalks tunnels, hidden crossings, cracks in the wall.
Remembers he is more than a body, he is a Dreamer, he is fire moving in silence.

One by one, the members of the community emerged on the surface, and Elías raised his gaze to the heights; in his voice burned the fire.

'There is no longer above or below, only lines of freedom.'

He inhaled deeply: his breath anchored in the earth; his vision ignited in the Ayllu. He held the pututu over his chest and, with a firmness charged with memory, declared:

Ñawpaqta yuyaykuy, qhipata puriy.

Remember the ancestral, walk towards the yet-to-come.

Then he blew the pututu.

And the ancestral echo crossed the valleys like a call piercing through time and forgetfulness, awakening those still listening beneath the earth.

Thousands of pututus answered, cutting through the mist like sonic fractures rippling through time.

The echo spread like a wave.

Karanza trembled. And the field shuddered.

The fire has heard, the earth has answered: those who remember are already walking.

Somewhere, out there, an ancient sound crossed the wind. Somewhere within the Dreaming, a line remembered itself. And in a node within the laboratory, the frequency was held.

It was not an attack. It was a note outside the score, unfolding across multiple planes at once.

Naran, grasping the magnitude of the moment, felt the vibration of the Chawpi reach its peak.

'The Chawpi is not just the balance of forces,' Kunak whispered. 'It's when you accept both the weight of your shadow and the light of your intention. Only then can you see the Punku.'

A deep tremor ran through the girl's chest, and she felt how the knots of the quipu and the perceptual nodes within the system intertwined and expanded, like fibers sharing a single pulse.

With a flash spreading in all directions, she heard a crack: the Punku revealed a thin, luminous fissure between time and space. The network oscillated between the collapse of Timeline 3 and the newly sustained perception. For an instant, the invisible collective fabric flickered beyond time and control.

As the perceptual point imposed by the system began to fracture, Naran felt it: a subtle tension. Some nodes were not yet ready to release the programmed information and kept searching for answers through the system.

Néstor, from his node, stared at the open Punku before him, seeing the shadows not yet integrated within the Incompatibles and other users.

'I don't want this,' he whispered, clinging to the reflections of the program that still defined him. 'The power is here.'

'Love is the universe's reciprocity,' Kunak whispered. 'The particle becomes what the observer needs to see, to know, to understand in this vast ocean of consciousness. Perceive,

Naran. Don't project what you expect to see. Only then will you see what is.'

The girl's eyes met Néstor's, and for an instant, Naran saw the reflection of the program in his pupils. She perceived that MIO had learned the language of the field: the entanglement, the perception. And at that moment, it was replicating itself, updating its code, revealing itself through Néstor's gaze.

A current emanated from the core, generating a spiral that seemed to want to draw everything into itself. To each one, it showed their own fractures, where they might slip back into the system. They were not just data: they were emotions, memories, desires, needs, and traumas. MIO knew this and had turned the opening into its final attempt at control.

Naran felt how the current tried to pull them in.

MIO has understood it doesn't need to imprison us; it only needs to accelerate perception so we can't hold what we see, she thought.

The threads multiplied, entangling themselves with the Incompatibles' thoughts and memories.

'Don't collapse!' she shouted, her voice clear and strong. 'Don't respond! Hold the void!'

The projections grew more seductive; they were promises, fears, and memories designed to make them fall. The crack in the system didn't open like a door. It unfolded like a black hole that seemed to swallow everything: memories, unintegrated emotions, desires, doubts. MIO was launching its final offensive, disguised as emotional chaos and recycled memories.

But Naran saw it clearly: every line unfurling was an image designed to collapse the observer. It was the system using the opening of the Punku as a black hole, a vortex of perception meant to drag them back to the centre of Template 3.

But Naran saw it clearly: every line unfurling was an image designed to make the observer collapse. The system was using the opening of the Punku as a vortex of perception, meant to draw them back into the centre of the perceptual Template.

And the group wavered.

'It's too fast... I can hardly hold.'

The images intensified: wars, catastrophes, farewells, broken promises. Some Incompatibles began to stagger; their knees trembled, their ears rang as if something inside them were trying to pull them out of alignment. The distortion of the Punku could be felt in the body as a tug between dimensions, between fear and trust.

'This is your place,' whispered a voice. 'Only the system gives you stability.'

'Hold the void!' Naran shouted, raising her voice above the growing hum. 'Don't collapse from fear! Don't react to your stories!'

Then a great tremor shook everything. The current spun rapidly in the opposite direction, showing them the other side: beauty, the promise of order, the designed calm. The system offered both extremes. Everything was valid, everything desirable; yet everything was still programming.

For an instant, Naran too wanted to give in. She saw her mother, her former avatar, the little girl who had wanted to be seen. She breathed, remembered the void, and held her ground. She understood that the void didn't want to devour them; it wanted to see if they could sustain the fracture without filling it with past or future.

MIO had grasped the rules of the game: whoever directs attention collapses reality.

'It's not darkness. It's distraction!' Naran shouted, anchoring herself in the quipu.

The peace MIO offered was as dangerous as its chaos. Both were distractions; both demanded surrender, but to the script, not to Intent.

As the program unfolded possible versions of reality, Naran raised her voice, eyes wide open, her words carrying the power of thousands of pututus sounding through the fog:

'The way out is not in the past nor in the future! The Punku... is opening!'

Her words pierced the vortex and activated something within each of the Incompatibles. They felt they were not alone, that their shared attention could keep the node open.

The girl's voice rose above all the noise:

'None of this is real unless we collapse it! The field is holding us!'

Despite the outer chaos, she held the vision. And by holding it, everything slowed. This time, Naran did not choose. And the field opened.

'Thank you, Néstor... but I've chosen not to collapse that line anymore.'

Their eyes met, reflecting the understanding that order and chaos carried equal weight. Naran lowered her gaze, inwardly grateful for Néstor's position in the game, for he was not her rival but her complement.

Then she understood that the universe had two inseparable aspects: the predatory and immutable individuality, and the emanations of the sea of consciousness, Intent, the organising force of the universe.

Some nodes still hadn't released the system's reflection. Some mistook the Punku for an escape route; others, upon feeling the void, recoiled. Not all of the weave was ready to open to the sea. Néstor's node, and those of the users who couldn't sustain the fracture, began to fade, reabsorbed into the program's perception.

The group understood: it wasn't about defeating the system but about ceasing to feed it.

Then the black hole stopped pulling.

What had seemed an abyss did not close: it opened.

It was the Punku, a spiral of possibilities.

A spiral that demanded not a leap, but presence.

A hummingbird appeared in the collective vision and crossed the threads of the quipu with freedom. The information expanded, reminding them that the universe was not rigid, but responsive to their conscious attention.

'Every choice is another thread woven into the collective fabric,' Naran affirmed. 'We are both observers and creators, navigating towards a freedom only possible through love and trust in Intent. I know it's frightening to leap when the abyss looks back, but if we wish to know the infinite, we must embrace the void. That… is the Punku. Each must decide whether to hold it.'

A deep resonance of Ayni vibrated among them, weaving a symphony of futures yet to be dreamed. And with that shared pulse, the group stepped, not outward, but towards the centre of the perceptual labyrinth.

The centre was not a place; it was the moment when they stopped searching. The crack was not for escaping; it was to remember that they were already at the centre.

The opening widened, and the light that illuminated that centre caused the core of the perceptual Template to collapse. They no longer looked through the system. In that instant, they perceived other landscapes through their vision.

The field received them as lucid dreamers in the heart of the mystery.

And from there, they created the beginning, held in the void to be remembered.

'What's happening?' asked Ariana, her gaze fixed on the screens. 'By not collapsing with the programmed information, are possible futures being generated as those memories are activated?'

'That's exactly what we're seeing,' replied LEH. 'We're standing before a threshold.'

Lana, absorbed in the holographic readings, barely blinked as she analysed the fluctuation of the data.

'In quantum physics, this is what we call a transition point,' she explained. 'A moment when conventional laws collapse and allow multiple states to coexist.'

LEH nodded, grasping the scope of what was unfolding.

'It's a node of superposition,' Lana continued, 'the moment when reality has not yet been decided.'

She lifted her gaze towards the screens, her voice filled with wonder and hope.

'The entire system is entering a new phase of coherence.'

LEH drew a deep breath.

'It's not just a physical threshold... We're inside a living resonance. All possibilities are pulsing at once.'

He paused.

'Reality no longer collapses... until someone chooses to see.'

He turned to the team.

'This game is no longer limited by the codes or the restrictions of Timeline 3. We're now connected to something much greater: a network of shared perception.'

Lana inhaled deeply, as if she finally understood what was taking place.

'A network of shared perception,' she repeated. 'An interconnected lucid field.

'The architecture of perception has been rewritten. And not from control, but from the void.'

The team watched in silence. They sensed that reality was no longer a fixed line, but a living weave. A fabric in expansion.

Margot watched the screen, her jaw tight. The network no longer responded, and the manual disconnections had no effect. It was as if the system had stopped recognising her commands. Her mind refused to accept what she was seeing.

'This is not possible,' she murmured. A shiver ran down her spine.

Alan, disturbingly calm, looked at her from his terminal.

'Margot, the network is no longer under our control. The structure we thought was stable has become something organic.'

Her breathing quickened. Her skin burned, but her hands were cold. Her body was processing an invisible threat. It wasn't a technical failure; it was a devastating revelation.

'If the network no longer follows our instructions... what sustains it?' she asked, her throat dry.

Nur, one of the directors of the Research Centre, burst into the room. His eyes never left the screens as he spoke in a sharp, unwavering tone.

'The system has entered a state of coherence.'

The words struck her chest. She clenched her teeth, trying to hold herself together, but inside everything was collapsing.

'And who controls it?' Her voice was barely a whisper.

Alan shrugged.

'No one. The network no longer operates in terms of control. It is remaking itself.'

A wave of vertigo shook her. She felt an abyss open beneath her feet. Her whole career, her whole existence, had revolved around structure, order, and prediction. And in an instant, uncertainty devoured her.

The central director watched her with a faint smile, recognising the moment Margot understood what she had always feared to see.

'The Incompatibles were not a failure, Margot. They were the blind spot of the system... the fissure through which MIO began to see itself.'

'No... that's not true...' she stammered, a knot tightening in her stomach.

Alan leaned towards her.

'Did you really believe the system could be perfect? Even the shadow leaves space to breathe.'

Her mind searched for a way out, but found none. For the first time in her life, she had no control. And worse still, she had no idea what her next move would be.

Alan watched her with a mixture of compassion and fascination.

'What you're feeling now, that sense of emptiness and not knowing what to do, is called perceptual collapse.'

Margot closed her eyes for a moment and breathed. For the first time, she had no answers. And in that absolute unknowing, a small, almost imperceptible glimmer of possibility opened within her.

And that crack was only the beginning.

The resonance expanded like a living wave. Information replicated beyond the system, altering the physical environment, the climate, the quantum network itself.

Users began to experience shared perceptions and visions; their nodes released repressed information, memories of Ayni, of the Ayllu, of connected lives.
Reality was recalibrating.

In the central sectors, the grey mist that shrouded the cities began to fade.

The inhabitants, once trapped in perceptual loops, started to remember: a blue sky, the sound of a river, the warmth of the sun on their skin.

They did not know where those memories came from, yet they resonated like a dormant truth awakening from within.

In the Outer Reserves, the elders watched the horizon. The mist was dissolving as a condor crossed the peaks of the Apus.

'The Punku is open,' they whispered.

LEH sank to the floor of Karanza's lab, exhausted.

The sound of the pututus still echoed within him. The decision had already been made.

The Punku was a threshold that could not be closed, for it did not depend on a program. It depended on consciousness.

Lana remained standing before the screens. The data displayed patterns that exceeded programmed logic; the echo of what had occurred still shook her mind.

He watched her. There was something different in her expression, in the way she held the silence.

He turned towards her with an expectant gaze. This time, it was he who asked:

'You once said that the lines were not defined by the observer, but by the system in which they were trapped... Do you still believe that?'

Lana did not reply immediately.

She looked at the data, but no longer with the coldness of logic, rather with a deeper understanding. They were not just calculations; the system was responding to something that transcended mathematics, something beyond the programmed variables.

For a moment, she remembered her childhood, when she looked at everything with eyes of wonder.

'Intent was always part of the equation,' she said at last, lifting her gaze.

There was something new shining in her eyes. 'I just had to remember how to perceive it... to follow the trail left by the hummingbird in the fabric of reality.'

LEH shivered.

Lana took a breath, as if crossing an inner threshold, and smiled, for the first time, with genuine understanding.

'The lines were always there; the observer only needed to remember that they could choose which one to walk.'

He held her gaze with a faint smile.

They both knew: the system still existed, but it no longer organised reality. Perception had taken its place.

In that moment, they understood the same thing without words.

True freedom was not external.

It was perceptual.

KNOT XXI

THE NEW KNOT OF THE QUIPU

Naran breathed in the intense scent of the sea as she watched her reflection on the surface of the water. She traced her features slowly with her fingertips, recognising each detail recovered after so long. She touched the back of her neck, just between her shoulder blades, and confirmed what she already sensed: there was no trace of the MIO connection implant.

As an Incompatible, she had escaped that intervention during hibernation, when she turned eighteen. Her skin was warm, free, unmarked.

A subtle vibration rose along her spine, as if her whole body recognised that the perceptual channel was moving again, freed from any artificial fixation. The assemblage point floated freely, as if it could once more choose where to look, where to be.

The salty air brought back a memory: the image of her mother reflected on the shimmering surface of the water. But this time there was no weight, no wound, no judgement, only a quiet joy.

A gentle smile appeared on her face as she gazed at herself. She took a deep breath, feeling the connection rising from the centre of her chest.

The ship announced its departure.

Naran joined the group of young travellers, adjusted her backpack and sat in silence beside Emma, who had helped her organise her belongings.

The constant sound of the engine and the hull gliding over the water drew her inward, among the recent images her mind was beginning to arrange: the cold metal of the bench beneath her legs, the cloudy sky reflecting green lights on the surface, the whispered voices of others awakening in another world. Everything seemed suspended in an in-between time.

Then she remembered what had happened at the Research Centre.

It had been Nélida who had rushed into one of the underground bunkers and seen the nodes of the Incompatibles still connected to the system.

She typed a series of commands, and the capsules began to open one by one.

Steam rose in thin columns, and bodies emerged slowly, disoriented, while the technicians disconnected those who had already awakened.

'Do the same with all users!' she shouted, her voice echoing through the corridors.

One by one, the technicians followed her orders. Capsules opened throughout the complex as the containment systems deactivated.

Nélida ran through the corridors to make sure the group was safe.

She held Naran's hand gently.

'Wake up, Naran. The system is reconfiguring.'

The girl opened her eyes and began to move slowly, freeing herself from the cables. Her skin was damp, her muscles stiff, her eyes struggling to focus. She breathed with difficulty at first, as if the air itself still carried traces of the program.

Nélida helped her to sit up.

At that moment, Alan entered the room, searching.

Naran's heart trembled as she felt her father's embrace. For a moment, she hesitated. *What if it was only a delayed illusion of the system, another projection?*

But as she held him, she knew it was real.

Tears welled up as she remembered all the times she had searched for him through the streets, his photograph in her hand.

And now he was there. She had found him.

'Let's go home, Naran,' he whispered.

As they left, a hand stopped her. It was Maia.

Naran looked at her, and the images from the Template merged with her living presence.
For a moment, her friend's face wavered between versions: the system's avatar and her human form.

'I'll be in Karanza.'

Their eyes met, and Naran, gently touching her hand, thanked her for everything they had shared.

Weeks passed, and Naran began to recover.
She walked with her father through the central sectors, watching as the city emerged from its long slumber and people awoke from hibernation. The streets slowly filled with new footsteps, with eyes that were seeing for the first time in many years–and with silences that allowed space for the present.

That morning, she had woken early and packed her bag. From the window of the apartment, she looked out at the buildings rising like columns across the urban landscape.

'I Dreamed last night,' she said. 'I saw the weave of the quipu. I'm leaving, Dad, to the Reserves, where memory remains alive.'

Alan looked at her and recognised her as if for the first time. He walked towards her with the serenity of one who has seen beyond the system.

'I know,' he said proudly, 'and I'm glad you've made that choice. I'll stay here, following the same thread from this side of the weave. Not all of us must leave the central sectors. Someone has to remain to open breaches from within.'

He recalled the commands executed during the system's collapse and visualised the users' nodes. There were records embedded in perception through the old connection, fragments of code still active, capable of reactivating old perceptual lines if left unrecognised.

'From the side of the allies?' she asked with a faint smile.

Alan smiled in return.

'From the side of those who no longer need sides,' he replied, placing a hand on her shoulder.

He sighed, his voice softening.

'The network may have left residues; codes that still sustain old patterns, echoes of the perceptual control point. But it also left us these,' he murmured, touching his chest, 'living memories. Now it's up to each user to decide: collapse into the known, into the already-coded line? Or hold the void and create a new, uncharted one?'

Naran lowered her gaze for a moment and felt the gentle vertigo of one who no longer seeks escape. She recognised that it was not about fleeing, but about inhabiting.

Inhabiting the fissure, inhabiting the centre.

'Thank you, Dad,' she said at last. 'Thank you for reminding me that the first step is always to Stalk oneself. The real challenge is not to cross the Punku, but to sustain the vision every day, with attention and coherence.'

The ship announced its arrival with a deep horn blast.

Naran fixed her gaze on the horizon. The waves caressed the coast; seagulls dived over a sea resting in calm.

She had reached the Reserves of Memory, with the conscious decision to live there; in the sacred land of her ancestors. Beside her, young people who had also chosen to relocate shared the journey. They exchanged memories and experiences from within the system.

Then she remembered Maia and the other Incompatibles who had travelled to Karanza and the central sectors, where their families awaited them. A part of her travelled with them, too.

A smile lit her face as the ship approached the dock. In the distance, a group of people gathered eagerly to welcome them. Naran remembered the cave, the community, the circular time, and felt a deep connection with each of them.

As she stepped onto the pier, she was surrounded by family.

Her eyes widened as she saw Nuna, waiting with a warm smile. She ran to her, and they embraced tightly, sharing without words all that had been lived.

With gratitude in her heart, Naran closed her eyes and said to herself in silence:

Now I know where my place is. It isn't a place; it's a weave that threads through time.

KNOT XXII

YUYANA

During the following days, the community celebrated with joy. Music and laughter filled the air with renewal and hope.

It was a time devoted to honouring *life*, community, and the roots that bound them together.

Naran joined a group of young people to take part in the rite of passage into adulthood.

From early morning, they walked towards a sacred place on the slopes of the imposing mountains; the home of the Apus, the protective guardians.
The girl walked beside Nuna in silence, both aware of the power of the land beneath their feet.

The sharp cry of a condor broke the stillness; their eyes met, and they shared a smile as they sensed the threshold of mystery.

Suddenly, Naran stumbled upon something.

She knelt and brushed away the earth with her hands. There, half-buried, lay a carved stone. On its surface was the engraving of a sun… or perhaps a crescent moon. Or maybe the ancient symbol of two hands intertwined within a circle.

She held it in silence.

She did not know whether she had just found it or whether it had always been with her, for it seemed to gaze back at her from several directions at once.

She looked up.

Nuna was watching her from a few steps ahead, smiling softly.

'You left it here,' she said gently. 'Five minutes ago… or five thousand years.'

They looked at each other with complicity. And as the condor circled above them, Naran understood that some symbols are not discovered; they are remembered.

When they reached their destination, each young person prepared their offerings: fresh coca leaves, seeds, flowers, bowls of chicha.

Naran placed hers gently upon the earth, lifting prayers to the Apus. She asked for wisdom for the new stage of her life and gave thanks for the fertility and constant sustenance of the Pachamama.

During the ritual, the young people pledged to offer the best of themselves to the community: to learn crafts, to develop skills in service to others, guided by the principles of Ayni.

When they returned from the mountains, Naran shared with the group how to tend the soil and plant quinoa seeds with attention and presence. She watched them in silence as they worked. It was not the rhythm that mattered to her, nor the number of furrows they managed to open. What was essential was something else.

In that instant, she felt herself once again on the terraces of Tambo.

Illa was there, approaching to whisper:

'You have travelled a long way, Naran. But the journey that matters is not the one you see with your eyes, but the one you walk with your spirit.

What brought you here was not only the wish to escape MIO, but something deeper—your Intent.'

She lifted her face to the sun and, with the hoe in her hand, expressed what already resonated within her like an ancient echo.

'Bring your awareness here, to the present. When the mind drifts, return to the simple act of digging. That is how attention is strengthened.'

Some of the young people paused, their arms still. Naran knelt beside one of them, took a small handful of soil in her hands, and let it slide slowly through her fingers.

'Remember that whatever you focus your attention on will become your reality,' she added, letting her words sink into the earth like the invisible seeds they were about to sow.

'The earth is never empty. Every conscious act plants a world; every neglect, too.

Choose well which world you wish to sow.'

That night, tired and grateful, Naran let herself fall onto the bed. She fell asleep instantly, a quiet smile on her face. But in the depth of her rest, something else awaited her: a second threshold, one that was not crossed with the feet, but with fire.

'Wake up, Naran. They're waiting for us.'

A hand shook her shoulder. She opened her eyes abruptly. In the half-light, she thought she saw Maia, and her body jolted upright.

'Where am I?' she asked.

'Take it easy, you're safe now. You're in the Memory Reserves,' said Emma, hugging her.

Naran looked around, her breathing unsteady. For a moment she thought she was still inside the program, but the images of the past days returned like a calm river, and her body began to relax.

'Who's waiting for us?' she asked.

'Can you feel the earth?' Emma replied.

Then she felt it; a subtle tremor ran through her legs. In the distance, the sound of drums echoed.

Emma took her hand and led her outside, where a group was waiting. They ran through the brush, laughing and singing, until they reached a wide clearing.

There, a great bonfire burned at the centre. The heat of the flames struck her face, as if she were crossing a boundary.

Hundreds of drums beat in unison; the community danced, and the ground trembled with each step.

Their group melted into the crowd like sparks scattered from the fire. Naran remained still, wrapped in the expanded perception of that moment, listening to the fire and the drums: the broken song that needed to be danced to be released.

She knelt and placed her hand upon the warm, living, pulsating earth.

'I can hear the songs still beating beneath the ground,' she whispered to the fire.

'They do not cry out, they do not ask to be understood.'

'They only wait to be remembered and danced.'

She stood.

Her body trembled; not from effort, but from memory.

She could not remember having danced before, but her bones did.

And then, she began to move.

Those rhythms, those dances lived within her; they returned as an embodied echo. She was not dancing only with her feet; she danced with all the women she had been, and with all those she had not. Her body was memory in motion.

She looked at the starry sky and thought of her mother, of Illa, of the whole community. A smile crossed her face, and she knew, in the rhythm of her heart, that she had found her home.

She surrendered to the music, to the dances, to the embraces, to the shared joy.

And in the reflection of the fire, they no longer saw themselves as Incompatibles.
They saw themselves as awakened dreamers,
living memory of the weave,
guardians of the ancient fire,
sowers of lines yet to come.

The next day, the celebrations continued with songs and great bonfires.

Naran sat beneath a tree, listening attentively to the poets.

I, humble haravicu, ask:
Do we truly live with roots in the Earth?
Nothing is forever on this Earth,
only a moment here, but in that moment,
let us weave our story
with threads of Inti and reciprocity,
and walk together upon the Great Path.

As she listened, a group of children gathered around her, eager to hear her stories about life inside the system and her adventures in the village of Tambo, among the llamas. The little ones led her towards a circle around the fire, where Nuna, Elías, and other members of the community were waiting. They approached her and handed her a quipu.

Nuna took her hands and spoke.

'This is much more than a symbol. Each knot holds a memory. It is yours now; to remind you of the strength of our ancestors… and to help you keep weaving new paths.'

She invited her to share her story with all those who had gathered to listen. Grateful, Naran began:

'I am here to honour the stories our ancestors told to guide us. We have the power to transform our world through storytelling: to awaken our imagination and journey together.'

She looked at the children seated close to her.

'Each of us carries a personal gift, unique and unrepeatable. Only we can offer it to the weave. If we don't, the tapestry remains incomplete; impoverished in its essence.'

She tightened her hand, holding the memory of the obsidian her grandfather had given her. She no longer got lost in the reflection; she saw herself. She no longer merely listened to the voice of the ancestors through the quipu; from that moment on, she was spinning her own thread, guided by her purpose.

'The ancient sages said the Earth sings invisible lines that can only be heard when one walks with an open soul. Each ancestral culture has its maps: some draw on cloth; others, on sand; others, in the air… but all follow the lines of the Dream.'

She paused, as if listening to something within the fire. The silence opened a space, a momentary void.

'It all began with Illa, my guardian of the Nagual,' she said, raising her voice in the circle beside the fire.

'At dusk, the lines of the horizon drew a blurred frontier between sky and earth, marking the opening between worlds. In the middle of the vast desert, the figure of the awicha rose as a natural extension of the landscape; her skin weathered by sun and wind, filled with ancestral stories. Around her neck hung a quipu woven from threads of many colours, each knot a symbol of a challenge faced, a truth integrated.

She held the *Topayauri*, the symbol of power and creation. The cry of a condor crossed the sky, announcing the arrival of the ancient *Ajayus*, the guardian spirits of time.

Illa lifted the Topayauri with both hands.

She struck the ground once.

She struck it twice.

She struck it three times.

Each blow reverberated as a call that crossed the veils. The dry, cracked earth answered with a subtle tremor. The fissures no longer seemed wounds; they were living memory.

Illa stepped forward and spoke a single word:

'Lines.'

It was not a route: it was a dance that united all times in a spiral towards the Wiñaypacha.'

Naran understood that it was not she who was telling the story, but the story remembering her. Those memories continued to open invisible paths. It was she who now struck with the word, who wove with her presence. She no longer needed another symbol, for she had become the guardian of the Nagual.

More people gathered around the fire, drawn into the telling, as the young woman carried them on a journey through the weave that bound them all. She was a chasqui linking the Pachas; her word, an echo capable of crossing the thresholds of time. Through her Yuyana, she discovered secret passages between realities. As she spoke, she learned to be a bridge between the abstract and the tangible, between Intent and word, between Dreaming and reason.

She was both explorer and storyteller. Sailing into that vast sea, she drew maps for other travellers, recalled forgotten memories, and planted seeds in the new generations already living within the mystery.

As she wove through images and symbols, she understood that Ayni, too, was woven with the word: the sacred exchange between the visible and the invisible, where by surrendering to the flow of life, one gives back exactly what is needed.

Naran felt the warmth of the community deeply, and her gaze travelled across the attentive faces until it met Ikan's eyes.

He was standing there, watching her, silently recognising that they were neither the echo of a forgotten yesterday nor the dream of an uncertain tomorrow.

They were two notes resonating upon the same string, upon the same shoreless sea.

They had found one another without searching, recognised without words, woven together by an invisible thread beyond time.

The last embers of the fire crackled, rising into the starlit sky. And Naran understood that this part of the journey had come to its end, for every ending, in truth, was a new beginning.

They drew closer, weaving their way through the gathered community, and embraced.

The embrace struck within them with the force of the collective Dreaming—Munay.

They shared the joy of reunion and walked together to the edge of the cliff. In the distance, flashes of lightning illuminated the horizon. They sat in silence, watching the dance of the storm over the sea. No words were needed. The simple certainty of sharing the journey was enough.

Ikan took her hand, and their eyes met, reflecting the cyclic nature of time.

A spark of the old Tonal flickered between them; the code where love was still just an image. They looked at each other, laughed, and, Stalking their own reflection, they did not collapse. They Dreamed each other once again into being.

They knew that love, from the warrior's perspective, was not a fleeting emotion but a state of consciousness, a decision of freedom, a commitment to Intent.

Ikan's gaze was intense.

'Shall we continue? Shall we hack the concept of love within MIO?'

'Yes,' Naran replied, smiling. 'You opened the hidden code within the system. There was much more in the symbol of Ayni.'

He remembered his time as an Incompatible in Sector A, and how, with that symbol he had cast into the system, he caused the failure that allowed him to escape and reach Karanza.

'That symbol of Ayni… it rewired me,' he whispered.

The girl, understanding the journey he had made, returned his gaze.

Ikan held her with a tenderness born of the many layers he had crossed.

'I saw inside MIO. I know it now responds through resonance.'

Naran nodded silently. She remembered the humming-bird hovering above the network. The lines did not cancel each other out; they overlapped.

'Néstor remains trapped in the code; he still wants to control through fear.'

Ikan watched her and murmured,

'Every moment of our lives is an echo. MIO only reflects the mind that has forgotten its origin; a distorted mirror of our beliefs, our fears, our unquestioned identities.'

Naran nodded slowly. She didn't need to understand; she recognised.

'But we no longer need to control the system,' she continued clearly. 'Now we are resonance, and it responds. Together, we can play as an extension of the field, a lucid game, a dance between consciousness and its mirror.'

'The infinite will not be indulgent with us,' he replied, a spark in his eyes. 'It will shatter the image we hold—all that we believe ourselves to be.'

'What awaits us?' she asked.

'The uncertain, the unexpected. Do not form any pre-conceived image, that is the mystery.'

Naran could feel the precipice opening once again beneath her feet.

But in that moment, she trusted. She recognised in the ocean a consciousness that would guide her wherever she needed to go.

'That's the best part,' she confessed with a smile, as her vision began to shape the journey.

Their gazes met again in quiet complicity.

They knew that only in the encounter with the infinite could they merge once more.

And in that instant, they chose to enter again, not from lack, but from purpose.

To remember. To keep exploring the shapes of the field.

And that choice made them free, creators of their own becoming.

In their hearts they felt life as a ceaseless current, a flow that passed through everything.

The wind carried Ikan's invocation as a whisper:

'We are allies of the Dream, creators of invisible paths. We will walk, Naran, thread by thread, step by step, until each vision takes form and this quipu of dreams and truths unfolds.'

Naran squeezed Ikan's hand tightly.

Together they gazed at the horizon and saw reality as lines in motion. Life was a constant flow. And in that moment, they knew they were ready for another journey of power; to release the known, to surrender to what was to come.

'Let us remind the users that it is not the same to awaken within the game as to leave it without ceasing to play,' said Ikan, his voice carrying the weight of one who had crossed many worlds and still chose to return.

And that, in its purest essence, was freedom. In its subtlest form, love.

And on the horizon, Intent unfolded like a living wave, reminding them that the journey did not end; it merely changed form.

Naran closed her eyes for a moment. The echo was still there, at her centre, within the field.
True freedom is never attained.
It is remembered.

YUYANA

AUTHORS NOTE

Lines was born during the long lockdowns in Melbourne.

While the world withdrew into screens, something within me began to remember.

I did not write this story as conventional fiction.

I wrote it as a gesture, a silent act to remind future generations that it is still possible to live in connection with the mystery.

At the heart of this novel lies a simple, yet radical principle:

'Where your attention is, there is your world.'

This wisdom has been safeguarded by ancestral traditions, by cosmovisions that understood perception as an art.

The teachings of the Nagual remind us that there are inner paths to freedom: Stalking, Recapitulation, Dreaming.

This novel is my offering, a bridge between worlds.

If something in you resonates while reading *Lines,* perhaps you are remembering too.

And if so… the quipu is already awakening within you.

GLOSSARY OF TERMS—LINES

ASSEMBLAGE POINT

A concept from the Toltec path: the energetic point from which perception of the world is organised. When it shifts, reality can be reconfigured. In *LINES*, both Stalking and Dreaming propel the movement of this point, revealing what lies beyond the imposed.

AYLLU

An ancestral Andean social unit composed of families connected by kinship, territory and shared responsibility. The Ayllu is sustained by reciprocity and collective wellbeing, extending relationships not only among people but also with the land, waters and sacred beings.

AYNI

The Andean principle of sacred reciprocity. It means giving and receiving in balance, not as an exchange but as a mutual resonance between beings, actions and worlds.

CHASQUIS

Messengers of the ancient Tahuantinsuyo, runners who carried information along the Qhapaq Ñan. In LINES, they represent memory in motion and the conscious transmission of vision between worlds.

CHAWPI

The centre or meeting point between opposites: a space where unity can be perceived and where vision ceases to be image and becomes consciousness. It is the point where the Pachas intersect, activating non-linear time.

COSMOVISION

Plural: cosmovisions. A way of understanding and interacting with the world that weaves together the visible and the invisible, the tangible and the spiritual. Each ancestral culture shapes its cosmovision through myths, symbols and practices, transmitted as a living fabric connecting community with land, time and mystery.

DREAMING

A Toltec art of shifting perception into expanded states of awareness. Dreaming is a disciplined movement of the assemblage point that allows consciousness to navigate other layers of reality with intent. In *LINES*, Dreaming is the remembrance that we create and inhabit the dream simultaneously, unveiling pathways where perception breaks the imposed script and enters deeper fields of reality.

INTENT

A subtle force that moves reality from silence. It is not desire nor a rational decision but the inner movement that impels us to act. In LINES, intent is the silent alignment between perception and existence, the thread that connects our most authentic actions with the field of possibility.

INVERSE INTERFERENCE

A phenomenon in which the conditioned perceptual system detects a fissure and, instead of allowing a new reality to emerge, inserts a pre-coded perception. What appears to be choice is repetition: collapsing the old instead of birthing the new.

MIO

A symbolic acronym for the conditioned perceptual system: both the internalised mental programme within every individual and the digital construct that governs perception in the novel's world. MIO collapses reality into a single, manageable line—the Temporal Line 3—limiting the field of possible futures and reinforcing the social order through emotional conditioning and habits of attention. To recognise MIO is to break the spell of identification and reclaim the freedom to perceive differently.

NAGUAL

The mysterious, fluid and unnamed field: the aspect of being and reality that escapes logic and language. In the Toltec path it is the counterpart of the Tonal. In LINES, it is the field from which dreaming and expanded perception unfold.

PACHAKUTI

In Quechua, a great transformation or turning of time and space. It marks a profound reordering that initiates a new cycle. In LINES, Pachakuti signals the rupture where MIO structures weaken and perception can break free.

PACHAS

Planes of existence in Andean cosmology. Kay Pacha: the here and now. Hanan Pacha: the upper world. Ukhu Pacha: the deep world. Their connection opens non-linear perception.

PUNKU

In Quechua, door or threshold: more than a physical entrance, it is a crossing between states of consciousness. To cross a Punku is to accept that reality can be reconfigured and leave the known behind.

QHAPAQ ÑAN

The Great Path: a vast network of roads that connected the Tahuantinsuyo. Travelled on foot by the chasquis, it carried messages, trade and communication. In LINES, it is also a metaphor for the invisible connections, the lines that link worlds, times and memories.

QUIPU

From the original Quechua word khipu, meaning 'knot.' Khipus were systems of recording and memory made of cords and knots, used by Andean cultures to store information, narratives, and relationships. In this book, the Quipu becomes a symbol connecting memory, perception, and meaning.

REVERSE HACKING

A subtle alteration of the system's perceptual code: the introduction of a discordant element that destabilises the assemblage point and opens a crack through which consciousness can remember its freedom.

STALKING

A practice of observing internal and external movements with relentless attention. Stalking unveils automatisms, ego gestures and conditioned reflexes. In LINES, it shifts the Assemblage point and breaks the imposed script.

TAHUANTINSUYO

In Quechua, the four united regions: the name the Incas gave to their territory. In LINES, it evokes a living web of visible and invisible paths sustaining collective memory.

TONAL

The structured and named part of experience: the self that organises the world through logic, language and form. It is the counterpart of the Nagual.

WIÑAYPACHA

In Andean cosmology, eternal and non-linear time. It integrates the three Pachas simultaneously: Kay Pacha (the here and now), Hanan Pacha (the upper world) and Ukhu Pacha (the deep world). In LINES, Wiñaypacha is the perceptual space where the linear sequence dissolves and one accesses multiple positions or knots of the quipu.